The
Restaurant
at the Heart of
the Lakes

ELLIE WOOD

The Restaurant at the Heart of the Lakes

Harper
North

HarperNorth
Windmill Green
24 Mount Street
Manchester M2 3NX

A division of
HarperCollins*Publishers*
1 London Bridge Street
London SE1 9GF

www.harpercollins.co.uk

HarperCollinsPublishers
Macken House
39/40 Mayor Street Upper
Dublin 1
D01 C9W8

First published by HarperNorth in 2024

1 3 5 7 9 10 8 6 4 2

A catalogue record for this book
is available from the British Library

ISBN: 978-0-00-862630-3

Printed and bound in the UK using 100% renewable electricity at
CPI Group (UK) Ltd, Croydon

MIX
Paper | Supporting
responsible forestry
FSC
www.fsc.org
FSC™ C007454

For my beloved Cumbria and the people
who make it my home.

Prologue

Anna Carleton knew the nickname they'd given her, though no one had ever called her it to her face – they'd only ever addressed her directly as 'Chef'. But she'd heard it muttered in the hush after they'd hastily silenced the radio, when she appeared on shift unexpectedly even though the rota said she was off. She winced as she recalled it. Despite the furnace-like heat of that kitchen, she'd made the atmosphere feel chill.

It had burned like ice on her bare skin when she first heard it. But since the night when everything had changed, she'd become softer, like frost slowly melting in spring sunlight. She was a different person now. When she recalled the boss she'd once been, she shivered. She'd thought being severe, even scary, was the best way to earn her staff's respect, but she'd been mistaken – nothing good grew in a climate of fear. She'd been so focused on getting to the top, she'd chosen the wrong route. After all, climbing to the summit of a mountain is much easier if you have a strong team around you.

She realised that now. But it had taken a life-shuddering shock. Pain twisted her lips as she remembered. She'd answered her buzzing phone – something she always scolded the other chefs for doing – when it rang for the third time in the same minute. She'd pulled it from her pocket and seen the name on the screen, tried to swallow back the terror that sliced through her in that split-second. Then, in the middle of a busy Friday dinner service on a warm summer evening in central London, her life had splintered like the ceramic plate she'd been holding. It had fallen from her hand as she'd taken the call, slipping out of her grasp like a lost last chance. And she'd stood there for god knows how long, surrounded by the people she spent every single day with, yet who suddenly felt like complete strangers, staring at the shattered moon of pale porcelain on the floor, trying to absorb the news.

1

'What do you think?' asked Dani, the pastry chef, yanking her into the present.

Anna's stainless-steel surroundings melted away momentarily as the honey hit her tongue. The taste took her back to that big basement kitchen where she'd barked commands at those below her . . . a real queen bee. She winced.

Dani bit her lip.

Anna blinked away the memory and broke into a smile. 'That's perfect.'

Dani grinned back at her. 'Really?'

Anna nodded, reached for a morsel more of the just-baked sponge to prove it. 'Well done,' she added, sprinkling deserved praise like seasoning. It had taken her too many years to find the right ingredients for a happy team, but she hoped she'd finally worked out the recipe.

'Cheers, Chef,' said Dani. She was already cracking on with the next part of her prep, concentrating on the bee pollen ice cream now, but her eyes were crinkled with satisfaction.

Anna surveyed the rest of the worktops, watching the hive of activity before her. She took in the hunched shoulders and shining knives, the selection of pans on the stovetop. The chefs moved round each other with steps that could have been choreographed. She glanced at the clock on the wall. Felt a small sting of annoyance. Where was the order from the farm? It should have been here well before now. She swallowed down a sigh. The slightest inconvenience could upset the smooth running of service, no matter how well rehearsed the whole show. She'd go in search of the produce herself, speed up the process, she thought, as she left behind the orchestra of cooking noises and stepped out into the blue-skied June day beyond the back entrance of the restaurant.

Hesta was hers, and that was both a blessing and a curse. She glanced back at the old stone building, a habit but not one of the ones she needed to break. She felt first a burst of pride that this bustling place belonged to her, then the familiar afterburn of burden. It was the first property that she'd actually owned, a dream she'd worked towards for her whole career. Her own restaurant. But over the years, what had once been a personal goal had morphed into something more. Become meaningful in a way she could never have imagined at the start. Greater than the sum of its parts. It wasn't about her anymore. That wasn't why she showed up in chef whites every day, though at the age of fifty-three she finally felt in the prime of her life. Since Hesta's doors had opened ten years ago, she'd felt the increase in responsibility weigh heavily like her cotton clothes were made of chainmail. The restaurant's name meant 'Have you?' in Cumbrian dialect, and what had been a quirky nod to the past was now a constant reminder of things she had to do in the present.

Right now, that was to go to Fell View Farm and figure out why on earth they'd failed to deliver the dairy goods she needed for the rest of the day not to be a disaster.

'Chef,' said Sally, the kitchen porter, head bent as she scurried past to go in through the back door, as though she'd half wondered about staying silent to avoid highlighting the fact she was late.

But perhaps that was a shadow Anna herself was casting on the situation. 'Morning, Sally,' she replied with a nod and nothing more, and Sally smiled as she disappeared inside.

Anna had learned not to let the inconsequential things cloud those that were important, to focus on the wood, not just the trees. No one could cook anything in that kitchen without Sally constantly working away, a cornerstone in the entire operation.

Anna turned back towards the lane. The farm was on the other side of Buttermere village, but still nearby, barely a ten-minute walk between hedgerows bursting with birdsong. The early-summer colours appeared brighter in contrast to the man-made appliances and silvery surfaces of Hesta's back-of-house industrial interior. The natural world enveloped her as she strode towards the farm, and she took a moment to focus on the sights surrounding her – without slowing down. Her tendency to rush about was too deeply ingrained. She looked at the vivid shades of brilliant green as the leaves danced on their branches like they were waving as she went past, and she breathed the scent of wild garlic, blown towards her in a blustery gust of breeze from the grass verges that brimmed with it either side of her. The last of the ramsons; a lush carpet of long flat leaves, studded with white star-like flowers, that was laid down by nature every spring. The unmistakeable aroma filled the shady banks and woodlands of her home at this time of year. She didn't need to look down to recognise it, as familiar as her mother's favourite perfume.

She twisted her head to gaze at the lake to her left, the landscape claiming her attention as though saving her from herself. The water glinted, celebrating the sunshine, always a gift in this part of the world, never a given. Anna felt the rays warm her face, reminding her how long it had been since she'd spent more than a few minutes outdoors. When was the last time she'd been down to the shore for a swim? She'd been too wrapped up in rotas and reservations and writing the new menu.

The farm came into view, but there was no sign of Rose or Will. She usually dealt with the daughter, had always found Will brusque, but perhaps he'd always thought the same about her. She'd already phoned twice to chase up the order – no answer – and had half expected to encounter one of them coming towards her on her way here. She'd been buying milk and butter from them right from the start, and had been loyal ever since. It shouldn't be a surprise that she needed them just as urgently as ever.

'Hello?' she called out as she entered the yard. Mud sucked at the soles of her shoes, mocking her impractical indoor footwear. She let out a groan. This was not how she should be spending her day. She'd have to change into the spare pair she kept in the staffroom before—

She gasped as a cockerel crowed close by. She clasped a hand to her chest as a clawing sense of irritation spread through her. She struggled to suppress it. She rang the doorbell outside the farmhouse and stood, hands on hips, waiting for someone to answer. When no one did, she walked round the side of the building. The tractor was parked over by the barn, their battered delivery van beside it. So surely someone had to be here. She shielded her eyes from the stark sunlight as she looked about. Beyond the old stone walls the fields were empty of their flock, the lack of white sheep-shaped dots making the square cubes of land look strange, like the blank faces of a dice with no spots.

Anna reached the shed at the far side of the farmhouse, heard a metallic buzz vibrating off the walls. Shearing season. She went inside, tried to shout above the noise of the clippers.

The man wrangling a ewe didn't look up.

'Excuse me?' Anna bellowed. Had he seen her come in? She saw the fleecy mass of sheep milling in the holding pen next to him and didn't envy the task of tackling them one by one. Too capricious a production line. She peered around the outhouse. There was no sign of anyone else. She watched as the farmhand gently wrestled the animal, saw it relax as he worked, skilfully shedding the wool in one complete piece. She could have clapped if she was that way inclined.

Then the humming of his machinery ceased and he stood up.

'Have you seen Rose or Will?' asked Anna, seizing her opportunity, raising her voice so it could be heard above the bleating.

But he was too busy corralling the shorn sheep into a separate enclosure. It looked like a different beast altogether without its furry coat, unrecognisable from the pillow-soft being it had been before, all angular bones and exposed skin. The man wiped his forehead on his sleeve. Then he tilted his head to one side and smiled as he met her gaze. 'You're Anna Carleton. The famous chef.'

Anna felt a flash of heat flood her cheeks. He reminded her of Dominik in a way. Similar height, strong build, a complexion created by the Cumbrian countryside. The comparison caught her off guard.

'Jackson,' he said, jerking his thumb at his chest.

He looked to be about the same age as Dominik had been back when she'd known him all those decades ago. Late twenties. Handsome, but not in the same way. No one ever could be.

He was staring at her, something she still wasn't used to no matter how many times she appeared in newspapers or magazines. She'd never think of herself as a local celebrity, but it didn't stop others doing so.

Jackson spread his arms out. 'I've been in here all morning. I haven't seen them.'

'Not to worry,' said Anna, turning to leave. He was already reaching for another baaing bundle of fluff, head bowed, attention back on the job. Dominik had been like that too, dedicated to the livestock and to looking after the land.

She took a deep breath of fresh air after being in the close, hot atmosphere of the animal shed. Then there in front of her was Rose, walking out of the milking parlour. She slapped her palms to her cheeks. 'Oh god – I forgot.'

Anna couldn't quite bring herself to say 'no problem': as she aged she had less time for untruths. She dipped her head in acknowledgement. But as Rose got closer, she noticed the girl's tired eyes and the pale palette with which exhaustion had painted her cheeks.

'I'll bring it over now,' Rose said, already starting back in the direction from which she'd come, as though life didn't allow her a second's pause to explain.

Anna found herself following her; she'd seen that expression often enough before, staring out from her own bathroom mirror. That feeling, the suffocating boa-constrictor squeeze of stress, was hard to forget.

Rose was marching at a pace even faster than her own.

Anna hurried to catch up with her. 'Is everything all right?' The cockerel cried out, as though ridiculing her question.

'Yeah, fine, sorry,' Rose replied without meeting her eye, making her way to the converted barn. She shook her head. 'This won't happen again,' she said sternly, more a reprimand for herself than a promise to anyone else. She stopped suddenly outside the big wooden double doors, turned to look at Anna. 'Erm, I know this isn't professional . . .' She flapped her fingers like she was physically sifting through words floating in the air, trying to find the right ones faster. 'I'm sorry to ask, but . . .' She bit her lip, appeared to be struggling with something much more difficult to get a grip of than the unpredictable sheep being grappled in the shed. 'Please could you give me a hand to load it all up?' A hawthorn-berry blush flushed her face at having to ask for help. 'Jackson's busy.' She jerked her chin at the outhouse. 'And Dad's on the quad . . .' She grimaced, a prickle of swallowed pride. 'Seeing as you're here and . . .' Her voice broke, her body betraying the boiling-point emotion bubbling beneath her skin.

'Yes, of course.' Anna stuck out her arms, struck by the urgency in Rose's tone. '*Two* hands. I'm no stranger to hard work.' She laughed; lifting a couple of crates was nothing.

A look of gratitude washed over Rose, but as Anna stepped forward to go through the doors, she noticed an undercurrent roiling in the young girl's eyes. As Rose smiled her thanks, Anna could see the doubt there, as clearly as if her pupils were the black dots of two question marks. *Do you really understand this pressure? With your smart restaurant and all those staff?* And Anna could see something else visible in

Rose's watery gaze. Something more surprising. The image of her own face shining back in miniature. This was *exactly* how she'd once felt.

'It's all ready to go . . .' said Rose, gesturing towards the belly of the barn as they walked inside, but Anna's sight took a moment to adjust to the contrasting light.

Rose was heading for the back wall, where a bank of colossal commercial refrigerators whirred white noise as though whispering a rolling to-do list.

As Anna's eyes adapted to the dimness, she noticed the newest member of the murmuring choir: a lead singer standing proudly at the front, shaped from aluminium and glass.

A gleaming ice-cream cabinet.

Rose was concentrating on counting quantities of milk and butter, fatigue causing her to lose faith in herself.

Anna frowned as she looked at the display case. No wonder the girl was feeling overwhelmed. Wasn't this too much to take on in addition to all her usual jobs?

But Anna would have been the same herself if she rewound the clock, she was sure of it. Rose was a fourth-generation farmer, and she was attempting to propel Fell View forward into a new era. It was an impressive plan, Anna thought, as she peered round at the rest of the equipment that had been plugged in and positioned about the place, realising now what was causing Rose to be under so much pressure. The start of a new venture was fraught with possibilities, both good and bad. She watched as Rose gripped the sides of a crate, arms tense with the effort of lifting it. But uncertainty was the heaviest weight in the world.

A rush of admiration mixed with concern coursed through Anna. She knew what it was like when work and life blurred into one. Ingenuity and necessity combined to make a powerful cocktail, but there was a point when it became toxic.

She approached the freezer cabinet, instinctively drawn to see what was inside – always a chef, first and foremost. Flavour combinations whirled in her mind at night; dreams were dress rehearsals for service.

'It's empty,' called Rose, coming back towards her carrying a crate. 'Can you grab the other one of these?' She motioned over her shoulder with her head.

Anna's gaze left the row of silver trays beyond the shimmering sheet of glass beside her. 'Yes, of course,' she replied. 'Have you started production yet?' she asked as she retrieved the second half of her order – a culinary enquiry was really the only valid reason to chat—

But Rose had vanished.

Anna went outside after her.

Rose was resting the rectangular receptacle she was holding on her knee, one foot on the back bumper of the van, as she unlocked the rear doors. 'Right, I'll drive this over straight away,' she said, taking the second container from Anna and sliding it onto the floor.

Anna craned her neck. The van was crammed full of all sorts of stuff. An open cardboard box was stacked with jars of what looked to be different kinds of toppings for the cones and tubs that would shortly be—

'Want a lift?' Rose slammed the back of the vehicle shut, curbing Anna's curiosity.

'Oh, that would be great – thanks,' she said.

Rose was climbing into the driver's seat, so Anna hurried round to the passenger side.

Anna opened her mouth to speak on several occasions, but silence seemed to have sneaked into the cab with them.

She couldn't quite think of the right thing to say. She had never excelled at small talk.

'Are you sure you're okay, Rose?' she finally said, as Hesta came into sight.

They were business contacts, not friends. What was she doing? As soon as the sentence was out of her mouth, she wished it would blow away straight out of the wound-down window.

But there was something about sitting side by side on the same journey that had persuaded Anna to ask.

She saw Rose's frame, rigid next to her, arms gripping the wheel as though she could steer the whole farm through anything if she held onto it tightly enough.

She gave a slight nod, not managing to mouth the word 'yes.'

'Just got a lot on at the moment.' Rose swept a sleeve over her face. 'It's fine.'

Not 'I'm fine', noted Anna.

'Well, if there's anything I can do.' She undid her seat belt.

Rose scrunched up her eyes, like that would force her tears back into her sockets, but one absconded down her left cheek, escaping the cuff of her jumper.

Anna's fingers hovered on the door handle; should she just get out and leave the girl to it? Or was there something she could do to *help*?

'The ice-cream project looks exciting,' she said softly, hoping positivity would encourage her to be chirpier.

But instead Rose completely broke down, folding her elbows across the steering wheel and resting her forehead on her arms, her body heaving out long-suppressed sobs.

Anna bit her thumbnail. She couldn't sit here all day, but equally how could she leave the girl in a state like this? She stared out at the blue sky scattered with sheep's-fleece clouds; the windscreen was a frame capturing this glorious summertime image. But here they were behind the scenes, where the reality of life was the precise opposite of picture-perfect.

Rose shifted in her seat and the van horn blared, making them both jump.

Then laughter stole in through the open window, dissolving a little of the awkwardness.

'Sorry,' mumbled Rose, sitting upright.

Anna was unsure whether she was apologising for the shock or for showing such an outpouring of emotion. Maybe both?

'Right,' Rose said, though clearly something was seriously wrong.

Anna took a breath, but Rose flung open her door, physically escaping the necessity to talk about anything more.

2

Anna shed the white chef's coat she'd worn to the farm and was reminded of the shorn sheep she'd seen earlier that morning as she shoved it into a laundry bag in the staffroom at the back of the restaurant. The memory of Rose crying was more difficult to shrug off. The image of the girl's shoulders wrought taut by overwork lingered as she swapped her mud-splattered shoes for a spare pair of kitchen clogs. In her clean outfit, she thought she'd feel refreshed and ready for the rest of the day, but she couldn't shake the niggling sense that she ought to do something. But what? Surely Rose had the support of her dad, Will. And they employed that farm-hand, Jackson, for a start. Perhaps there were others. It wasn't her place to get involved. Fell View was a supplier, and one that kept itself to itself, slightly apart from the rest of Buttermere, tucked into a fold in the valley.

But even when she was back beside the pass in the midst of the hiss and sizzle of the lunchtime service, she was unable to shift the snapshot of Rose's wrung-out body slumped over the dashboard—

'Try this.' Dani held out a teaspoon.

Anna wasn't normally the one taking instructions, but she did as she was told. Her focus was usually Sabatier-sharp, but today she wanted someone else to take control. What if that was what Rose was wishing too? Everyone needed a little assistance at some point, after all.

She put the curl of butter Dani had handed her in her mouth, expecting to savour a swirl of soft summer sunshine but instead spluttering as a wave of salt hit her like she'd swallowed a gulp of sea water.

She spat it into the bin.

Dani raised her eyebrows. 'Same reaction I had – except I swore.'

'Thanks for sharing the experience with me,' said Anna, shooting her a sideways glance. She took a swig of water, trying to wash the tingling sensation from her tongue.

'We're gonna have to pull it.' Dani flicked a hand towards the door that divided the kitchen from the front of house.

Anna nodded, eyes watering as though she was still caught in the undertow. 'It's already on the tables?' Her tone alone asked, 'How many times have I told you to taste *everything* first?'

Dani slunk away to inform the Maître D, more sheepish than the ewe at Fell View.

Anna sighed. Great. Someone must have already complained. Asked one of the staff to send it back. She imagined a customer buttering a broken-off piece of freshly baked loaf before biting into it – and cringed.

Hesta was supposed to provide the very finest cuisine – Anna prided herself on using prime Cumbrian produce, locally sourced ingredients – but right now it wasn't even offering the bare minimum required of an eatery. The food ought to at least be *edible.*

Whatever was going on with Rose and Will further up the road was in danger of impacting the restaurant's reputation. Her name too; they were inextricably entwined, as synonymous as the Lake District was with water. If Hesta was affected then so was she, and vice versa. And she'd sacrificed so much to get here. She braced herself against the pass, as though she could extract some of the metal's strength.

She was jolted back to the present by the muttering of the mini printer regurgitating diners' orders.

She resolved to speak to Rose, as she plucked the scrap of paper from the mouth of the electronic device. She couldn't afford for Fell View's errors to affect her business but, beyond that, blunders as big as messing up the entire batch of butter could be dangerous. Farms weren't the setting for fairy tales. If they were, she and Dominik would still be together.

3

The four-hour break in between lunch finishing and dinner starting was when the other chefs left the premises – carried on with the rest of their lives, picked up their kids from school, perhaps crossed paths briefly with their partners as they came home from work, if they weren't also operating on hospitality's split-shift schedule – and Anna was alone with her thoughts.

It was close to four o'clock now. The countertops had been scoured and gone were the shouts and steam of mid-service. At this time, and late at night, when the last diner had long gone and the front-of-house staff had disappeared, the kitchen was a silent stainless-steel temple. Usually, she relished the opportunity for contemplation, appreciated the peace. But today she was craving fresh air.

She opened and closed chiller cabinets, checking stock, making sure everything was correctly labelled, and recalled the chorus of ice-cream-making apparatus up at the farm. The beginnings of a headache throbbed at the edge of her vision like a thunderstorm on the horizon. Just as she was about to slam the fridge door, she saw the rows of golden roundels that Dani had stayed late to create. Enough to see them through that evening and the following day. Anna made a mental note to add an extra hour to her timesheet. Her shoulders lowered as she closed the door, as though someone had literally lifted a load from her. She would be totally lost without her team.

She completed her post-service rituals, grabbed the well-worn wicker basket from the back room, and stepped into the surprisingly cold afternoon. Even the sun was on a break, barely visible behind a vapour-gauze curtain, suspended in the sky on a hammock of cloud. She took a deep breath of first-of-June-scented air. Notes of fresh green foliage and impending rain.

She tried calling Rose's phone but reached voice mail. The drone of the new units arranged in the barn echoed in Anna's mind. She walked briskly along the lane towards the farm; figuring out the best way to tell Rose about the unpalatable butter was more complex than putting together an entirely new menu. She'd have to carefully formulate exactly what she was going to say, but how? Her words only seemed to flow when good food was involved.

Soon the fields that fringed Fell View came into sight as she rounded the corner. But there was something she had to do first. She diverted down a wild and weedy bridle path, far enough away from the few cars that hardly amounted to traffic, till she was among the filigree fronds of the freely growing grass. It was in secret-seeming places like this, hidden in plain sight, where the best foraging was to be done. She began filling the wicker basket she'd brought with her, eager to finish the task ahead of the imminent downpour. Clouds collected above the mountains like they were having a meeting, deciding when to burst. She carefully cut the lace-like heads of the creamy-white elderflowers. It was important to pick them when the buds were newly opened on a fine, still day. Dominik had told her that. She lay them gently in the bottom of the basket one by one, and as the frothy-blossomed bouquet became bigger, ideas began to bloom in Anna's brain. It was when she was surrounded by the dynamic magic of the countryside, watching the flora and fauna unfold as the four seasons unfurled one after the other, that she came up with her best recipes. Elderflower champagne sorbet. Crisp sweet-batter-dipped fritters. She bent closer to gulp a lungful of the refreshing elderflowers. Their citrusy smell was a tonic.

Then she leaped upright as the roar of a quad bike ripped through the calm air before coming to a stop at the entrance to the bridleway before her.

Will's knuckles were white on the handlebars, his hair a mass of tousled strands resembling the knotted tangle of grass at Anna's feet. His face was red with rage and a day of being out on the wind-whipped hills. ''Scuse me. What are you doing?' The engine rumbled a low background growl.

Anna held up her basket like she was surrendering a weapon.

'This is our land,' stated Will with a tilt of his chin.

'I know, I asked Rose if I could . . . I mean I've always . . .'

The fragrant hedges flanked her like a natural fortress, defending her.

'We run the farm jointly. The decision is both of ours.'

His arms were stiff, unmoving, as though demonstrating his stance on the matter.

'Right, well, I'll go then.'

17

Suddenly the lane was like a runway, the luminous elder-flowers lighting the way for her to leave.

'Would you like these, seeing as they're yours?' She offered him the bunch of fresh florets, sending a waft of their summer-fruit scent into the deepening sky.

The aroma seemed to sweeten him slightly.

'No. Keep 'em.' His voice had softened.

'I'll find them elsewhere from now on.' Anna stomped her way back onto the road.

Will sighed, loudly enough that Anna heard it over the reverberating sound of the motorbike. 'Sorry, I'm . . .'

'Being ridiculous?' suggested Anna before she could prevent herself, the grumble of the vehicle seeming to lull, rendering her voice audible. Perhaps she'd said the words with the same force as she felt them.

Will's face was moon-pale like a chastened child.

'I've picked very little of what is growing, and have left plenty for the wildlife, and as far as I was aware, I had the permission of Fell View Farm.'

Will opened his mouth.

'That bridlepath is a public right of way,' Anna continued, flinging out the arm clutching the basket with a flourish.

Will gave a nod. 'Right you are.'

'If I'd done something wrong, I'd apologise,' finished Anna, stepping into the halo-gold glow of the headlamps.

'Look, I take it back.' Will's fingers let go of the handlebars, as if relinquishing control.

'It's fine. There are lots of other places I can go,' said Anna from where she stood in the spotlight, staring back at him fiercely. 'But, by your own logic, you're equally responsible for the late – and faulty – food order we received at the restaurant this morning.'

'What do you mean?'

Anna was satisfied by the confusion in his voice, the fact that his high horse had transformed back into a four-by-four.

'You and your daughter are jointly accountable for that. You said so yourself.'

'Eh?'

'Both of you must have decided that butter delivery was fit for purpose – which it was not.' Her lips were pinched like some of the salt taste was still in her mouth.

'I don't know about this.' His palms were back on the bike's handlebars, but he was struggling to grasp the situation.

'If I can't rely on the quality of the produce to be consistent, I'll have to pull the contract.' It wasn't a threat; she spoke the truth. Hesta's name was at risk.

Will's brow crumpled. 'Please don't do that. We can refund you for—'

'A restaurant is only as good as its worst meal.' Anna's mantra could have been inked on her skin.

Will dipped his head. 'I don't know how that happened.' He might have apologised but the words were drowned by the grizzle of the quad's engine. 'We *need* your business . . .' he said, his desperation loud and clear. 'Supplying Anna Carleton is . . . well, if that stops, we'll lose other accounts.'

Anna could sense him spiralling as keenly as if she was watching him ride a helter-skelter.

'Rose has been distracted with one of her schemes.' A flash of irritation crossed Will's face, like lights flickering before a power cut. He lacked the energy to elaborate.

Anna raised her eyebrows. 'I saw the ice-cream machine when I came round to chase up my order.'

'I've told her to stop.' Will shook his head.

'I thought it was a partnership?'

'We can't afford to be messing around . . .' He exhaled, scraped a hand through his hedge-straggle hair. 'We have to focus on the farm, stop faffing about with pipe-dreams.' A glimmer of fatherly pride replaced his frustration, like the rosy rays of dawn after the darkness of night. 'She's a clever girl but we can't cope with any more on our plate.'

'It's a good idea though, diversifying, bringing the farm into the modern day . . .'

Will visibly bristled like his back was covered in hedgehog spines. 'We're going to sell it, all that equipment.' The storm-cloud expression was back. 'Shouldn't have bought it in the first place. We don't have the money and she doesn't know what she's doing when it comes to . . .'

'If there's anything I can—'

Will cocked his head, saying, without even speaking, 'You're a chef, not a farmer, for goodness' sake.'

Usually people treated Anna with reverence, smiling when they encountered her, like she was a standing stone on a mountain summit. They would whisper, 'Look, it's Anna Carleton' when they spotted her out and about in Buttermere; locals liked to think they were part of her inner circle purely because they lived in the same place. But not Will. Although Fell View and Hesta belonged to the same landscape, and each embodied the same principles, championed Cumbrian food, he always seemed to give the impression he disagreed with what she did. It was as though he believed her elevated dishes were a desecration of decent meat and veg. But he'd never even been through the restaurant's doors.

'I'd better get back.' Anna glanced at her wrist, the universal mime for mentioning the time; she didn't wear a watch. Her natural habitat was the kitchen, and it had a clock.

20

'Aye, I've got milking to do.' He gave a parting nod and the quad bike snarled before he disappeared out of sight.

The restaurant was packed, even though it was a Wednesday night, and when Anna sent the last main course over the pass, she and the other chefs gave a sigh of relief. She helped with the clean down, then left Dani in charge of any remaining desserts, and said goodbye to Sally, who was midway through a metallic mountain of pans, on her way out. Trusting her staff to do their jobs in her absence was something she'd realised was crucial; looming over them in her uniform like a snow-capped peak wasn't helpful. And working every second of the day wasn't good for anyone – she'd discovered that herself the hard way. An executive chef, worn-down and waxy-faced, could burn out as quickly as the waning flame of a tea light.

Anna checked her phone in the back room. There was a message from Rose saying she'd drop off a replacement order of butter when the evening service was over. Anna might be done for the night but did Rose ever get to stop? She pulled on her coat and walked out of the door, passing the pair of candle lanterns that stood either side of Hesta's entrance as the final flicker of fire left one of the wicks.

Anna shoved her hands in her pockets. Should she wait and speak to Rose?

The van swung into sight before she had chance to decide.

Twilight was descending on Buttermere and Rose was a silhouette as she stepped down from the driver's seat. But dusk wasn't to blame for the fact she was a shadow.

Anna took the box Rose handed to her. 'Thanks.'

Rose's arms went limp as she let go of the crate, like a little more energy had left her body. 'I hope it didn't cause too much trouble.'

21

Anna let the sentence disappear into the dark. 'I saw your dad.'

Rose's forehead crumpled. 'He didn't come round?'

Anna shook her head. 'I was picking elderflowers in the lane.' She left out the confrontation, figured Rose had enough reasons of her own to disagree with him, without Anna adding to the inventory.

'He said you're stopping with the ice cream?'

Rose folded her arms. 'No, because it never even got started in the first place.' Her eyes shone in the amber light of Hesta's window.

'I thought it was a good idea.'

'Well, Dad didn't, so . . .' Rose glanced at the scatter of stars that seemed to have come out to support her. 'If we don't do something, though, that's it – we'll have to leave the farm . . .' She searched the canopy above, as though there was a constellation called courage. 'We can't make a living like this. The price of milk . . . the cost of—'

Sally slipped out of the back door and jumped, surprised to see her boss still standing there.

'Night,' she murmured as she shuffled in the opposite direction, pulling her jacket round her.

Anna raised a hand. 'See you tomorrow, Sally.'

She turned back to Rose. 'D'you want to come inside for a sec?' She understood how Rose thought about Fell View; Anna felt the same about Hesta – as though the very stones of the building were as much a part of her as her own blood and bones. She knew how much the farm meant to Rose; that it was a physical connection to the time when there were three of them who lived there.

Rose sagged against the outside wall.

'You run the farm between you, though, you and Will.'

Rose looked at her in the fast-fading light. 'Dad says how can we set up a second business when we can't manage one.'

'If you've got a plan, I could look over it.'

Rose looked like she'd been about to say something but thought better of it. A retort about it being a completely different kind of venture from Hesta, perhaps.

'It's not on me at the moment,' said Rose, standing upright again.

'No. I know – can I just put this box down?' Anna started to make her way towards the rear of the restaurant, glancing over her shoulder at Rose. 'Come in for a minute. Try some of the syrup I made with your elderflowers. I want to know what you think.'

Rose frowned, confused. 'You're one of the best chefs in the country, why would you want *my* opinion?'

It was only once Anna had squeezed a small stripe of the delicate sauce onto a spoon for her and she'd tasted the perfectly balanced elderflower flavour that the first shoots of excitement began to grow within Rose. She realised Anna hadn't wanted her advice at all. She was showing her that it was possible to create the incredible out of the ordinary.

4

'What do you reckon?' Anna's expression remained neutral. She wasn't one for excessive smiling, and the sound of her laugh was rare, reserved for when she really meant it. Her emotions matched her cookery in that respect: every element was on the plate for a reason, there was nothing extraneous or just for show.

'It's . . . *delicious*.' A spark of life seemed to have returned to Rose, as though she'd taken a medicinal dose of delight. '*Really* delicious. I don't know how else to describe it. Different. Like nothing I've had before.'

Anna dispensed a drizzle for herself, sampled the restorative shot of concentrated countryside. 'And to think it comes from a humble hedgerow, hey?'

'Well, I imagine you do a fair bit of wizardry to get it into that gel.' Rose regarded the translucent tube as though trying to figure out the background workings of a magic trick.

'The flavour itself is mainly nature's doing, though.' Modesty was the secret ingredient in Anna Carleton's food; sustainability was her hallmark.

Dani wished them both goodnight, without giving any hint that Rose's butter blunder had been the last thing she'd needed in an already busy day.

Anna waved 'bye' and gave a grateful bow of her head.

Rose was looking at the other containers on the work surface in front of them, reading the black-ink letters on each label.

'Have a try of this one and see how it compares.' Anna upturned another squeeze bottle and presented Rose with a glistening deep-red viscous disc this time.

Rose took the spoon; the ruby-jewel sphere sat in the centre of it like a precious stone. 'Oh wow – that's incredible,' she said as the rich-fruit flavour rolled around her mouth. 'Very . . . *vibrant*.'

'Same plant,' said Anna, gesturing at the first flask.

'Really?' Rose peered at the contrasting colours of the containers each condiment had come from.

'The first one was made from the flowers, the second from the berries,' said Anna.

'That's amazing.' Rose angled her head as she listened.

'A taste of summer, and a taste of autumn,' continued Anna. Speaking the information out loud was like bringing a little bit of Dominik back. Her mum had sparked her love of cookery, but it had been him that had taught her everything she knew about foraging; he'd explained the contents of the wild larder that lay beyond the bricks and roads of Buttermere and stretched out towards the horizon as far as you could see. He'd shown her the treasures that were unburied, there for the taking, and shared with her those that were cleverly concealed and so even more rewarding. He'd understood that some things required a little more care and attention to blossom to their full potential – helped her see that plants were just like people, in that sense.

Rose was still rapt by the array of culinary creations on the worktop. 'They're both so . . .' She bit her lip as she rummaged for the right word. 'Fresh.'

'Mother Earth's menu is always changing. That's what keeps it interesting: it shifts with the seasons.'

Rose's eyes roved over the other receptacles like an avid beachcomber.

Anna was pleased to see energy fizzing from within her once again, wondered whether Rose's plan to future-proof the farm was perhaps being reignited. She hoped so; she identified with the girl's fighting spirit, admired her enterprising attitude. 'What do you think so far?' she asked, hesitant to ask about the paused project outright in case Rose wilted right there and then.

'Phenomenal, to be honest,' replied Rose. 'Very inspiring. I love the way you take such simple stuff and –' she splayed the fingers of both hands at the same time, as though she was releasing a giant dash of fairy dust – 'transform it into things that are so surprising and wonderful . . .' She trailed off and a cloud of confusion came to hover over her face. 'I don't really understand why you're showing me all this, though – people book to come here months in advance, travel from the other end of the country to eat your food.' She flung out an arm in the direction of the back door. 'I've seen customers – and locals – clamouring to catch a glimpse of Anna Carleton at work.'

Anna felt her cheeks scorch like she was standing too close to a searing-hot stove. She'd never become acclimatised to the concept of fame, always experienced a prickle of discomfort when it was referred to in the same breath as her name. The price she'd paid to get to this position wasn't something she wanted to celebrate.

'I think opening an ice-cream parlour is a great idea.'

Rose straightened up as Anna batted the topic of conversation back to her, like the steel surface between them had become a ping-pong table. 'I appreciate that. It's a compliment, especially coming from Anna Carleton, but we're not going ahead with it.' Rose sighed.

'But I think I can help you figure out a way to make it work.' Anna put her hands on her hips. 'I understand that a business needs to be profitable, that numbers need to stack up,' she added. 'We can look at profit margins and all that sort of thing—'

Rose held up her palms. 'Look, it's really kind of you to want to get involved, but we can't . . .'

Anna felt her face smart. 'I wasn't meaning . . .'

'No, I know your advice would be invaluable.' Rose shook her head. 'I didn't mean it like that, but I'm sorry, we just can't afford it.'

'But—'

'However much it was. I've already spent enough – did a three-day course on how to make the stupid stuff that cost an arm and a leg, and Dad's right. How do we know we're ever going to make money, let alone recoup the expenses of setting it all up? What's going to make people come to our spot for ice cream rather than any of the other places out there?'

'Well, this is what I'm saying. There's so much that is right on our doorstep.'

'And what you do is unreal. Actually mind-blowing.'

'I didn't mean pay me for anything.'

'What?' Rose paused for air. 'I don't understand. You're —'

Anna flinched in anticipation of hearing her name echo about the kitchen cabinets again.

'You were going to give your time – your expertise – for *free*?' Rose screwed up her features. 'Why on earth would you do that?'

'What if I wanted to?'

'For what reason?'

It was Anna's turn to struggle with serving up a suitable sentence. She swallowed. 'To give something back.' The Buttermere community had saved her, after all. Being back here, the place she'd been brought up and now called home, had brought her to life again.

'The offer is there, anyway.'

Rose was silent.

The gastronomic gadgets surrounding them seemed to hum in unison more loudly, as though in solidarity with the ice-cream-making instruments up at the farm.

'Didn't mean to interfere,' said Anna. 'I guess I tend to get very passionate when it comes to food.' She started to tidy away the squeeze bottles of sauces and syrups.

'It's been so interesting seeing everything,' said Rose. Her insides were a coil of uncertainty. What if Anna had a point? she wondered. Here they inhabited a foodie's fantasy land. A natural paradise of flavourful ingredients grew all around them. An entire pantry providing speciality produce. Rose pictured a cookery show where the chefs had a fully stocked store cupboard at their disposal. There were so many unique plants and herbs to choose from. Showcasing this was what Hesta did best, but what if the same ethos could be at the heart of Fell View Farm too? Wasn't being mentored by Anna Carleton too good an opportunity to turn down?

'Wait a second,' Rose mumbled.

Anna stopped packing things away. 'Oh, of course,' she said when she saw the sticker on the front of the container she was holding. 'I should have known this one would be of most interest.'

Rose squinted to look at the label, but Anna had already upended the bottle and was squirting a glossy circle of scarlet sauce onto a clean spoon. 'Probably be your favourite, seeing as it's made from your namesake.'

Rose raised her eyebrows.

'Here.'

Rose tried to form a definition befitting the ensuing taste sensation; it wasn't like anything she'd tried before and totally unlike either of the elderflower inventions. 'Tastes tropical. Fruity.'

'Rosehip syrup,' said Anna, replacing the cap on the nozzle of the container.

An unignorable idea began to burgeon in Rose's brain.

'Made from wild roses,' said Anna.

Rose's eyes shimmered.

'Right, that's enough of that. And I won't mention any more about ice cream.' Anna mimed drawing a line in the air with the squeeze bottle. 'But if I hear of anyone wanting some equipment on the cheap, I'll let you know. The team have lots of contacts. The catering industry's a small world really . . .'

But Rose wasn't listening. She couldn't help envisaging two words emblazoned across the chiller cabinet that currently stood in the outhouse up at the farm. She imagined them stamped on stacks of cardboard tubs that would then be crammed with orbs of ice cream. She could see them written on flyers and, if she really tried hard enough, in the heading of a feature in the local newspaper.

Wild Rose Ice Cream was about to be born.

5

'Thank goodness for that,' said Dani, with a grateful glance up at the ceiling, as though the extraction system was a portal to the heavens. 'The last lot was like something made from Morecambe Bay.' She stuck out her tongue in a grimace and shuddered, then immediately began slathering a hunk of bread with the rest of the tester pat of butter she'd broken into, spreading it generously on a slab of sourdough, now she was sure it was safe to consume. 'Better just double check it's definitely okay, though.' She gave a muffled laugh as she bit off a chunk. 'You're always telling me to taste, taste, taste, aren't you, boss?'

Anna shot her a sideways look.

'Well, I can safely say this batch passes my strict quality checks,' declared Dani with a lick of her lips.

'Good, let's hope the problem's sorted and it doesn't happen again.' Anna shut the fridge door, as though physically closing the chapter where something inedible had come out of Hesta's kitchen. Her shoulders relaxed slightly as she

31

slid the sheet of yellow-gold ingots onto the side to soften a little before the lunchtime service.

'So, what was all that about last night, then?' asked Dani, through a mouthful of churned cream and crumbs.

They'd worked together for so long that Anna still understood. 'I was explaining the different things we make, why foraging's at the core of what we do, how much variety—'

'Giving away our secrets?'

Anna shook her head. 'Showing a little hint of what's possible, how many options there are if you only look for them.'

'Why? Don't people usually pay for that?' Dani was frowning and chewing at the same time, used to multitasking. 'Thought you had to get a table at Hesta for an insight into that stuff. Or work your socks off back here.'

Anna raised her eyebrows as Dani took another huge bite of bread. 'It's obvious something's awry – orders are coming in late and, when we get them, they're completely wrong—'

'Urgh,' interjected Dani, shivering at the salt-spiked memory.

'Will is always hostile—'

'Thinks what we do is hoity-toity – heard him say it with my own ears,' said Dani.

Anna's eyes widened. 'What?'

'I was walking back to my car one afternoon and he said it to my face . . . I mean, I had blocked his gate by parking in front of it, so he wasn't best pleased, but—'

'Anyway, I just thought there might be something I could do to help,' said Anna, not quite sure why she was explaining herself to her pastry chef, but somewhere along the way, Dani had become a friend not just an employee. 'Rose seemed to be struggling, and I thought I might have the answer.'

'And do you?' asked Dani, when she didn't elaborate, savouring the delayed start to her working day.

The other staff weren't due in yet, and it was during moments like these that Dani tended to grill Anna, asking quick-fire questions that no one else would dare brave but seemed to blaze on her lips like hot chilli.

'I don't know. But I can share what I *do* know. Might as well be of use to someone else.' She swallowed. For the smallest fraction of a second, she thought she'd experienced a little of what it would have been like to have a daughter when she'd been teaching Rose about the versatile wild with its aromatic plants and gemstone berries. 'It's my passion, turning humble shrubs into something that can take a meal to the next level.'

'Is Rose jacking in farm life and coming to work here, then?' asked Dani.

'No.' Anna openly looked at the clock.

'What then?' pressed Dani.

'She wants to make ice cream—'

'Ooh.' Dani's features melted slightly beneath the spotlights.

'I thought I could be a sort of . . . mentor to her maybe, if she wanted.' Why was she telling Dani all this? Her eyes flicked up at the wall once again: they had a fully booked restaurant to cook for in a few hours' time. 'I can't help thinking I haven't always made the right choices, and this might be a chance to do something good.'

Dani pouted, either because she was contemplating Anna's words, or because the final morsel of butter-coated bun was gone.

'*The Compassionate Chef*,' she said, sweeping a hand through the air. 'Isn't as catchy a title as Jamie O's TV series, you know.'

Anna smiled despite herself. 'Right, enough of your jokes,' she said with a shake of her head.

Dani dissolved into laughter.

'*I* need to be getting on.' Anna straightened up.

'Wait a sec,' said Dani, suddenly serious, as though the sourdough had soaked up her silliness and left her sober. 'We're doing the summer menu now, aren't we?'

Anna looked like she'd just eaten a block of the salt-butter. 'Yes, of course, same as we have been doing all week.'

'Well, then,' said Dani, pausing to relish her boss's reaction. 'We don't need the elderberry or the rosehip syrup, do we? They're not in the new dishes?'

Anna narrowed her eyes. 'No.' It took her early-morning mind a few seconds to piece together what Dani was saying. 'I could give them to Rose to try with her ice cream, you mean . . .'

Dani put her fingers to her mouth in a chef's kiss before disappearing off in the direction of her pastry section.

Anna ran through the bookings for that lunchtime, taking note of diners' special requests and shouting them out to Dani, as well as any birthdays or anniversaries too, feeling a swell of satisfaction that Hesta had been chosen as the place to mark such memorable occasions. A ripple of warmth, like the afterglow she experienced post-swim on the shore of Buttermere, spread across her skin, and the thought of the oak-tree-lined track alongside the lake reminded her . . .

'I need to go and get some more wood sorrel,' Anna called over to Dani. The lemon-apple tang of the leaves made such a delicious dressing, perfect with fish, and the flavours were finest when the plant was freshly picked.

'Bring me back a treat!' Dani replied, like a lover whose other half was off to the corner shop.

As Anna changed in the staffroom, she contemplated the switch to the summer menu. Despite the issue with Fell View, the new dishes were going smoothly. Everyone had pulled together yesterday to put on a fine performance. In Anna's all-time favourite restaurant review, the critic had said Hesta was multi-sensory theatre, where the chefs told stories of the Lakes, bringing alive the heritage and putting wild food at the fore, with the seasons as the inspiration—

'Sally's not coming in today.'

Anna jumped at the sound of Dani's voice from the doorway. She turned round.

'Just had a text.' Dani held up her phone.

Anna blinked. 'Why hasn't she rung me?'

Dani shrugged. 'Says she's sick, and she's sorry for the short notice,' she read from the screen.

Anna's shoulders sank. Sally's role was integral, the equivalent of slick stage mechanics: the whole reason the rest of the production worked.

'Thanks for letting me know,' she said. She'd have to be KP tonight. She couldn't risk roping someone in on night two of the new menu.

Dani went back to the kitchen, leaving Anna lightly marinating in irritation. The restaurant was only open five days a week, so the staff could have a proper break and the rest of the time Anna could rely on them to be on their best form. This core belief was the foundation she'd built Hesta upon. If the team was strong, the show could go on. Of course, the staff's wellbeing came first and foremost, but a last-minute illness was nevertheless inconvenient—

'Want me to go and get the wood sorrel?'

Anna started and spun round to see Dani standing there again.

'Is that any help?'

Anna shook her head. 'It's fine.'

'Sure? I don't mind.'

'I'll go. Thanks, though.' It wasn't that she didn't trust Dani to come back with the right plant – with its distinctive trio of green leaves atop a red stem, sorrel was simple enough to find – and she knew her pastry chef would come straight back, not be tempted to make the trip take twice as long, but Anna felt she ought to bear the ultimate responsibility. There were too many lookalikes lurking, concealed amongst the bushes and trees, pretending to be harmless, to send someone else. It was easy to be fooled, even for someone as well acquainted with the foliage-strewn woodland floor as Anna.

Outside, the storm of the night before had subsided into soft cashmere clouds.

Anna wound her way towards the lake, then along the pebble-and-earth path, as familiar to her as the carpet in her front room, perhaps more so.

Beneath the ancient oaks, she bent to pluck red stems of wood sorrel. The little heart-shaped leaflets closed up when they were parted from the ground, like miniature valentine's cards from past relationships. She held one in her palm, watched as it folded in on itself, wondered if she'd done the same in the years since she'd last seen Dominik.

Out here, away from the chop and crackle of the kitchen, in the fragrant forest air, was when she thought of him most.

She started to make her way back and, as the woodland met the fields, she noticed a figure in the distance crouched beside a tumbled crumble of rock rubble: a dry-stone wall rendered unrecognisable by the storm. As she got closer, she could see it was Jackson mending it.

'Hi,' she said, when she was nearer.

She thought he hadn't heard her when at first he didn't look up, he was so engrossed in the process, but then he stopped sifting through the assortment of stones and glanced up at her. 'Morning.' His gaze went to the basket, and beyond her, to the woodland route she'd just taken, and back again. 'What is it you were after this time?' he asked, cocking his head to one side.

She tilted her heart-shaped hoard towards him.

'Hearty meal you've got there,' he said with a nod but no smile.

She was probably holding him up, she realised. 'I'll let you get on,' she said as he started rebuilding the breached boundary again.

Anna surveyed the scattered rocks as she carried on walking, watched Jackson turn a slab over in his hands. She looked over her shoulder, saw him slot the piece of stone in place, hiding its ugly rough edges and facing the smooth, even side out towards the world. It was an art form as well as a skill.

A thumping sound reverberated about the surrounding hills and she looked upwards, wondering where it was coming from. The sky was spun grey wool and the air was still, in contrast to the night before. As she revelled in the silver light, she spotted it: the insect-like whirr of a helicopter glinting above her.

Guests winging their way to Hesta, no doubt, Anna thought, risking a grin now there was no one around. People coming to her restaurant. Such sightings in the village were scarce, but once in a while a rush of rotor blades and a blast of breeze would herald the arrival of high-fliers to Buttermere. She wondered which of the names on the reservations list travelled by private aircraft as she took a last few lungfuls of the Lake District afternoon, before slipping inside the back door to the kitchen, ready for a busy lunchtime shift, and forgetting all about it.

She was standing at Sally's sink, with the roar of the spray tap in her ears, when it happened. Normally she'd have been beside the pass, at the interface between front and back of house, so she'd have heard her Maître D the first time he spoke to her. But it was only when Ovie shouted her name above the kitchen cacophony for the third time that he managed to get her attention.

'What is it?' Anna turned round, saw his solemn expression, knew it was something serious, and steered him to the silence of the office.

'There's been a crash,' he began. 'A helicopter . . .'

'*What?*' Her eyes widened as his words whirled in her head like the spinning wings of the aircraft she'd seen earlier. 'The people on board – are they *okay*?'

But she didn't wait for his answer, had to find out for herself. She was propelled towards the back door, fuelled by disbelief and a need to know whether they were all right. *Her* customers, who, only an hour or so beforehand, had been seated at one of the restaurant's tables.

How had it happened?

The Lake District could often look like the backdrop to a film, but Anna didn't want to see a disaster movie. Not here in Buttermere.

She knew the people's names, which made it so much worse. Had checked the bookings before the pre-lunch staff briefing, seen Ovie's scribbled symbol, a capital H within a circle, the universal sign beside a table for three. He'd have let Will and Rose know in advance, of course, made a note to pay them for the inconvenience of guests landing on their ground. People who'd come here for a memorable time and had got what they'd hoped for in the most terrible way. A whole *family*.

Please let them be okay.

She scanned the field next to Hesta. There was no sign of anything, only a vast expanse of green, but the ruined stone wall where she'd seen Jackson working away that morning now seemed like an omen of the wreckage to come.

Her stomach swirled like she'd been thrust into a turbulent sky as she made her way closer to the farm.

She heard a siren sound in the distance, the urgent wail of emergency resounding around the valley as it grew closer.

She reached the track leading up to Fell View, and there it was. In a grassy pasture just beyond the farm buildings. An ugly mangle of metal, no longer an enviable emblem of wealth and luxury.

The helicopter was now a lump of crumpled debris.

Anna stood still, shocked by the speed with which a dream-seeming day could disintegrate into a nightmare. Life could switch so suddenly. In an instant.

Anna looked back over her shoulder. The site of the crash was only a few hundred metres from the patch of turf that formed a rural landing pad beside the front door of the restaurant. The aircraft must have started its return journey, only to fail in flight. It hadn't got far. How high had it been? Were the passengers . . .?

She swallowed, unable to help imagining the scenario, yet struggling to contemplate the horror of it all.

An ambulance swung up the road, coming to a stop at the scene, semi-obscuring her view.

A second set of flashing blue lights followed the first, a police car this time, which careered past her up the rough driveway.

As Anna entered the yard, she saw Rose and Jackson walking towards her, away from the shiny man-made shell that hovered between helicopter and coffin, leaving the experts to do their work.

Their fire-ash faces stared at her.

'What happened?' Anna asked. She pointed in the direction of the reflecting lights and ricocheting shouts.

Rose blinked back at her. 'I heard the noise, like a really loud thudding, when I was in the barn. It seemed too close, I could tell something was wrong, and when I came out I saw it come down . . .' She peered behind her as though she still couldn't believe the scenario that was unfolding, then looked back at Jackson, as though now they were bound together by that moment.

'I was so worried . . . for a second I thought it was going to hit you in there.' His eyes were wishing wells, full of thankful tears. 'Thank god it didn't.' He blew out a breath of relief.

'Yes, thank goodness,' murmured Anna. Grief had flowed through her body like blood, she knew the feeling better than any other, but her heart flinched at the idea of Will losing Rose. Her chest squeezed as she thought of the child and its parents who'd boarded the helicopter that morning and flown to Hesta in a billow of anticipation.

'They'd been to the restaurant . . .' said Anna, trying to explain why she was there. 'Do you know if . . . are they . . .?' She trailed off.

'I don't know,' said Jackson.

'It just plummeted down,' said Rose, one hand raised to indicate the aircraft's trajectory. 'D'you think it'll be . . .'

The word 'fatal' hung like fog.

It was a moment before anyone spoke, could see a way to continue through the murk of uncertainty.

Then a flurry of activity, medics and uniformed officers in a hurry.

Anna craned her neck, caught a glimpse of the ambulance doors being flung open. But she quickly averted her gaze, unwilling to be a spectator, aware she would have hated someone witnessing her worst-ever minutes.

Rose put a hand on Jackson's arm; he seemed even more shaken than she was, thought Anna, perhaps as he'd seen the event unravel in real time.

'He was the first one to reach them,' Rose explained, glancing up at him as she spoke. 'He called 999. I was in too much of a state.' She shook her head, as though admonishing herself. 'Thank god you acted quickly.'

But Jackson wasn't looking back at her, his eyes were now puddles in a flood. His cheeks glistened with tears and he rubbed at his skin fiercely with soil-stained fingers.

Anna turned away; she wouldn't have wanted people watching her cry.

Rose wrapped him up in a hug, a spontaneous show of empathy, before swiftly stepping back, as though realising their bond was only based on being in the same place at the same time.

'I'd better get back,' said Anna.

Jackson mumbled something inaudible over the howling sound of the ambulance siren starting up again.

'Sorry?' Anna waited for him to repeat whatever he'd said.

Rose twisted away to acknowledge an approaching police officer.

Anna gave Jackson a small smile, but he was glaring back at her, the damp sadness all but disappeared. 'Good riddance, that's what I said.'

A stab of surprise made her stomach clench.

'They wouldn't have been here if it wasn't for you.' He fixed Anna with a furious stare.

'Jackson!' Rose reprimanded him; her attention returned to the two of them as the policewoman retreated.

'It's true,' said Jackson, with a tilt of his chin.

'It's not her fault,' said Rose, folding her arms. 'They want to speak to both of *us*, actually,' she added. 'We were the ones who were there when it happened.'

'I'll leave you to it,' said Anna, raising a hand, as though in half-surrender.

'Bye,' replied Jackson, in a tone that was just and so on the right side of polite.

Rose frowned at him. 'She's not to blame, okay?'

The worms-squirming sensation in Anna's abdomen eased a little as Rose defended her.

Jackson gave a humourless laugh. 'Why are these people here?' He spread his hands wide towards Anna, demonstrating that she was the answer.

'What she does is incredible.' Rose pointed a forefinger in Anna's direction. 'No wonder they come from all over. And Buttermere would be a *very* different place if Hesta didn't exist.'

Jackson drew himself up to his full height, as though he was an inflatable that Rose was pumping up with each breath she took.

But Rose continued before he could open his mouth. '*We* wouldn't survive for a start, without selling to Anna and being able to say we supply the best restaurant in the Lakes. Plus, I'm in the middle of trying to set up an ice-cream business – you know that, Jackson – and we need customers for that to work.'

Rose's last words rolled round Anna's head. So, she was carrying on with the venture . . .

'Just think of all the visitors Hesta brings in,' Rose continued.

But her words seemed to have made him balloon-like, ready to pop.

'I'd rather not. We can do without them trampling around the fields, looking at us like we're part of a country show, here for their entertainment,' Jackson said. 'We've got enough work on without dealing with folk like that. A farm isn't all fluffy animals and frolicking about. This lot isn't just here for a cute photo—'

Anna raised both hands this time. 'Look, I'm sorry for coming over. I just wanted to make sure—'

'You hadn't lost a couple of rich customers and their spoiled kid,' Jackson cut in. 'They'll be fine. Time they came back down to earth, anyway.'

'Jackson!' Rose's eyes were wide.

He fell silent, as though he'd shocked himself. 'They're meant to be coming to a sustainable restaurant,' he spat. 'Yet they *fly* here!'

'How people travel about is on them and no one else,' Rose said, gesturing in the direction of Hesta. 'If they want to come by helicopter, that's their issue.'

'*She*'s the root of the problem,' said Jackson. He nodded at Anna. 'With your fancy foams and froths and finicky bits of food.'

'You should write reviews.' Anna raised her eyebrows.

His face flamed. 'I've had enough stupid questions and silly comments from people coming to your place to last me a lifetime. I'm not below them because I'm a farm labourer and I'm not in finance or something flashy like they are.'

Anna's shoulders sank. 'I know that. I'm not your enemy, Jackson,' she said gently. 'I know you think I am for some reason, but I'm on your side. Buttermere is my home too. I've always tried to do what's best—'

'Can we stop this now, please?' interrupted Rose. 'I don't know about you both, but I've got a lot to do today once we've dealt with all this.'

'Absolutely.' Anna bowed her head. 'Let me know any news,' she added in a low voice, with a last glance over at the rumpled hull of the helicopter.

'I will,' replied Rose. She turned to Jackson, but he was already marching off in the direction of a uniformed officer to give his statement.

6

'There you go.'

Anna's dad handed her a cup of tea, in the mug she always chose whenever she was there, with the frieze of wild strawberries. Her mum had bought it for him, a token to mark their china wedding anniversary when they'd been married for twenty years, and Anna had taken to using it whenever she was at her dad's house, as though it could somehow turn tea for two into three.

'Thanks.' She clasped the warm drink as though it was winter, and a sigh slipped through her lips when she smiled at him in thanks as he slid a plate of shortbread biscuits onto the coffee table, sugar-dusted oblongs with dimples like dominoes. 'What a day.'

'Gosh, it was awful about that helicopter . . .' said her dad from over by the fireplace.

Anna nodded. She'd spent the remainder of service making sure everyone else was okay, reassuring her staff and the rest of the diners, but afterwards she'd needed the comfort of her childhood home. She reached for a biscuit, telling herself sugar helped cure shock.

She tucked her feet up beneath her on the sofa and settled back against the cushions. She was a little girl again when she stepped inside this house, a daughter, Robert and Marion's child, and her stresses and responsibilities seemed to be hung up at the door along with her jacket, temporarily suspended, waiting for her to pick them back up when she left. She watched her dad fiddle with the fire, the amber flames that flickered in the grate illuminating the years that had crinkled his face. Everything else in the room was still the same; it was as though time might be rewound if they only tried hard enough, kept the smallest details identical to before, continued the rituals they'd always shared when there was one family member more.

A monsoon of memories rained down on her each time she came, even now. She looked around, at the damson-coloured curtains and undisturbed rows of books, and felt as though she was drifting through the past on an upholstered life raft. Her dad stayed kneeling by the hearth for a moment, as though in prayer, the old, cold cottage yearning for a lit log burner even on an early June night like this, as though it didn't have the heart to be cosy without Marion. The warmth had left the walls once she'd gone.

Robert scrambled upright and sat down in an armchair opposite Anna. He was motionless for a minute, afloat in the silver-grey ocean of carpet her mum had chosen, as though afraid to move in case he should sink.

'You okay, Dad?' asked Anna, proffering the plate of biscuits. He reached out and took one.

'I think I need to do something, Anna,' he said as he bit into it.

The crumbs of shortbread felt like sand in her mouth at the crack in his voice. 'What do you mean?'

'I'm just . . .' he flailed a hand, like a drowning man.

She took a sip of tea, choked as it scalded her throat.

'Just what?' she asked with a cough. She set her mug down on the coffee-table island between them.

'You know, coasting along.' His hand flopped down, dangled off the arm of the chair. 'I bob about, here and there, but . . .' He flapped his fingers like he was trying to steer a boat without an oar.

Her eyes filled like sea water rising up a pair of portholes. Her dad was rudderless, marooned without her mum. It had been a long time now, but it didn't get easier, Anna knew that. He did his best to keep busy, but without the routine of work, his emptiness seemed to have escalated. She pushed herself off the sofa, stretched her arms out to hug her dad. Life spread round the gaping hole a loved one left behind, but the gap was always there. Grief was a whirlpool, waiting to suck you down at the most unexpected moment.

Robert gripped his daughter tightly. 'Being retired is worse somehow,' he said into her hair. 'More time to think . . .'

Anna nodded, breathed in her dad's aftershave before she let go again. 'Is there something you've got in mind?' she asked, back on the sofa now, clutching a scatter cushion to her chest with both arms.

'I don't know yet.' He shook his head.

She wondered what he'd been thinking about. Travelling? Moving to a different house?

Her stomach churned like she'd been hit by a wave of seasickness.

'Anyway, I'm fine,' he said, the most-told lie, his parental instinct to protect his daughter from the harsh truth kicking in. He slapped his knees. 'Tell me something good. What else has been happening with you?'

Anna searched for something more cheerful to say but the image of the helicopter crash was still circling in her head.

'Fell View Farm are going to start doing ice cream.'

'Ooh.' A hint of a smile. For a second, his seventy-five years melted to single digits and he was young again. 'Well, that's exciting.'

'They haven't properly announced it yet,' she said, adding a sprinkle of secrecy to make him feel special. 'So don't tell anyone.'

Her dad opened his mouth, then closed it again. His unspoken sentence swilled round the room: *Who am I going to tell?*

The absence of her own mum made Anna think of Rose – it was worse for her: her mother wasn't dead.

'I've offered to help with it,' Anna continued, letting his unsaid words drain away. 'Rose is in charge and it's clear she could do with a hand.'

'That's nice.' Fatherly pride made Robert's eyes wide. 'In what capacity?'

'Milking the cows.'

Anna let his ripple of laughter wash over her, cherishing the sound.

'Only joking.' She reached for a second biscuit. 'I'm the Official Ice Cream Taster,' she declared.

A wave of chuckling from her dad. 'I want that role.'

'It's already taken, sorry,' said Anna, mid-chew. She turned to grin at her dad but he'd sunk into silence once more.

'It's okay, you can have the job,' she said.

He gave a smile, but she could tell it was only on the surface.

Anna carried on. 'I've actually said I'll help with flavour development,' she said. 'That's if Rose wants me to. And Will allows it.'

'That's a great idea. No one could be better in that department.' He nodded at her.

Anna tipped her head to one side. 'Well, I'll do my best. I've got lots of things I think would be good to try out, and there's something really exciting about that.' She realised she was fizzing over with the anticipation of getting started. Being up at the farm earlier, and hearing Rose say she was going ahead with the plan, must have had that effect.

She leaned forwards. 'I'm hoping, if we use local ingredients and have really interesting combinations, that might just give Fell View an edge over the competition.'

'You're very good at working hard, Anna.' Her dad's forehead creased. 'But it's a lot on top of everything else . . . you don't want to go back to where you were before.'

They trod carefully through the silt of the past, doing their best not to dredge up too much.

'I'm not a business partner or anything, but I know plenty about foraging – I've already shown Rose a couple of things – but there's so much more out there, right outside their door, and all year round. It's the freshness of everything, the unique taste.'

'Ooh, what kinds of things are you thinking?'

Anna's face glowed with the heat of the fire and the enthusiasm that burned inside her. Foraging was how her passion for cooking had begun; the focus was on the Lake District landscape that she loved. The place that had rescued her.

'Bilberry pie ice cream.'

'That sounds delicious.'

'Blackberry and crab apple.' She clapped her hands together.

'Wowee.' A glimmer of delight in Robert's gaze. 'They talk a lot about vegan options now. But you'll have thought about that.'

'How does wild mint sorbet sound?'

'Amazing.'

'Or honeysuckle.'

'Really?'

Anna nodded. 'It's delicious – very delicate – and you only need a few of the flowers. Oh, and meadowsweet sorbet – has a scent similar to almond.'

'You've thought of everything.'

'Not quite. That's just the beginning. It'll all change with the seasons . . .'

'When will it open?'

'I'll have to ask Rose.'

They were thrust back from the oasis of their imaginations into her dad's living room.

'Let me know,' said her dad. 'And if you hear any more news about the people in the helicopter . . .' he added, as though their bump back to reality had reminded him.

Anna nodded. 'Of course.' There was something more she wanted to say, that feeling of being a kid again making her want to spill out her worries to her dad. But he had enough to deal with. 'Right, I'd better get going . . .' She stood up.

Robert rose too, with the ease of someone much younger.

'Bye, Dad.' Anna hugged him, gripping him tightly as though they were about to be winched from the scene in a sea rescue.

'You're not responsible for what happened today,' said Robert.

50

Anna pulled back. Her thoughts had travelled across to him without her permission, invisible stowaways.

'That's not what everyone thinks,' she said, remembering how Jackson's rage had blazed like the wood burner beside them. 'They wouldn't have been in Buttermere if it wasn't for me. They were coming to my restaurant.'

'It was an accident. They could have been off anywhere.' Her dad took both her hands in his, transferred the words in his head with a gentle touch. *Sometimes it's no one's fault.*

'Oh my god, did you actually see it?' said Dani, the second Anna stepped over the threshold that evening.

'No.' Anna shook her head, read through the reservations again, trying to retain the information; she'd been through the list once before, but remembering what was important felt like wading through a flood, filtering the flotsam and jetsam.

'I couldn't believe it when I went home – I saw the farm all cordoned off, police tape everywhere . . .' Dani soaked up drama like sourdough dunked in soup.

'Not nice when they'd been here, though, is it?' said Anna, trying to reel her back in.

'Yeah, but, if I trip up on the way to the corner shop, it's not the village store's fault, is it?'

Anna looked up from the bookings sheet.

'Anyway, my cousin's in the police, and she's not really meant to say anything, but . . .'

If she was anything like Dani, she couldn't help herself, thought Anna.

'She was driving the patrol car when they got the call.'

'And?' Anna put down the reservations spreadsheet.

51

'She said they're going to be all right.'

'Oh my god.' Anna sighed.

'Shaken up but minor injuries.'

Anna slumped against the side of the workbench. Most of the time, Dani's serving of gossip was an amuse-bouche Anna could do without at the start of each shift, but tonight she couldn't have been more grateful.

'Oh, thank goodness.'

'She wouldn't tell me any more than that.' Dani wrinkled her nose like she'd been denied the final episode of a TV show. 'I mean, can you imagine the moment you realise it's coming down, falling out of the sky?'

Anna had felt something like it, a stomach-dropping sensation, but when her feet were still on the ground.

'Evening,' said Sally to the two of them as she slouched though the door looking like she'd been found in a hedgerow along with the elderflowers. Her creased clothes, scruffled-up hair and dark-circled eyes didn't paint a portrait of fine health.

'If you're not better, you honestly shouldn't be here,' said Anna as her KP shrugged off her jacket.

'No, I'm fine,' said Sally. 'Promise.' She gave a smile that wouldn't convince a stranger.

But Dani had bigger issues to discuss. 'Did you hear about what happened today?'

Sally grasped her jacket to her body. 'No, what?'

Anna watched her as Dani relished the chance to repeat the events up at the farm. Sally looked uncomfortable, like she was struggling to stay upright. A kitchen was no place to be when you were unwell, thought Anna. There was nothing worse than being blasted by heat, forced to stand when all you wanted to do was—

'Can I sit down for a second?' Sally said suddenly. 'I feel a bit lightheaded.' She stumbled into the staffroom.

Anna went after her and would have been followed by Dani if the saucepan containing the watercress velouté hadn't started to bubble over.

Sally doubled over on the back-room stool; her folded jacket clamped to her tummy like the fabric might transform into a hot-water bottle of comfort.

Anna crouched next to her. 'You can't be at work when you're in this state,' she said.

Sally hung her head.

'I appreciate that you wanted to be here, though. See how you're doing tomorrow.' Anna filled a glass of water for her. 'Everyone gets sick sometimes. But can you text *me* next time, not Dani, so I can get someone from an agency lined up to cover the shift? Otherwise, it makes it very difficult—'

'I'm sorry, I was hoping I'd be feeling all right by then.' Sally took a sip of her water.

'It's okay,' said Anna.

'You need some sugar,' declared Dani from the doorway. 'Have one of these.' She offered Sally a container of pine-needle-infused biscuits. 'Should help if you're feeling a bit fuzzy.'

The citrus scent of the fir trees from the far side of the lake wafted towards Anna. She closed her eyes, momentarily transported to the shore of Buttermere. The cookies were her invention; she'd shown Dani how to make them just like Dominik had explained the best way to harvest the evergreen fronds—

'Want one, boss?' asked Dani, with a rattle of the biscuit box.

Anna opened her eyes. The sweet, woodland aroma still fragranced the air but she shook her head to dispel the memory and stood up; she left her private life outside these four stone walls, reserved thinking of him for the sliver of spare time she spent away from Hesta, after the evening service, in the small hours when there was no one around to see her but the silver-faced moon.

'I'll have yours then,' said Dani with a shrug, putting a pine biscuit between her teeth before snapping the lid back on the box.

Anna turned back to Sally. 'Keep in touch, okay?'

Sally nodded, but it looked as though Dani's edible remedy might have made her feel worse rather than better.

'Is there someone who can come and get you?' asked Anna, hoping she wasn't going to have to offer to take Sally home, despite them already being a staff member down. Sally had mentioned her partner in passing – Steve, was it? – but Anna had enough to keep track of here at the restaurant, so she left general chit-chat to Dani. She wasn't at ease discussing the relationships of others when she had nothing to share in return.

'No, but I'll be fine – promise,' replied Sally. 'It's not far to get home.'

'Do you want me to run you over?' said Dani. 'So to speak.'

'No, definitely not,' said Sally, as she got to her feet, her words garnished with vehemence. 'I'm honestly all right now.'

'Well, let me know how you're doing,' said Anna. She glanced at Dani. 'We'd better get back to work,' she added, jerking her head towards the kitchen. *We've a lot to do*, was written on the wall along with the staff rota.

Sally winced like a pine needle was stuck in her throat. 'Sorry,' she murmured.

Anna exhaled. Tiptoeing around the emotions of others was an intricate dance she was still doing her best to master.

54

No sooner had Sally left, than Ovie appeared; his presence always signalled some sort of news. Anna searched his expression, took in his quick-blinking eyes and clamped-together lips, and braced herself for something bad, touching the wooden desk even though she'd never believed in good luck.

Dani's gaze swivelled between the two of them, and she stood unmoving as though her shoes had sprouted roots.

'Marcus Bradley is on table four.' Ovie's voice was hushed, his tone low.

'You're joking!' Dani screeched. She sped back into the kitchen as though her chef's clogs were skates.

Anna pressed her palms together; she tried to reply but nothing came out, possible responses getting stuck like they were trapped in a blocked piping bag.

'We literally found out when he walked through the door just now,' said Ovie, as though Anna had spoken.

'And you're sure?' asked Anna, finally forcing out a few whispered words. It wasn't that she doubted her Maître D, but this day was one she'd both anticipated and dreaded in equal parts.

Anyone else in the restaurant world might have taken the comment as an insult to their experience, but Ovie understood the gravity of the situation. 'Absolutely certain,' he said.

Anna swallowed. 'The booking would have been under another name . . .' Of course it would. It was a superfluous sentence – Ovie knew that was the case as well as she did. But saying it aloud was her way of attempting to emulsify the terror and excitement surging through her body. She ran through checklists in her mind. She was all too aware of the power one person and their pen had to make or break a restaurant. Depending on their opinion, a place like Hesta could be catapulted to the top or sent plunging from public favour. And no matter how many great write-ups she received, her position never felt any less precarious. It could only take one bad article to start the downturn. Anna knew how easily dreams could shatter.

They'd practised and trained and briefed the rest of the team for this precise scenario.

Time and time again.

But she and Ovie both knew that tonight's set-up was one they hadn't prepared for.

Ovie met her gaze. 'Sally's not in tonight.' A statement as obvious as Anna's had been. It was as though he had struggled to suppress what he really wanted to say, had chosen something safer, instead of screaming *What are we going to do?* like Anna wanted to, too.

Anna shook her head.

Ovie raised his eyebrows.

Dani skidded back into sight, framed by the door, her face bechamel pale. 'I can't believe this is happening,' she said. 'It's going to be a car crash without Sally.'

'Thanks for the vote of confidence,' said Anna, the helicopter wreckage flitting into her mind. She pursed her lips. 'Please can we *try* and remain positive, particularly around the rest of the team.' She jerked her chin towards the restaurant.

Dani vanished back into the kitchen, but Anna could hear her swear-word-peppered speech from the staffroom.

'Please tell me *you're* not going to pot wash on the most important—?'

Anna put her hands on her hips. 'What else do you suggest?' she said to Ovie. She glanced at the clock on the back wall. 'Service is about to start.' She paused, deciding not to say aloud again the name of one of the most famous food critics in the country; it was like lighting a flare and telling people not to panic. 'Guests are arriving. There's no time to sort a replacement. I can't take any other chef off their station. You know as well as I do the KP is crucial to the whole process.' She blew out a breath. 'There's no plate of good food without clean pots and pans.'

Ovie hung his head, as dismayed as if she'd just fired him.

Anna sighed. 'I thought you'd have a little more faith.'

Ovie looked up. 'This isn't a time for blind belief, Anna – I'm all for being optimistic, you know that – but I don't see how we can give our best performance without you at the pass.'

'I have to trust the guys out there to do their jobs.' Anna flung out a hand in the direction of the kitchen.

Dani came careering back into the room. 'Check on!' she called, holding aloft a slip of paper.

'Oh god, I wasn't there to take the order . . .' Ovie hurried back to oversee front of house.

Anna followed him, marching into the kitchen to begin service, conscious this shift could decide Hesta's fortunes for the next few weeks, months, or possibly years – everything she'd worked for, day in, day out, for decades, distilled into a newspaper column designed to entertain readers, not reflect the efforts of Hesta's staff.

Dani thrust the order slip at her.

Table four.

One scallops with sorrel pesto and one watercress velouté to start.

One lamb with wild mint and one pea and artichoke risotto with ramsons for the mains.

All different dishes, never a duplicate. Bradley would be purposefully tasting and testing across the whole menu, trying to see everything that Hesta had to offer.

Anna nodded at Dani. 'We do the same as we always do, okay? We cook our hearts out.' She paused; if Hesta was slated, she truly would feel like her insides had been served up for the newspaper readers' amusement. But it was her role to rally. She glanced up, raised her voice to address the rest of the team. 'We treat Marcus like any other diner. We do our best, as usual. We stay consistent. The meals that go to table four will be the same standard as for any other guest.'

'Yes, Chef!' chorused the faces before her, above the hiss of searing-hot butter and the burble of saucepans on the hob.

Anna opened the dishwasher and a billow of steam fogged her vision. *Focus*, she told herself as her mind drifted again to front of house, while her body worked away back here, balancing two jobs at once. She'd see-sawed constantly throughout service, swapping between being head chef, presiding over the pass as much as possible, and supporting the others by standing in as kitchen porter. As the vapour cleared, she could make out Ovie standing in front of her like an ominous apparition. She searched his expression for clues.

'Table four has just gone,' was all he said.

Anna stood upright, allowing a little of the tension to leave her shoulders. Marcus Bradley had left the building; there was nothing else that could be done now apart from wait.

Dani appeared beside them once the mist had dissipated, as though they'd conjured the Ghost of Gossip. 'So, what's he said to you, then?' she asked Ovie, neck outstretched as though she'd evolved to eavesdrop.

'Nothing, that's part of his *job*,' Ovie replied, emphasising his last word to indicate Dani should concentrate on hers.

She was undeterred. 'What, zero?' She frowned. 'Must have given away something, surely. He's a food writer, not an actor.'

Ovie shook his head. 'There's no point trying to guess.'

Anna was inclined to agree with him. Reviews were subjective. If she'd personally served Marcus the most inventive, flavour-packed menu she'd ever created, it still might not be to his taste. She'd been crushed by critics in the past, even before she had her own place. A negative article could leave scars that lingered like burn marks.

Not knowing when to expect the impact was the most painful part. Would it be in the paper that weekend? Or published in several Sundays' time, when the memory of tonight had faded slightly, making the shock cut a little bit deeper? The torturous interlude had now begun, and no one, probably not even Marcus, knew when the piece would be printed, shared across social media, and murmured around Buttermere and beyond. The stark black and white marks would be imprinted in Anna's head, as hard to remove as if they were written in permanent ink on her skin. Somehow the good reviews didn't sink in the same. Kind comments were much harder to keep in mind.

Later, when everyone but her had left, Anna went through to the main part of the restaurant, walked past the table where Marcus Bradley had weighed his words. The dining area looked out across the lake, which reflected the glow of the low building. She fixed her attention on the warm gold light, told herself that an upbeat attitude reaped rewards in the long run, but her gaze kept drifting to the dark patches of water, where it was impossible to tell what lay beneath, and, as she stood in front of the glass bifold doors, looking out at the blackness, a wave of doubt rocked her. The world didn't always work like that.

7

Anna counted the bowls on the stainless-steel shelf in front of her, and failed to squash a sigh when she saw that one was missing already. She dipped her head in mourning. It had only been a week. She'd commissioned them from a potter in Ambleside, specifically for the new menu. She studied the rest of the dishes on the shelf, each one an artwork in shades of Shimmering Lake. Her scowl slipped slightly as the glazed surfaces glinted under the ceiling lights and she was reminded of Buttermere glimmering on a warm day. She recalled the moment she'd taken them out of the box for the first time, peeling away the protective bubble wrap to reveal the blue and green colours of the pottery beneath. Every piece was different; the same way no two dawns were identical. She'd set them down one by one, examining them in reverential silence. They were even better than she'd imagined, the perfect vessel for the velouté.

'Hello?' came a voice from the back, jolting Anna from her thoughts.

Was that Rose? she wondered.

'In here,' Anna called with a glance at the door that led into the staffroom.

'Sorry, were you just about to go home?' Rose was barely visible behind a stack of plastic containers.

Anna wracked her brain: she hadn't ordered anything from the farm—

'The very first batch of Wild Rose Ice Cream!' announced Rose. 'Just made,' she added as she dumped the tower of tubs down on the worktop as though she was in her own kitchen at home.

Anna felt a ripple of something unfamiliar, an emotion she imagined might be similar to maternal pride.

'I haven't tasted it yet,' said Rose. 'I had to come and show you straight away,' she continued, face chef-pink like she belonged there beside the shiny metal cabinets.

The strange sensation swelled in Anna's stomach. She smiled, eager to see what was inside the containers. 'Go on then, tell me what we've got.'

Rose opened the first tub. 'Elderflower ice cream,' she declared with a grin.

Anna grinned back, pushing the memory of her unpleasant encounter with Will from her mind. At least Rose was making use of the flowers that grew in the lane. 'Sounds fabulous,' she said, reaching for spoons.

'Your idea,' declared Rose, and a rowan-berry bloom reddened Anna's cheeks as she reached up for two of the new ceramic bowls – the inaugural production run of Wild Rose Ice Cream deserved a bit of ceremony.

'They're beautiful,' breathed Rose, bending like she was looking at a row of paintings in an exhibition.

'Do you want to do the honours?' asked Anna, raising a spoon as if it was a pair of scissors poised to cut a red rope.

Rose nodded, standing up straight to soak in the moment. She scooped a delicate curl of glistening ice cream into each dish, then handed one to Anna.

The summer-sweet scent filled her nostrils, making her shoulders relax. She lifted her spoon to take a mouthful.

Rose was ice-sculpture still beside her, and Anna realised she was awaiting her opinion the same way she herself anticipated Marcus Bradley's review.

Anna wondered how best to describe it as the elderflower flavour burst across her tongue. *Zesty and fresh.* The consistency was perfect too. She'd be pleased if she'd made it herself, in fact. It was certainly fit to serve in the restaurant. An idea fizzed at the edge of her mind. She set the bowl back down.

'What's wrong?' asked Rose with a frown. She peered at the ice-cream swirl in Anna's dish. It was starting to melt now, like sun-softened snow.

Anna was over by an enormous silver chiller unit and Rose wondered whether she was about to pull out a professionally made version, like someone presenting 'one they made earlier' on a cookery programme.

But she came back with the sauce bottles Rose remembered from the last time she'd been here.

'Elderberry syrup,' said Anna, squeezing a double circle in the base of each of their bowls with a twirl of her wrist.

The garnet-coloured drizzle took the dish to the next level.

Rose laughed with delight. 'It looks like it could be on the menu here!'

She was digging in now, her ice cream streaked with pink like a blushing sky at sunset. 'That's amazing,' she said, mouth full.

Anna slid the bottle towards her. 'Take it. And the rosehip syrup too.'

Rose raised her eyebrows, still eating.

'We're not serving them at the moment. They're yours.'

Rose shook her head.

'Make use of them. Please.' Anna took a bite from her own bowl of ice cream. 'The balance is spot on. Not too sweet. Still subtle. Tastes like the Lake District in June.'

'Right, that description's going on the label,' said Rose.

Anna smiled.

Their dishes were empty.

'What's in the others?' she asked with a tilt of her head. She tried to think what else was in season.

'Oh, that's elderflower ice cream for you,' replied Rose. 'If you want it . . .' Her smile had faded, as though she was unsure what she'd been thinking, giving something she'd made to a world-class chef. 'You probably don't,' she muttered. 'It was meant to be a sort of thank you, but now it seems silly . . .' Rose wrinkled her nose.

'But this is the start of your business,' said Anna. '*You* keep it. Can't have an ice-cream shop without any ice cream!'

'Okay,' said Rose to the floor tiles.

Anna hesitated. 'But if you insist . . .' She reached for the boxes.

Rose's face lit up like a fellside in full sun.

'Dani'll definitely want to try it. She loves using foraged flavours in her desserts.' But there was someone else Anna thought might appreciate it even more. 'Let me know what other varieties you make.'

'I will,' replied Rose. 'Right, better get back.' She glanced at the clock.

'Me too,' said Anna. It had been a long shift.

And, as Rose drove back to Fell View Farm, and Anna closed up the restaurant, over in Manchester, Marcus Bradley was giving his write-up of Hesta a final read-through before he pressed 'send' to the newspaper. Satisfied with his work and picturing it in print on a double-page spread laid across a Sunday morning coffee table, he clicked to submit his article.

8

Sally had her hands cupped over her face like an oxygen mask. When she peeled her palms away, her skin was paler than when she'd collapsed onto a chair the night Anna had had to step in and be KP in her place. 'Please tell me you're winding me up,' Sally said, eyes huge beneath the kitchen spotlights.

Anna shook her head. She'd waited till Sally had been back at work for a few days, and seemingly in better strength, before she broke the news about their formidable visitor.

'I can't believe it.' Sally shook her head. 'I'm so sorry I wasn't there.'

'So were we,' said Dani, coming to stand beside her by the enormous commercial sink.

'You couldn't help it,' cut in Anna. 'We did our best in the circumstances.'

'Oh *god*,' wailed Sally, covering her face again. 'If he rips us to shreds, it'll all be my fault.'

'No, it won't,' said Anna before Dani could speak. She kept her voice calm, hoping she too would believe her own words if she said them with enough conviction. 'It wasn't ideal being one down, but I think we maintained our usual standards.'

To her dismay, this seemed to upset Sally more.

So you can manage fine without me? was written in crinkles on her forehead.

Anna put her hands on her hips. 'Look, it wasn't the night any of us would have chosen if it was up to us.' She drew in a breath. 'But some things are out of our control.' In life, it had taken her a long while to accept that fact, though knowing it to be true didn't make it any easier to come to terms with at times. 'Marcus Bradley's opinion is one of those things. All we can do is carry on being the best we can possibly be.'

Ovie appeared on the other side of the pass.

'Don't tell me, the King's booked in this afternoon?' called Dani drily.

'Nothing would surprise me anymore,' murmured Anna with a wry smile as she went over to speak to her Maître D, but Sally didn't laugh.

'At least I'd be here this time, if that really was the case,' she said, the forlorn furrows of her frown even more pronounced. 'I feel like I've let everyone down.'

'Hey, hey . . .' said Dani, leaning against the edge of the sink next to her. 'We just wished you were here, that's all,' she continued, in a gentler tone than she usually used in the kitchen. 'These things happen.'

'Thanks,' said Sally with a small smile, somewhat startled her colleague even had a low-volume setting.

'I'm going to make a coffee,' said Dani, standing upright. 'Do you want one?'

'Thanks, but I'm okay.' Sally blew out a breath.

'*Boss? Hot drink?*' Dani bellowed over to Anna, back to her booming self.

'What did I do with my water bottle?' Sally said to herself, looking around to check she hadn't accidentally put it down somewhere in the kitchen. Her mouth was dry and she felt too warm all of a sudden. She went back into the staffroom to search for it.

Dani stuck her head round the door. 'Sure you don't want anything, Sal? Ovie's offered to make us one from the proper machine out the front—'

Then she caught sight of Sally, and shock stole her speech.

The secret screamed so loudly it was hard to believe the room was silent.

Anna tilted her head skywards as she waited for her dad to answer the door. The air was still, as though Buttermere was holding its breath, hoping that the glorious weather would continue. This afternoon was postcard perfect. Lambswool wisps of cloud slowly slid across a vast canopy of blue.

'Anna, hi.' His eyes no longer smiled when his mouth did.

She stepped forward to give him a hug, squeezed him tight to make him feel her love. Sadness hung like aftershave in the air, invisible but there, and his shoulders were hunched like he was permanently braced for bad news.

'How was work?' he asked as he led the way down the hall.

Anna saw her face in the wall mirror as she passed, wondered whether, now she was older, she resembled her mother more and it was too much for him to bear.

'It was okay, thanks,' she said, following him into the kitchen. 'Fairly smooth. Forty in for lunch. Still waiting on that review from the critic that came in a couple of weeks ago.'

She felt as though they were talking to each other on opposite sides of a pane of glass sometimes; like he had to

68

try extra hard to listen, and she had to make more effort to be heard.

She held up the canvas bag she was carrying, changing the subject. 'Homemade ice cream from Fell View Farm.'

'Oh, very nice.' He was reading a script, now, for someone playing a character who was completely fine. But acting wasn't his talent.

Anna tried a different tactic. 'Have you heard from Matthew recently?'

If Anna was the night sky, seen with predictable regularity, her brother was a shooting star, glimpsed rarely, with little warning, yet never failing to spark an expression of wonder on their father's face.

'Yes, he rang!' A twinkle in Robert's eye as he stirred the tea, reliving the memory. 'Only a short conversation . . .'

Brief, like a meteor sighting, thought Anna.

'But he seemed really well.' Robert beamed.

Anna knew with complete certainty her dad loved them equally, was proud of them both, no matter what, but there was something about the fact that Matthew had fulfilled his father's unpursued dream that bonded them together in a different way. Everyone always said Anna was her mother's daughter when she was growing up, and sometimes she wondered if she reminded her dad too much of her mum. Robert looked as though he was about to say something else, but he carried on making the tea instead. 'The helicopter incident made it into the Manchester Evening News.'

Anna took the mug he handed her. 'Did it?'

Robert nodded. 'Matthew said he was going to ring you . . . It's difficult when you're on such different schedules, isn't it.'

That was the accepted reason, the line the three of them repeated to each other to make it true.

'Passengers survived, didn't they, but it was a hell of a close call, apparently.'

Anna cupped the mug with both hands to counteract the chill that crept over her. She didn't want to think about the crash. It could have been so different. Deadly. Her throat constricted as she took a sip of her drink and she spluttered. In a way, anyone coming to Hesta formed a connection with her. They'd decided to visit because they'd liked the sound of her menu, or heard about her reputation as a chef, or admired the philosophy behind her food. Perhaps all three. Eating at her establishment meant a link had been made. After all, relationships were forever being forged around dining tables, whether in a restaurant or at home.

'Still looking into the cause, it said.'

Anna's stomach dropped like she was sitting in a simulator, experiencing the scenario for herself.

'Life can change in a split-second.' Robert shook his head. All conversations led back to Marion in the end.

'Fancy some ice cream?' asked Anna, more for a change of topic than because she really felt like any. 'Elderflower flavour.'

It was when they were settled outside on the bench in the back garden, that her dad dissolved like his uneaten ice cream.

'What is it, Dad?' she whispered, though she knew the answer, just not the solution.

His gaze was on the gravel pathway that led down to Marion's herb garden.

'I don't know what to do with myself.' His head drooped like a plant without water. 'Retirement was something your mum and I talked about like it was a film we'd one day go and see together.' His lips twisted. 'I never imagined I'd be here on my own, and for so long.'

Anna looked at the now-liquid ice cream in her dad's dish, so different from what it had been before. She didn't know what to say, felt the barrier between them on the bench. She put a hand on his arm, to breach it.

Sometimes she wished Matthew was there to share the task of filling the gap their mum had left. But Anna couldn't blame him for not being here now, when it was her who hadn't been around when Marion was alive.

9

Anna was looking for chanterelle mushrooms in the woodland beside the lake when Dani rang. It was mid-July, though you wouldn't know it from the way the wind teased the trees, tugging at their leaves and making their branches tremble, as though taunting them for thinking it was summer. Anna crouched when she saw a cluster of egg-yolk-coloured funnel-shapes beneath one of the trunks, and smiled when she breathed in the faint apricot smell. *True chanterelles.* Sometimes it could be hard to tell the difference, the false kind were such good imposters, even for an experienced collector like herself. But the feeling of alighting on a patch of real chanterelles – especially her first ones of the season – was hard to beat. One of the best-flavoured wild mushrooms to be found, they were Anna's favourite for the fact their little yellow trumpets seemed to cheerfully declare that there were little pockets of brightness to be found in every day if you only looked hard enough.

She was picturing them pan-fried in butter, imagining their fruity, peppery taste, the perfect accompaniment to sole—

The sound of her mobile ringing made her jump, it seemed such a contrast to the serene surroundings of the lake shore.

'Have you seen it?' Dani asked, dispensing with any form of greeting in her urgency.

'Seen what?'

Oh god. Sunday morning. She'd almost forgotten, it had been that long ago – it was strange how time could carve a concern so all-consuming into only an occasional thought – but now the moment of judgement was here, her shoulders tensed at the sudden weight of anticipation as to what Dani was about to say.

'So you haven't read it? I mean, bloooody hell!'

Was that good or bad?

'Big double-page spread – impossible to miss it.'

'Do you want to tell me what it says—'

'I can read it out, if you want? Got it here in front of me. Big picture of you – the one with your arms folded, from a while back, when you're looking a bit younger—'

'I'm not bothered about the photo, Dan. Can you just give me the gist of the *words*.'

'So, you don't want the whole thing, then?'

'You know what, can you just send it to me?'

'Okay, will do. Doing it now.'

Her phone bleeped, but she didn't have the chance to open the message before Ovie called too. He hardly ever rang her: it had to be about Marcus Bradley's review. Did that mean it was bad? She'd be seeing Ovie soon enough when she got into work—

'Fully booked for the rest of the year!' he said with a whoop, his smile so big it was making itself heard on the phone.

'Seriously?'

'Yes, no space left – except for the locals' table, of course.'

'That's brilliant!'

A third call was coming through to Anna's phone. She took her ear away from the screen to check the name, but it was an unknown number she didn't recognise.

'Sorry, Ovie, someone else is ringing me . . .'

'Okay. See you in a bit – to celebrate!'

Yes, thought Anna as she clicked to answer the unidentified call, she definitely owed the team a thank-you. A glass of something sparkly to mark their hard work. Sally would be so relieved—

'Is that Anna Carleton?'

'Speaking.'

'This is Flick from Grinfluence.'

Grim what? 'Sorry?' Anna didn't understand any part of the sentence that had just been spoken. Flick talked with the speed of someone who was already irritated at having to make a phone call in the first place.

'Felicity Townsend, here, from Grinfluence Agency. I sent you an email . . .'

Maybe the business name looked better in writing, but it really didn't work on the phone—

'. . . but I thought calling was quicker.'

Flick clearly didn't even have time to use her full name.

Anna rested her back against a tree trunk, seeking something solid in the madness of the modern world.

'We've got an exciting proposal for you!' Insincerity made her voice a squeal.

Anna winced. 'Oh, thank you, but we're—'

Flick cut her off, her determination barely concealed by her sing-song tone. 'The chance of a brand partnership with

Olivia Lawson.' She enunciated her client's name so Anna knew she was meant to have heard of her.

'Sorry, who?'

'The influencer.'

'Right.'

'She'd like to come to your restaurant!'

'We'll be delighted to welcome her to the Lakes. I do just need to say that we're currently full until—'

'Perrrfect!' interrupted Flick, elongating the vowel as she exhaled, satisfied she was getting somewhere. 'So, in return for dinner, drinks et cetera, she'll post about her visit on all her social media channels.'

'We don't really—'

'She'll be coming next Friday night, around seven, unless her event in the afternoon overruns or the traffic from Manchester is *terrible*' – she gave a brittle little laugh that was meant to bond them, as if they were friends discussing their commute – 'So if you could reserve the table for the whole evening . . .'

It wasn't a question: according to Flick it was happening.

'We're completely full, I'm afraid,' said Anna. 'Every table is taken for the next six months. We've been—'

'This is for *Olivia Lawson*,' said Flick, all camaraderie evaporated like steam from the jaws of an open oven.

'Thank you for thinking of us—'

'It's an a-ma-zing opportunity for you to boost your profile and build a much bigger platform for . . .' – a pause while she clearly checked the notes on her laptop – '*Hesta*,' Felicity said, like she was wrinkling her nose while she spoke.

Well, Anna wasn't impressed by *Grimfluenza* either. 'As I said, thank you for the offer but—'

'Olivia has four hundred thousand followers!'

'That's lovely for her.'

'Her endorsement can make *all* the difference!'

With hindsight, maybe Anna ought to have given Flick's statement more consideration, but it would soon be lunchtime, and she had to get back to the restaurant.

'I'm sure it can, I honestly am, but I've really got to go, otherwise there'll be nothing for guests to actually eat, which is our main concern as a restaurant.'

'Think about it – imagine if Hesta went *viral*!'

Anna grimaced; that really didn't sound appealing in the context of food . . .

'Thanks again. Bye.'

Anna clung to her basket of joyful-looking chanterelles as she made her way back to the village, as though by grasping onto nature she could wipe away her interaction with the artificial Flick.

It was only when she arrived at work that she learned her new acquaintance had already tried her pitch on Ovie.

'A lady called *Click* or something rang to speak to you,' he informed Anna as she went through to the front of the restaurant to see the fully booked reservations system for herself. 'Let me see . . . I wrote it all down.'

'Yes, she got my mobile number somehow.'

Ovie looked appalled, like a goalkeeper who'd failed a save. 'I'm *so* sorry. One of the more junior staff might have given it to her when I was away from the—'

'Don't worry,' said Anna, noticing he had the newspaper open on the front desk. The pages with Marcus Bradley's review stared up at her.

She flinched at her picture. The photo was from when she was head chef in London all those years ago. Arms crossed.

Face stern. Heart unbroken. She hadn't agreed to pose for a head shot since, so they'd had no choice but to use it. She always said she wanted the food to be the star, not her.

'You haven't read it yet?' Ovie pulled her back to the present. The expression of pride in his eyes made her chest squeeze as he handed her the article.

'A REAL FIND' declared the headline.
Hidden in the heart of the Lake District is Hesta, run by Cumbrian chef Anna Carleton.

The ink blurred, and Anna blinked furiously at her own unexpected emotion. That description meant more than any award. Buttermere was where she belonged and Hesta was her home. The staff had become an extended family.

She looked up. Ovie was immersed in reading the column all over again. There was a buzz about the restaurant, the collective kind, the type felt at midnight on New Year's Eve, where everyone was united in good spirits and possibility fizzed about the walls of the place.

She carried on reading.

It was, in short, the greatest, tastiest show on Earth . . . Tables face the sensational view of Buttermere, a reminder for the diner that nature is the focus here . . . Carleton takes familiar fruits and vegetables and turns them into something spectacular . . . I think my hunt for the best restaurant in the UK is finally complete.

Anna felt a hand on her shoulder.
'Well done,' said Ovie.

The words seemed to echo in time with her heartbeat. No one ever said that. Maybe they assumed they didn't need to anymore. But Ovie never guessed at anything.

'Thanks for being with me on this journey,' she said.

His eyes shone in the light from the window.

Ovie had been more of a brother to her than Matthew, in many ways, but Anna understood why. Matthew had done what he could to carry on.

A car horn blared outside, breaking Anna from her thoughts. She saw Will on his tractor through the glass, raised her hand to wave, but he was glaring at the driver of the vehicle in front. 'You can't park there!' she heard him shout.

'I'll go out and help,' said Ovie, diplomatically, disappearing out of the door with the speed of an expert bomb diffuser.

In the briefing before service, Anna thanked the entire team because, just as each brick made up the building they were standing in, each person present played their part in making each customer's experience special.

'Is it true we're getting champagne at the end of our shift tonight?' asked Dani beside her.

'A glass not a bottle,' clarified Anna as they made their way back to the kitchen.

'Not for you, though, Sal,' Dani said, then shut her mouth as if she'd shocked herself.

Anna turned to look at her KP.

'I guess I wasn't there that night, so . . . that's only fair,' Sally muttered, her eyes swivelling from Dani back to her boss.

Then Ovie appeared at the pass.

'Don't tell me,' called Dani, 'Beyoncé's booked in for lunch?'

But there was no trace of a smile on Ovie's face. 'Will wants to speak to you,' he said to Anna. 'And he won't take no for an answer.'

As soon as Anna left, Sally turned to Dani. 'Don't say anything,' she hissed. 'Please.'

'All right, all right,' Dani replied, checking to make sure her rye bread mixture had risen. 'That was a genuine mistake, I didn't mean to—'

'I need this job, Dan,' whispered Sally, eyes wide. 'You've no idea how much.'

Anna came back through the double swing doors.

'What did he have to say, then?' asked Dani, dusting the surface of the rye loaf with flour.

'Blaming me for the village being busy.' Anna started cleaning the chanterelles, the gentleness of the process forcing her to calm down. 'Doesn't seem to understand that you need *people* to buy *ice cream.*'

'Hope you told him that,' said Dani, scoring the top of the bread as though it was responsible for the comment rather than Will.

Sally took the bowl that Dani had just tipped the rye dough from and carried it over to the sink, trying to tear her gaze away from the rounded mound of uncooked bread that now sat on the side, swollen to double its original size and about to face the fiery heat of the oven beside them.

'Ooh yeah, it's the real stuff,' said Dani, having grabbed an open bottle from an ice bucket and yanked it out by the neck to check. 'You taught me the importance of quality control, boss,' she said to Anna, who shot her a sideways glance.

'Where's Sally?' Anna asked Dani, who was already taking a swig of her drink before the toast had even been raised.

'Gone home. Said she was shattered and she'd slip out the back.' Dani sighed. 'God, that's good,' she added, taking another gulp. 'Does that mean I can have hers?'

Anna rolled her eyes, then noticed Ovie giving her a nod to signal everyone had a glass of bubbles in their hand.

Anna cleared her throat. She wondered where to start, probably should have thought about her speech before now, but the evening service had been hectic and the main thrust of gathering everyone together was really to say a simple thank you . . .

A sea of silent smiles stared back at her.

She'd never been particularly comfortable with public speaking, but it was important to celebrate these moments with her staff. She should have tried harder to make people feel valued in the past . . .

She squashed the thought. She was here in the present, and her team were waiting for her to talk.

There was an anticipatory quiet about the restaurant, like a surprise party about to erupt. She desperately wanted Hesta to be a happy place. Guests often came to celebrate, mark special occasions, but she wanted the staff to come to work and enjoy what they did too. She looked over at Ovie, urging her on with a tilt of his glass, and felt a swell of gratitude that he'd been here for so long, come from London to join her on this journey. Then Dani, busy downing her wine, but as dedicated and hardworking as anyone Anna had ever met.

Anna opened her mouth to speak – just as the still-room window to the side of her splintered into a thousand shards.

10

A cocktail of expletives came out of Dani's mouth as a jagged stone smashed onto the floor of the restaurant. Shrieks of shock reverberated around the walls. Faces were frozen with fright.

'It's all right,' Anna said, holding up her arms as though she could physically quell panic.

'You don't sound convinced, boss,' mumbled Dani, her voice muffled by her fingers.

Anna's heart thumped as she saw Ovie slip out of the front door to search for the culprit.

A vibration of nervous confusion had replaced the congratulatory mood of only a few minutes earlier.

Ovie returned. 'There's no sign of anyone in the lane.'

'I think if they'd wanted to say hello they'd have used the front door,' muttered Dani.

'Probably just kids getting up to mischief,' said Anna loudly, so everyone could hear. But it was never as easy to create calm as it was to destroy it.

She'd always thought of Hesta as a haven, but perhaps to others it symbolised something else. *Who would do such a thing?*

'I used to get up to all sorts of stuff when I was a teenager, but I'd never have done anything like this . . .' Dani murmured.

'I'll call the police,' said Ovie.

Anna nodded. 'Thank you.'

The other staff began to slip out now, keen to make their way home all of a sudden.

Anna surveyed the debris with a shake of her head. 'God, what a mess.' She saw the sky purpling outside the window, like it too was bruised. She felt wounded; an attack on Hesta was an assault on her and everything she'd worked for. She turned to look at the huge slab of rock that lay on the cracked cream floor tiles. The craggy stone seemed such a stark contrast to the carefully curated surroundings of Hesta's interior. She squatted down, leaned so close to the soil-caked surface she could smell the damp earth, and suddenly she understood. This wasn't the hijinks of village kids at all. It was a missile made from nature. A rock grenade. Someone was sending her a message. *But why?*

'Are you okay? Is *everyone* okay?' asked Rose the next morning, dropping the crate of butter and milk she was delivering down on the worktop with a bang. Anna was reminded of the night-splitting sound of the stone exploding through the window in a firework of glass shards.

'We're all fine,' replied Anna, voice hoarse from lack of sleep. Her brain felt like it had been in Rose's ice-cream maker, her thoughts tumbling round nonstop. 'No one was hurt.' Except for her.

'Phew.' Rose's frown faded. 'Do you know who did it?'

Anna shook her head. 'I thought it might be kids pranking about. Start of the school holidays—'

'My cousin says there've been other incidents like it.' Dani came over to pluck some butter from the crate. 'In other parts of the country, though. High-profile restaurants targeted by activists.'

'Really?' Fear had furrowed Rose's brow again.

Anna put a hand to her chest, as though she'd just been punched. Was that what had happened?

'Suppose Hesta is the most famous place in the Lakes.' Rose turned to face Anna, but she couldn't smile at the compliment. Blood pounded in her ears.

'The better-known the restaurant, the more press coverage, I guess,' added Dani.

'But what have they got against here?' Rose's palms were upturned like she wanted a written explanation from those responsible.

Anna was touched by her outrage.

'Well, even your dad says it's *hoity-toity* . . .' Dani leaned against the countertop, taking the opportunity for a break seeing as no one else was doing any work. 'So clearly not everyone is a fan.'

'But he knows how many people depend on Hesta,' murmured Rose.

Dani tilted her chin to indicate the crate of dairy produce from Fell View and folded her arms pointedly.

'I'm sorry,' said Rose, glancing from her to Anna. 'He's just stressed and worried—'

'And angry that the lanes get clogged with people coming to visit Hesta, when you're actually going to need all those customers to buy your ice cream.' Dani pursed her lips.

'All right, Dan,' said Anna, raising a hand like she was reaching to turn down the heat of a hob. 'Do you want to unload the rest of the—'

'I'm just saying, if that's how *he* feels, imagine how other people who don't really have a clue about what we do can get worked up.' Dani reluctantly began to unpack the containers of milk. 'Doesn't matter whether or not we're the real root of the issue, they need something to vent their frustrations on.'

Anna flinched like she'd touched a scalding pan. She understood how easy it was to channel energy in the wrong direction. She'd done that herself in the past.

'Look, we don't know who it was,' she said. 'Could be a group of environmentalists making a stand, but—'

'We're the greenest restaurant there is, so they need to get their facts straight!' Dani slammed the door of the fridge in a retaliative protest of her own.

'The most important thing is to stay true to what we do,' said Anna, her hands on her hips. 'And not give in to bullying.'

'Too right, boss,' said Dani with a nod.

'Anyway, how are things with you?' Anna said to Rose, changing the subject in the hope that Dani would cool down. 'How's Wild Rose coming along?'

Dani turned back to her section, having subsided like choux pastry that had expended all its steam.

Rose blew out her cheeks. 'I wanted to try and get open before summer's over but there's so much to do.' She picked up the empty crate. 'Hopefully by September so we can catch the end of the season.'

'Well, let me know if I can help with anything.' Anna smiled but then an image of Will's furious face found its way into her mind. 'Otherwise, best of luck with it all.'

'Thanks,' said Rose, forehead wrinkled with worry, her default expression.

Anna felt a pang of almost parental concern again, like pinpricks puncturing her skin, as she watched Rose walk towards the back door. But the future of the farm was between her and her father. She thought of her own dad. They'd had their tensions once upon a time. But now she was much older, she understood more. When she worried about him, it gave her a sense of how he'd felt back when she was young. She pictured him now, had an overwhelming urge to give him a hug. And as she heard the van engine roar up the road towards Fell View Farm, an idea began to form.

11

In the first week of August, the weather was soup-simmering temperature. The back door of the restaurant was permanently flung open in a hopeless attempt to coax air into the furnace-hot kitchen, and, even very early in the morning, standing anywhere near the stove was an endurance exercise.

For Anna, the heatwave was an unwanted gift, like a Christmas present she didn't want to receive but knew others would be thrilled to have. After a stifling night spent slow-cooking on top of the sheets, lying awake right into the small hours, Anna decided to get up and go down to the lakeshore. Finding a slice of time to go for a swim seemed to have become increasingly difficult, like trying to divide up a cake into too many portions, but now here she was, standing on the edge of Buttermere, ankle deep in the silver-lining of the scorching spell: a chance to be here, seeing the summer in all its shimmering glory.

The water was calm, Fleetwith Pike perfectly reflected in its pink-hued surface. The sounds of dawn circled her, and she stood completely still, soaking it all in. People travelled from all over to come to the Lake District, and she was lucky enough to call it home. 'Why did I ever want to leave?' she whispered to the hills. But on her return here, she'd had an entirely different perspective from the one she'd had when she left – as though she'd retraced her steps on a walk, and seen the view behind her for the very first time.

The wakening day was so breathless, each sound and movement seemed magnified. She heard the distant drum of a woodpecker, as nature's orchestra warmed up for the day ahead. A duck drifted across the shallows, destroying the flawless mirror-image of the mountains, oblivious. It was so easy to tear through life without realising the repercussions, Anna thought, as Fleetwith Pike fragmented in front of her.

Then the distant rumble of a tractor started up from the fields behind her, pulling her back to the moment.

She'd stripped down to her swimming costume on the pebbled bank, tried not to think of the rock that had been thrown through the restaurant window as she'd crunched across the sharp stones with bare feet. No one had been caught, and the mystery looped round and round in her head like a swooping bird.

She waded into the lake, and the cool water welcomed her with rose-gold ripples. With every stroke, it was as though she was pushing aside her thoughts, leaving them in a heap on the shore with her clothes. She concentrated on the sensation of the water surrounding her, felt her heart beating faster with the effort of propelling herself on. That was how she felt in the kitchen too – she had to be moving forward so she knew she was *alive*. If she stayed still, she'd sink.

But time was as liquid as the lake when she was swimming, in contrast to when she was at work. Out here, supported by the water, she had no sense of the seconds and minutes passing. It was as though the world was suspended.

She left the cold caress of the lake, striding out of the water with droplets clinging to her skin as though begging her to stay. She wrapped herself in a towel and took a last lingering look at the sweeping mountains before her: a landscape that was constant, ancient, and had taught her so much. The forests and hills had shown her what resilience looked like, and the importance of patience. They'd inspired her appreciation and respect for the wild.

As she walked home, the noise of the farm machinery grew louder, gradually swallowing the tranquil atmosphere as she drew closer. Anna felt her shoulders tense at the thought of encountering Will.

But he was at the other end of the field, far beyond the dry-stone wall beside her, busy cutting the grass to make silage, already preparing for the winter. She and Will really weren't so different, thought Anna, though he'd never agree – both of them always looking to the seasons ahead, governed by nature in their own separate ways.

Maybe it was the elation she felt after her swim, or the fact that embracing the blazing-hot weather, instead of grumbling about it, had made her see that sometimes you didn't need to alter a situation, only your point of view, but suddenly she felt a rush of inspiration. It was still very early, and she didn't need to be in work for a couple of hours yet. Perhaps it was time to breathe new life into her kitchen at home and make something so utterly different from her usual style of cooking that even the thought of it made her smile.

She wasn't feeling quite so sure about her idea when, a little while later, she was crossing the field where Will was climbing down from his tractor cab. She'd timed it right, at least, she thought as she trod carefully through the cut swathes. The air seemed unnervingly still now the engine was silent, as though the countryside was holding its breath. Had he seen her? She didn't know. What had she been thinking? The joy she'd felt in the aftermath of her swim had faded like something left out in the sun. Now she felt foolish as she traipsed towards him, palm slick against the handle of the basket.

He was hunched like he was hauling the whole of Fell View Farm behind him wherever he went.

Anna wished she'd stayed well clear, got on with her own day.

He was close enough for her to make out his expression, but it didn't mean she could read it. His eyes were squinting against the brightness, or because he couldn't bear the sight of her?

What should she say?

But he spoke first. 'No help from Rose this year, thanks to you.' He wiped his sleeve across his forehead.

Anna swallowed.

'She's in that barn, head in the clouds.' Will flung his hands in the air, like the sky was equally to blame. He heaved a huge sigh.

'I was just coming to see if—' began Anna.

'You can poke your nose in a bit more?' cut in Will. His words were sharper than the shingle on the lakeshore. 'I'm a pair of hands down because my daughter is set on some pie-in-the-sky plan.' *And it's your fault*, said his glare.

Anna flinched at his coldness, despite the warmth of the day.

'So, unless you can drive a tractor, I'm afraid I need to be getting on.' He glared at the grass-strewn ground around him.

'Right. I see. I just brought you some cake, for if you're having a rest,' Anna said, bracing herself for a blaze of anger as she realised that assuming he had time for a break was like striking a match near tinder-dry hay.

But it never came. His gaze went to the basket, then back to her face, and he didn't say anything, as though surprise had stolen his ability to speak.

'And some cordial – thought you might need a drink,' Anna finished. She set the basket down in the sliver of shadow cast by the tractor.

Will coughed, as though his throat was as parched as the summer-baked soil. 'Thank you,' he mumbled at last.

Then Anna turned and began to make her way back from where she'd come.

She was nearly back at the lane when he called to her. She looked over her shoulder to see him shielding his face with a hand.

'Do you have time to stop and have some too?' he said, squinting against the sun.

She hesitated, momentarily still as the push-pull of staying or going rendered her motionless. She hovered by the boundary wall. Dani and the other chefs would be at the restaurant soon. But what if there was a small seed of hope that, one day, she and Will could, if not find common ground, at least exist side by side happily like the lake and the land?

She nodded slowly. 'Okay.'

'We can sit in the corner, there's some shade there,' Will said, gesturing with his free hand to where two dry-stone walls joined; the other was holding her basket.

They sat down, Fell View Farm sprawled out in the distance, and Anna half expected him to launch into another rant about Rose and the ice-cream venture, seeing as the barn where she would be was directly in front of them.

But he didn't.

'This is . . . very kind of you,' said Will, with all the ease of someone regurgitating gravel.

'You don't know what it is yet,' quipped Anna, risking a small smile at him as she reached into the basket.

Will gave a little laugh, low and almost like it had escaped before he could stop it.

Anna met his gaze: greeny-grey eyes she'd never been near enough to notice before.

She poured cordial into two cups, then topped them up with sparkling water. 'Elderflower pressé,' she said. 'Thought it might be refreshing.' She offered him one of the drinks which glinted and fizzed in the sunlight.

'There's a theme to this picnic,' Anna said, with a glance at Will as she started to unpack the cake. 'This is elderflower sponge.' She heard Will's intake of breath at the sight of the glistening icing and the smell of the sweet-scented sponge as she peeled back the wrapping.

'Look at that!' He was grinning, and Anna saw a glimmer of the man he must once have been.

'Bit rustic, but should taste good,' she said, cutting a generous slice for him.

'Are you joking? This is *luxury*,' he said, taking the wedge of cake she handed to him. 'Thank you.'

'Well, you provided the elderflowers, so it was a team effort,' she said, with a sideways look at him.

Will spluttered, mouth already full. 'It's delicious,' he said through the crumbs, but a frown wrinkled his forehead as he said it, like a storm coming after sunshine. He was silent now, chewing more slowly.

Anna took a sip of her drink, felt the bubbles froth on her tongue. She surveyed the farm from where they sat: an idyllic-seeming sprawl of buildings set in the August-bathed valley bottom. But its pastures stretched in every direction as far as the eye could see, right up to the fell tops where the sheep were tiny white dots. The sheer scale of the place made Hesta look minute. And Will and Rose didn't have a team of people to help them. It was only recently that Anna had seen Jackson there as an additional pair of hands. She couldn't imagine the work involved in running everything, the endless list of tasks that needed to be done to make sure the livestock were well taken care of and that the farm kept going. She looked over at the cow shed, where hundreds of cattle were milked twice a day, then back at the enormous field before them, which Will had just mowed.

'Still need to row all this up by myself,' he said, following the line of her gaze to the cut grass on the ground. 'Then, after it's wilted, Jackson'll help me do the rest.' He blew out a breath, as though bracing himself for the long day ahead.

Anna knew how silage was made. The image of the harvester regurgitating the forage always reminded her of a mother bird feeding its chick. Buttermere was a small village and she'd caught glimpses of the process over the years, seen the growling machine threading up and down the field, chopping up the swathes and then spitting it out into the trailer being driven alongside. But she'd learned how it was done long before that. She'd spent that sun-soaked summer out in the fields with Dominik, and the aroma of freshly mown greenery that perfumed the morning air around her now took her right back in time. She closed her eyes briefly as she remembered the grass sticking to their clothes, his laughter on the breeze. She thought how she still measured the year in the rhythms of the farms around her. She told herself it was because Hesta was in sync with the growers they relied on – but she knew it was the echo of Dominik's words that made each changing season bring another rush of memories.

Will began talking again, more comfortable now he was telling her about farm processes and equipment he was familiar with, rather than making small talk.

Anna nodded as he spoke, taking in the wrinkles round his eyes and the week or so of salt-and-pepper stubble on his jaw. He was miming the process of both vehicles moving in tandem now his hands were empty. He glanced across at Anna and caught her looking at him.

'Oh, it was beautiful, by the way, that cake,' he added, and she didn't know whether he was blushing or sun-flushed from being outdoors since daybreak.

'I'm glad you enjoyed it,' she replied, watching the sparkles dance in her drink.

'I heard about the incident at the restaurant,' Will continued, as though realising he'd got carried away talking about himself. 'Terrible business, that.'

'So it wasn't you then, putting a rock through the window,' said Anna with a wry smile.

Will let out a sigh laced with a laugh. He studied a blade of grass that he rolled back and forth between his fingers, as though his body was unaccustomed to being still. 'Look, I don't mean to be . . .'

'Difficult? A total arse?'

'Ouch.' He picked up his cup, looked into it like it was a miniature wishing well. 'It's just a lot, sometimes.'

'Tell me about it.'

'What, with your fame and fortune? You must be kidding.' He either rolled his eyes or glanced up at a bird flying wild and free in the sky above.

'It's not a picnic all the time,' she said, draining the last of her elderflower pressé. 'I'd better let you get on.' She wrapped the rest of the cake back up and got to her feet. 'I'll leave this here,' she said, pointing at the basket. 'Sounds like you might need it later.'

Will scrambled upright. 'You're going.' His tone was as flat as if they'd left the top off the fizzy water.

'My restaurant doesn't *entirely* run itself.'

Will pursed his lips.

'Good luck with the rest of it,' Anna said, tilting her chin in the direction of the field, before turning to make her way towards the gate further along the wall.

'Thank you,' she thought she heard him murmur, but she couldn't be sure as a car grumbled along the lane beyond, reminding her that Buttermere was coming to life and customers would soon be on their way to Hesta. She raised a hand in farewell, not looking back to see Will staring after her with a crumpled brow.

'Christ alive, it's boiling in here.' Dani stuck out her tongue to illustrate her point, seeing as her hands were full with a loaded baking tray. 'Could have left these *outside* to bake,' she said with a jerk of her head at the rows of golden biscuits set out neatly on the metal sheet she was holding: hazelnut tuiles. Anna's eyes roved over the curved discs delightedly. The hedgerows were bursting with the creamy, earthy nuts come August, and the smooth, buttery sweetness was one of Anna's favourite flavours, especially in desserts. 'Well done, Dan,' she said with a nod at the crisp arcs that were so light and thin, the real skill was in not snapping them before they were served. 'They look perfect.'

'Cheers, boss.' Dani grinned back at her. She slid the tray of tuiles onto the side but the atmosphere seemed barely any cooler than the oven. 'Bloody hell, it's hot. I feel like *I'm* being cooked today.'

'I don't think even that would shut you up,' muttered Anna under her breath.

'Heard that,' said Dani, crunching down on a tuile; the only time she wasn't talking was when she was eating.

Ovie appeared at the pass. 'Ready for the staff briefing when you are,' he said to Anna.

'Bet you're wishing that window was still out, hey Ove?' bellowed Dani. 'To get some *breeze* through there.'

Ovie acknowledged her joke with a smile. 'No, I'm pleased that's all fixed and, hopefully, behind us.' He shook his head sadly, as though the incident had been a violation of his own home. He probably spent more time here at Hesta than in his actual house, realised Anna.

'My cousin said there's not really a lot they can do,' said Dani, folding her arms either because she enjoyed being an authority on the topic or because that was the only way to ensure some of the tuiles actually made it to the diners. 'Doesn't look like it was an organised thing – no one's owned up to it and surely that's the point of a protest: you want to get your message across or whatever.' She subsided into silence as she tried to put her finger on the rock-thrower's reasoning.

'It'll be kids messing about and they'll be back at school and out of mischief soon,' said Anna.

'I hope you're right,' said Ovie. 'There's enough excitement in your dishes without the need for such drama.' He dipped his head at Anna.

She batted the air. 'One good review from Marcus Bradley doesn't mean we can be complacent,' she replied.

'Morning,' said Sally, her face visible from the staffroom door. 'Sorry I'm a bit late,' she added, ducking back out of sight as though disappearing from a firing line.

Anna glowered in her direction as she tried to work out what was wrong. 'Right, I'll see you out front in a minute,' she said to Ovie with a clap of her hands. Her gaze went to Dani, who leapt into action, or at least stopped leaning on the work surface looking longingly at the tuiles. Their just-baked fragrance still scented the air, but it didn't sweeten Anna's attitude towards Sally's lateness. She struggled to hide her annoyance as she strode towards the staffroom to confront her kitchen porter.

'Boss,' said Sally as she came back in, tying her apron on and fixing a hesitant smile to her face.

Anna noticed the quaver in her employee's voice, and her stomach dropped like she'd slipped suddenly back in time. She swallowed, catching herself. She wasn't the same now as she had been back then. She clenched her jaw, bit down on the words she once would have said.

And then Ovie swung through the double doors, suit crisp but forehead crinkled. 'I've got Felicity Townsend on the phone for you,' he said to Anna.

She felt a flash of frustration creep up her neck. *Not again.*

'Won't take no for an answer,' he added, adjusting the tie he still wore despite the hot weather.

So Anna followed him through to the restaurant, leaving Sally to heave a sigh of relief that she wasn't the focus of her boss's attention anymore.

Service had finished, and Anna was busy doing a stock take, when there was a tentative knock on the back door. Anna looked up from the order sheet she was filling in, as Rose called through to the kitchen. 'Hello?'

'Hi,' replied Anna. She saw Dani wave goodbye out of the corner of her eye, followed by Sally, who seemed to shuffle out after her as though she knew Anna had wanted to speak to her. She sighed.

'Is this a bad time?' asked Rose, rubbing her eyes as though tiredness was something that could be wiped away like a tear.

Anna saw the shadows that seemed to have settled under the girl's eyes, gradually staking their claim to her face. 'No, as long as I phone this in before I leave, it's fine.' She put down her pen. 'What's wrong?'

Rose swallowed, as though otherwise her troubles might gush out all at once. 'I can't do it,' was all she said, before she covered her face with her hands.

Anna took a step towards her, unsure what to do. She looked around at the sterile surroundings of the comfortless kitchen. 'Hey, hey,' she said softly, but the harsh lights stripped any solace from the room. The sharp lines and hard surfaces seemed to semaphore the message that the world was an inhospitable place.

Rose's fingers were still cupped over her eyes as though she couldn't bear to look at any more bleakness.

So instead of steering Rose into the staffroom, with its health-and-safety-warning covered walls, Anna ushered her into the restaurant.

There was only Ovie left at the front desk, but discretion could be the name of his cologne, he was so adept at being tactful. He barely moved his head to maintain the illusion it was just the two of them, simply gave Anna a small smile as a silent sign of support.

Rose stopped crying, as though she couldn't squander the chance to see inside Hesta's dining room up close no matter how upset she was. Her eyes widened at the contrast between this side of the double doors and the other.

'Why don't you sit down,' said Anna, indicating a chair on table six. It had the best view of the restaurant and faced away from the black abyss of the midnight lake. Anna always found that window to be a mirror for her emotions, an enormous looking-glass that magnified her feelings and reflected them back at her.

Rose felt the moss-soft material of the back of the chair as she sat down, smoothing her fingers over the fabric like a child reaching for a comfort blanket.

'Right, tell me what's happened,' said Anna.

'Nothing,' said Rose, about to put her elbows on the table-cloth, but stopping herself. 'That's the problem.'

Anna frowned, and her face looked even more rumpled next to the wrinkle-free tarn of white linen that lay between them.

'I'm not getting anywhere,' continued Rose. 'I can't do it. It's not possible on my own.'

'No, probably not,' said Anna, matter-of-factly.

Rose sat up straight with surprise.

Anna recognised that stubborn spark of fiery fight. Rose wasn't really ready for her ice-cream dream to be snuffed out. 'I mean, I don't think anyone succeeds at anything without having some assistance along the way.' She saw Ovie raise a hand to wish her goodnight, then glide towards the door with the grace of a suit-clad swan. 'We all need help at times.'

'Even *you*?' Rose sniffed.

Anna nodded. '*Especially* me.'

12

That night, Anna's sleep was a restless swirl of ingredients, and when she woke, it took a few seconds for her tired brain to decipher which of the fragmented recipes were figments of her fitful imagination, and which were the actual flavour combinations she'd suggested for Wild Rose Ice Cream.

Leaving without even her customary cup of morning coffee, she went down to the shore. Now, with the lake lapping about her shoulders, the conversation was as clear in her mind as the water that enveloped her.

She could just about see the crab apple tree on the fringe of the farm in the distance. Its branches were so heavily laden with fruit, it reminded Anna of Rose, and how weighed down she'd felt the previous evening.

They'd stayed in the restaurant till the moon stared straight through the enormous window at them, its lunar features frozen in an expression of shock, as though at the lateness of the hour.

Anna floated onto her back, looked up at the sunlit summer sky. Brightness followed dark every single day, reminding her that, even when things felt black, there were always better times on their way. Nature had so many lessons, she thought, turning over and starting to make her way back to solid ground. She hoped Rose was feeling more sorted this morning. They'd put together a list of seasonal ice-cream ideas, scribbling down taste pairings to experiment with on the back of an old menu. Then they'd covered the crucial elements of Rose's business plan, Anna guiding her round potential pitfalls like an experienced hiker navigating the best route up a mountain.

'I mean, I don't exactly have a map to success,' Anna had said as she stifled a yawn.

'But you do,' protested Rose. 'Look at all this!' she said, glancing around Hesta's dining room like she was in a cathedral-cave of wonder.

'Yes, but I'm still learning things every day,' said Anna sagely. 'I haven't always done things the right way.'

It had almost been dawn by the time Anna had gone home, but instead of feeling hollowed out with exhaustion, she felt energised and invigorated. She was fusing her passion for food with something purposeful, helping people, and as she'd slipped into dream-steeped sleep, she'd felt the smallest taste of being complete.

She passed by the field where she'd sat with Will the previous morning, wondered whether he knew Rose had been to see her, and felt furrows of doubt crease her forehead. But then she saw the crab apple tree, much closer now, and noticed that its boughs weren't as loaded as they had been before. Some of the fruit had been picked, and Anna smiled, hoping that Rose was feeling much lighter too.

At four o'clock, the blistering heat had diminished enough to make Anna crave being outdoors again. The last trickle of customers had left, and the restaurant was quiet and still, like a chattering stream run dry. She wandered towards the woods, seeking the shade of the parasol-like canopy as much as the porcini mushrooms that grew beneath the trees. She bent to inhale the fresh-soil smell, and thought of the first time Dominik had told her about the interwoven network they formed with the tree roots underground. The 'wood wide web' he'd called it, and she'd laughed, the kind of light, heartfelt giggle she'd let out back when she was that girl but hadn't for a long time since.

But it wasn't Dominik's face that appeared in her mind for once. Much to her annoyance, it was Will's. Why couldn't they have the same mutually supportive dynamic demonstrated by fungi and forests? she wondered, scraping the dirt from the stem of a mushroom and shaking her head. There was a lot that could be learned from the wild.

She was careful to only pick a small portion of the porcini she found, but decided she'd make a risotto with some of her haul for the staff dinner before service. She could almost taste the firm meaty flesh as she thought about sautéing them that evening and her stomach rumbled as she walked back in the direction of the village.

'Nice one, Chef!' said Dani as she spied the nut-brown dome-capped delicacies sizzling in the pan. 'Ceps!'

Anna pondered the fact there were different names for the same flavoursome mushroom. *Penny bun*, in English, because with its rounded top it looked like a just-risen roll. What was it that Shakespeare said? 'A mushroom by any other name would taste as sweet'?

'They're my *favourite*,' added Dani with a fist pump.

'*Everything's* your favourite,' shot back Anna.

Dani plucked one of the uncooked porcini from the container on the worktop and ate it fresh. 'Mmmm,' she said, closing her eyes.

'Save *some* for the customers, please, Dan,' said Anna. She shook the pan and the butter sputtered like a sparkler.

'Risotto, Sal?' bellowed Dani as the kitchen porter came through the back door.

Late again, thought Anna, resisting the urge to glance up at the clock. She needed to speak to her; she'd do it after the dinner shift, not before. First things first: they needed service to go smoothly.

'I'm not hungry, thanks.' Sally replied.

'I don't know what that feels like,' said Dani, standing over the stove in anticipation.

'Have you already eaten?' asked Anna, looking over her shoulder. The last thing she needed was one of her staff fainting from lack of food and the stifling heat. They were on their feet all night, and they had a good six-hour stint left ahead of them at least.

'Er . . . yes,' came Sally's reply.

Anna narrowed her eyes. Sally was wearing a baggy hoodie; despite the fact it was *boiling*. But it was Dani who looked more uncomfortable; her gaze stayed on the saucepan. She was suspiciously quiet, thought Anna, as she stirred in the rice. She had the distinct feeling she had stepped into the middle of a recipe for disaster.

Suddenly, her resolve to wait till the end of the night vaporised. She set the risotto aside, unconcerned if it spoiled, and folded her arms. 'Right, what's going on?'

Dani visibly swallowed.

Sally steadied herself against the sink. 'Look, I'm really sorry . . .'

Anna raised her eyebrows, waiting for her to continue, but then all at once she understood. Pieced together the ingredients.

'She's pregnant,' blurted out Dani, before clamping her palms over her mouth. 'Sorry but it's dangerous not to say, Sal,' she added with an apologetic glance at her colleague.

'I can explain,' said Sally, clutching her stomach as though shielding her unborn child from any blame.

'So that's why you've been late.' Anna's mouth twisted as she spooled through all the signs.

Sally nodded. 'I had appointments . . .'

'When were you going to tell me?' asked Anna.

Sally fiddled with one of her sleeves.

'I mean, you've told Dani, it would seem.' Anna flung a hand in her direction.

Sally gave the pastry chef an anguished glance. 'I didn't, actually, she just found out . . .'

'And when was *I* going to find out? I mean, it's pretty important in this environment, Sally.' Anna resisted the urge to bang her fist down on the worktop. *How could Sally put her in this position?* If something happened to her or the baby . . . it didn't bear thinking about.

'How far along are you?' asked Dani, as though the question had been expanding inside her.

'I'm twenty-eight weeks,' Sally replied. She stripped off her sweatshirt and blew a sticky strand of hair away from her face. She sighed, as though revealing it was at least a little bit of a relief.

Anna uncrossed her arms, swept a hand over her face.

'Please, I'm totally fine,' said Sally.

'Why didn't you say?' asked Anna. 'I have a right to know at this stage.'

'Because you're AC!' replied Sally, the forcefulness of her voice surprising her.

Anna shuddered as though a blast of freezing air had swept through the room. It had been a long time since anyone had called her that. *AC: ice cold, like air-conditioning.* She gripped the edge of the work surface. 'I see,' she murmured, almost to herself. Her gaze was on the floor tiles, as though a portal to the past had opened up right there before her.

The silence that followed made it feel like time was suspended, as though the nickname had blurred the lines between then and now. Eventually Anna spoke again. 'How did you know about that . . .?' she asked Sally, squinting at her, still wincing at the memory.

'Dani told me.' It was Sally's turn to feel shame make her cheeks flame. 'Sorry,' she added with a glance at her colleague.

Dani grimaced. 'Ages ago. Back when Sally started . . .'

'I'd heard it before, though,' confessed Sally. 'Catering industry's a small world.'

'Right.' Anna rubbed her temples.

'I still came to work here,' added Sally, a weak smile on her lips.

'You said you didn't have a choice,' chipped in Dani, still smarting from her earlier comment. 'That you needed the job.'

Anna tried to tear her thoughts back to the present. She needed to *focus.* 'Right. I need to do a proper risk assessment before you continue a minute longer. If I haven't made sure everything's safe for you and then . . .' She paced to the other side of the room as though the consequences could be left there instead of rolling through her mind.

Sally looked stricken. 'No. You can't tell me to go.'

'I haven't got a choice,' said Anna. 'I'm going to have to ask you to leave.'

'What?' Sally clung to the side of the sink. 'Please. I'll be careful. I wouldn't put my baby in harm's way.'

And what about me? Anna wanted to say. Sally hadn't spared a thought for her, or Hesta. 'I'll be in touch in due course,' was all she said. She strode over to the staffroom door to show Sally out.

Sally was sobbing now, great spasms of panic wracking her body. '*Wait—*'

'I don't have *time* to,' said Anna, glancing at the clock: five p.m. What was she supposed to do now? Guests would start arriving in an hour. They had a fully booked restaurant that evening. 'Dani, can you finish the staff food and serve it up?' she called. 'I'll be back soon.'

'Where are you going, boss?' Dani shouted from the stove.

'To get a temp KP. I did it last time but I can't keep doing it.'

Sally looked like she was about to pass out. 'Please,' she said, following Anna through to the back room. 'I'm fine, I promise. I'm only six months, I'm fully capable—'

'You can't do *anything* till I've got a proper grasp of all this,' Anna cut in. 'And a plan in place – you shouldn't be lifting heavy things; we'll have to look at your hours, think about reducing them—'

'No!' Sally interrupted.

Anna stared at her. There was something Sally wasn't telling her. She could sense it, like an aftertaste of untruth. 'What is it?' she demanded, fear of not having all the facts making her feel suffocated, like she couldn't breathe. 'Come on, Sally. How can I make sure you're okay when you're not talking to me?' It was taking every ounce of her effort not to raise her voice.

Sally screwed up her face.

'Please, Sally,' said Anna, careful to keep her tone level. 'This is *serious*. There are hazards *all over the place* – it's a commercial kitchen . . .' She just stopped herself from adding *for Christ's sake!* Frustration was making her head ache. How could Sally behave like this, after all she'd done for her? Anna had taken her on and trained her and—

'Steve and I have split up. I can't afford not to work.' Sally sank down on a chair in the staffroom like a fallen soufflé. Tears streamed down her face in rivulets of sorrow. 'I haven't been here for a full year . . . I won't be . . . eligible for . . .' She said in staccato breaths.

Anna put a hand on her shoulder. 'All right, come on. Let's take a moment.' She sucked in a deep lungful of air, then blew it out slowly, and did it again, until Sally did the same. A slight breeze stole in through the open door, as though the countryside could sense when it was needed, and the scent of cut grass and warm greenery reached them. The summery aroma seemed to calm Sally slightly, and Anna herself felt more grounded again.

Until she caught sight of the clock on the staffroom wall, and a surge of stress pulsed though her veins.

She had to get going. 'You can stay here if you want, till you're all right to drive, but don't go into that kitchen, okay?'

Sally gave a nod. Her head hung low as though she couldn't lift it with the weight of sadness that pressed down on her.

Anna raced across the village, but the further she got from the restaurant, what had at first seemed like a good idea, gradually congealed, like a takeaway meal deteriorating as it travelled. So, by the time she knocked on her father's door, she almost couldn't bear for it to cross her tongue, and nearly turned back.

But he answered like someone receiving a bouquet they hadn't been expecting. 'Anna, hi,' he said, with a smile of surprise. But it slipped away when he saw the sheen of stress on her skin, the tension in her shoulders.

'Is everything okay?' he asked, opening the door wider and stepping aside.

Anna stayed standing where she was. 'Er . . . it depends – what are you doing?'

He glanced back down the hall, let the emptiness of the rooms speak for him, so he didn't have to say 'nothing' out loud.

It was as though he kept the house quiet so he could hear the ghosts of happy times past, thought Anna as she met his gaze. 'Is there any chance you could help me?'

'Now?' Robert looked at his slippers, then back at her face.

'Actually, no – don't worry. It's ridiculous.' Anna sagged, resting her hand against the outside wall.

'Are you on the way to work?' asked Robert, peering down at his watch. 'Gosh, yes, it's later than I thought . . .'

'Well, that's it.' Anna fiddled with one of her earrings; the same gold studs her parents had given her for her twenty-first birthday. 'I've come to ask a favour, but it's stupid . . . I just didn't know what else to do.' Standing in front of her dad, she felt like a child, at fifty-three years old.

He waited for her to continue, but was already sliding off his slippers and putting on his shoes, so she carried on.

'We don't have a KP for tonight and we've got a fully booked restaurant.' Anna blew out a breath. 'Any chance you want a job for the night?'

'Oh, *right*.' Robert stopped still. 'That's definitely not what I thought you were going to say.'

Anna batted the air like she could whisk the conversation away and start again. 'Yes, I don't know what I was thinking.'

'I thought you were going to ask me to fetch something or . . . I mean, I'm not really . . .' He waved his hand as he searched for the right words.

'No, I know,' cut in Anna. She shook her head. 'It's not your place to come and pot wash.'

Robert held up a palm. 'No, that's not what I meant at all.'

'It was a silly idea.'

'No, it wasn't – I just haven't worked in a professional kitchen. I don't want to, you know, let you down.'

'You would quite literally be doing the opposite.' Anna rubbed her brow. 'But it's all right, I can do it myself,' said Anna.

'I know you probably can,' said her dad, shutting the door behind him. 'But sometimes it's nicer to have some help.'

Anna smiled back at him. There was that feeling again, as though the years had been peeled back and she was a little girl once more.

They made their way back to Hesta, walking side by side along the lane, sandwiched between hedgerows that spilled over with summer.

Anna tilted her head to look at her dad beside her, his pace matching hers as they strode along. He wasn't staring down at the ground like he usually did as though searching for traces of where Marion once stood; his chin was tilted upwards, and his gaze was on the shining windows and solid stone walls of Hesta, as it came into view round the corner.

'There should be some spare chef whites you can wear, and I'll show you how everything works—' Anna stopped talking as she saw that Sally was still there, sitting in the back room, face blanched and a tissue balled in her fist.

'Um, good evening,' said Robert, raising a hand to greet her.

Sally's eyes refilled with tears.

'This is my father,' said Anna, introducing him with a flick of her wrist. 'He's going to cover for you tonight,' she said, careful to emphasise that no one was being replaced.

Sally sniffed.

Anna handed Robert a set of clean clothes. 'I'll whizz through the health and safety stuff too,' she said. 'But Sally's the master, so ask her anything you want to know quick, before she goes,' she added, but when she turned to give Sally a reassuring smile, she was already gone.

'How are you finding it?' asked Dani a while later, depositing a pastry-flake-caked baking sheet beside Robert at the sink.

'Just about keeping up, I think,' he replied, puffing out his cheeks as he rinsed a saucepan.

'I need that,' Anna shouted over to him, arm outstretched.

'Yep.' Robert flung a tea towel round the pan's shiny sides, drying it as fast as his fingers would allow. 'Here – Chef.'

'Bossy, isn't she?' Dani yelled with a companionable grin.

Anna was back over by the pass, so engrossed in making sure service was running smoothly, she didn't notice that Robert's smile stretched all the way to his eyes.

13

'I don't know how you *do* it,' said Robert, looking up at the star-scattered sky as they wound their way home. 'Day after day.'

'And night after night,' added Anna, glancing up at the moon, which gazed down at them open-mouthed as if what happened on Earth was a mystery. 'Thanks for this eve,' she said, watching him walk beside her, his silver hair bright in the moonlight. Age had decorated him in shades of platinum, as if making the point that growing old was a privilege.

'I enjoyed it,' he replied, turning towards her. 'It was nice to be part of it all.'

Anna smiled, but a plethora of unspoken thoughts exploded in her head.

'Your mum would have been very proud,' he murmured, his eyes meeting hers.

Hot tears muddled Anna's vision. The lane beneath her feet blurred.

'But you know that.' They were almost at her dad's front door now. 'Don't you?'

Anna blinked and his features came back into focus.

'She was *always* so proud of you.'

His face distorted once again as her eyes welled. 'I'm not sure.'

He put an arm round her shoulders and squeezed, as if love could only travel by hug.

'I wish I'd not gone.' The words that had whirled in her mind but she'd never said aloud.

'To London?' said Robert, moon-bathed in midnight.

Anna nodded. She'd left, and not looked back. And then never got to see her mum again. Now, all these years later, her own skin was gradually being reupholstered with wrinkles, while Marion had never been granted that honour.

'Oh, Anna,' said her father, cheeks glistening with sympathy. 'You did *right*. Your mum wanted you to live your life.' His lips trembled. 'I should have let you do that too . . .'

Anna felt a sharp pinch of pain in the part of her heart where Dominik lived.

They were outside his house now.

'Do you want a cup of tea?' he said, as he patted his pockets for his key.

Anna's eyes ached with tiredness, but the adrenalin-drenched demands of service meant that sleep was always out of reach for at least another hour. 'Yes, please,' she replied.

Once they were inside, she sat on the sofa while Robert pottered about making their drinks. She felt too exhausted to summon up anything to say till he was settled opposite her in the armchair. But when he came through to the living room, there was a restlessness about him that couldn't be explained away by the fact he'd worked a shift in the rush and bustle of Hesta's kitchen.

'There's something I want to show you.' He was delving in the bottom drawer of the bureau, his back to Anna.

111

'Maybe I should have told you sooner, but I didn't want to . . .'

The words 'upset you' hung in the air like a cobweb. 'It just never seemed the right time, but hearing you say you shouldn't have gone to London, when we were talking on the way home . . .'

Anna inched forwards in her seat, nervous now. She didn't feel in full enough strength to deal with something unsettling. Longing and regret loomed larger in the small hours of the morning; everything seemed darker when the sun wasn't shining.

Her dad turned round, a full-to-bursting folder held in both hands. Her pulse quickened. She couldn't face a file of photos of her mother. Why had he decided to share this with her now? There was something about the middle of the night that made everything feel like it wasn't real life; in its silent, still centre, time seemed almost suspended.

Anna gripped the edge of the sofa cushion. Fatigue screamed through her bones, yet her heart was pounding. It was a disorientating combination, like being strapped into a ghost train on an after-hours ride. She dreaded being confronted with a heap of pictures of Marion. It hurt too much.

Robert looked up at her. He was kneeling next to the coffee table now.

He pulled out the contents of the folder, and Anna frowned. It wasn't full of memories of her mother at all. Spread out before her was a collection of articles about *her*.

She reached out and rifled through the cuttings – newspaper columns and magazine features. One with the same image that had been used alongside the Marcus Bradley review.

'She was so proud of you,' said Robert, his voice breaking, as though to match his heart.

Anna's gaze roved over the sheets of paper, all carefully arranged in date order, the last one from the year her mum had died – she immediately flicked right to the back, as guilt seared her heart, turning her attention to the first article instead. A snipped-out page from *Cumbria Life*. The time she'd won a Rising Star award when she was twenty-four. The photo they'd printed was one she hadn't seen for more than three decades. She wiped her eyes as she looked at her dark hair pulled back in a work-ready bun, the bright eyes that belied the nerves she'd felt that day. The arms-crossed, back-straight pose she'd chosen to signal she meant business, but there was a hint of a smile on her lips too. She'd been less fierce at the beginning, before sheer determination had started to be confused with steeliness. In the picture, she was standing in front of the sturdy stone wall of a building that was as recognisable to her as if the background had been Big Ben. The place she'd eventually come to name Hesta. *Buttermere's Brightest Star*, read the strap line.

Anna Carleton, who was born here in the Lake District, receives highly coveted Rising Star accolade for becoming the youngest-ever female head chef in the country. Anna, who runs Apogee restaurant in London, attended the prestigious ceremony in Mayfair along with a whole host of famous names and notable figures in the culinary industry. Anna said she was honoured to be acknowledged, and humbly added that she 'still had a long way to go . . .'

Why had she always thought going a long way was the answer? Why had she only realised she wanted to be back here once it was too late? Anna wondered, as the sound of her dad pouring tea tugged her back to the present.

'She was proud anyway, before all this,' said Robert, waving a hand at the chronological compilation of cuttings. 'Not because of what you'd achieved or where you'd set your sights for the future, but because you were forging your own way, doing your own thing.' Robert passed her a cup of tea, but Anna put it back down on the table, torn between looking through the rest of the articles and closing the folder completely. She knew the arc of her own career, didn't need reminding of the sacrifices she'd made.

'I didn't find it for quite a while,' he said, with a dip of his head. 'But she'd kept everything – every tiny little mention.'

'Not the bad ones, I bet,' said Anna.

'Oh, no, she'd curse the critics who said anything negative,' said her dad, with a chuckle.

Anna smiled at the thought of it as she flicked through the folder for a final time, before it was buried back in the bureau. She paused as she was leafing through the pages, spotted a piece about her keeping rooftop beehives in the capital.

There's a big buzz surrounding Anna Carleton at the moment and customers are swarming to the Mayfair restaurant she runs, but now there's another reason that everyone's talking about this pioneering head chef. Anna has brought Cumbrian bees to the capital's skies, and is setting a fine example of sustainability right here in the heart of the city . . .

The Lake District had always been an inspiration for her. She'd been guided by the seasons that were so distinct back home, and it had shaped her style of cookery. But somehow it all only truly made sense against the backdrop of Buttermere. The wild beauty of the Cumbrian landscape was a better canvas than any expensive urban surroundings.

'Don't regret going to London,' said her dad, leaning forward.

'I just wish I could have had more time with her.' Anna sighed.

'I know, so do I.' Robert nodded.

'Why didn't she *say*?' said Anna, the sentence suddenly bursting out of her.

'I think she thought she was doing what was best,' explained Robert.

Anna slid the article she'd been reading back into the folder, but it wasn't as easy to push her emotions back inside her body.

'She was trying to protect you, in her way,' said Robert.

Wasn't it strange that you could be so sure you were acting in the interests of the people you loved, when all the while you were doing the opposite? thought Anna.

'I wish I'd known. I'd have done things differently.' Anna looked at the strawberry motif on her steaming mug.

'She wouldn't have wanted that. It's the reason she didn't say . . . to any of us.'

'Did you have any inkling?' asked Anna. She'd always wondered, never had the nerve to ask until now.

Her dad's head bobbed up and down slowly. 'Yes . . . in those last months, though I don't think I wanted to admit it to myself.' He hunched over his tea, hands curved round the cup for comfort.

Anna wondered when exactly it was that she'd realised her parents were just people, with their own private thoughts and complex personalities, like her.

'As soon as I found out, I said we should tell you, but she was adamant. Didn't want to throw you off course.' Her dad gave a sadness-laced smile.

Back then, ambition had burned in Anna's belly but, unbeknownst to her, time was melting away like a lit candle.

'But Matthew was still here, it was different for him. He got to be with her.' Anna rubbed her temple. 'I don't know how he didn't *realise*, though.'

'He was busy being a teenage boy. Your mum wanted you both to live your lives, not mourn hers before you had to. She wanted to see you and Matthew in your element, know you were happy.'

'I wasn't happy,' said Anna, the words surging out of her like steam escaping a saucepan. 'I thought I would be, but I wasn't. All this –' she flipped through the contents of the folder, the clippings flashing like slides in a reel of her life – 'was my dream at one point but—'

She stopped as something caught her eye.

A pale-blue envelope among the cut-out articles. Anna pulled it out. Her name was written on the front in her mother's handwriting, along with her last-ever London address.

'What's this?' she asked.

Robert shook his head. 'I don't know. I wasn't aware it was in there.'

Anna gripped the envelope in both hands, felt the thick square of card beneath. She imagined Marion holding it, penning the letters in scribbled loops, and her eyes watered. 'Do I open it?'

'Well, it is for you,' said Robert, putting his cup down.

As she gently tore it open, Anna pictured her mum doing the reverse, sealing it shut, all those years ago. Why had she never sent it?

But the birthday card inside was inscribed with a date Marion would never see, realised Anna, unprepared for the

116

gut-punching impact of a full page of her mum's hand-written words. She swallowed. 'She was still thinking of me . . .' Anna murmured, looking up at her dad with tear-tingled eyes.

He nodded and came to sit beside her on the sofa. 'She must have put it in here, hoping that one day you'd read it.'

Anna blinked and her mum's scrawl swam back into view.

To my dearest daughter, Anna,

Wishing you a very happy birthday. I do hope it is. I know you'll probably be working, but hopefully we'll get to speak to you at some point. I am looking at a wonderful picture of you as I write this, the one where you're squinting in the sunshine when you're about six years old and splashing about in the lake with your brother. You were always such a strong, determined, little girl. Don't ever stop following your heart.

I hope you know how much I love you. Knowing you're following your dreams in London makes me very happy. No one works harder, but remember to stop and look up and appreciate it all once in a while. Be proud of yourself too, I couldn't be prouder of you. I loved you from the moment you were born, my brilliant little girl. Life rushes by so fast, I don't know where the years have gone. But I'm so grateful to have had you and Matthew.

Your dad and I love you both so much. I know I've said that, but remember he's only ever tried his best too.

I love you,

Mum xxx

Her dad's head had been bowed as he sat beside her, but he looked up as Anna flung her arms around him and hugged him tightly, the birthday card on the seat cushion next to her, as though Marion herself was there right beside them.

14

'Why didn't she post it?' asked Anna, overcome by an urge to talk through all the things they'd never spoken about, as though the dead of night was when such things could be shared.

'I think she must have written it well beforehand, knowing what she wanted to say, but also that she might not be able to for much longer.'

Anna slowly tucked the card back into its envelope, and Robert hoped that some of the pain, and the blame his daughter had felt for being absent, could at last be put to bed.

Anna reached for the folder, and gazed inside as if it might turn up another secret. For the few moments it had taken her to read the card, it had seemed almost as though Marion was there. Anna had been able to hear her mother's voice, nearly as clearly as if she'd been speaking the sentences aloud in person.

She took the file back over to the bureau and knelt beside the burnished walnut wood of the bottom drawer. The inside was cool and dark and coffin-like. 'What else is in here?' asked Anna, digging around amongst the scattered piles of ash-thin paper.

'Things I couldn't face sorting. Old bills and stuff that probably needs shredding.'

Anna slotted the folder back on top of a stack of similar-looking coloured wallets, and couldn't help noticing what was written on the front of the one below. She pulled it out and stared at the four capital letters inked in marker pen: *FIBS*. Why had her mum hidden a file of *lies* in the family furniture?

'Did you know this was here?' asked Anna, holding it up to show her dad.

'What's that?' He bent forward to peer over her shoulder, his eyebrows crinkling as though they were conferring with each other. 'Fibs?' he said with a frown. 'Doesn't mean anything to me. Not sure I like the sound of it, though.' He went to sit down, as if physically taken aback at the thought Marion had kept certain things private.

No matter how close you were to a person, were there always some unvoiced secrets concealed somewhere? wondered Anna.

Robert rubbed his chin. 'It's your mother's stuff, so maybe we should just leave it be.'

Anna brought the file over to the sofa, rested it on her knee. 'But why's it with my things – that she wanted me to find – then?'

Robert yawned, as though his drained brain couldn't reason with any reliability at this hour. 'Wouldn't she have told me, if it was something she wanted us to see?'

'Well, maybe not if it wasn't to do with you, and it was meant for me,' said Anna.

Robert settled back in the armchair, relieved at the idea that the fibs inside the folder might not affect him. He didn't want any part of his life with Marion to have been a lie. 'Then it's up to you,' he said, with a tired nod.

Anna looked at her dad, his eyelids as heavy as his heart. 'I should let you go to bed.'

'No, it's okay,' he said, using yawns as punctuation now. 'Nice to have your company.' He reached to put their cups back on the tray, as though by keeping moving he could stave off sleep.

Anna flipped open the folder, not so much out of curiosity as a need for more connection with her mum. When she'd seen all the photographs and features Marion had saved, Anna had felt a closeness to her that she'd been craving for the last thirty years.

But the contents of the cardboard wallet weren't at all what she was expecting, despite the fact she didn't know what she'd presumed to find. There weren't any pictures of the past. The collection of printed documents inside was purely concerned with the future.

Anna started to skim-read the sheaf of official-looking papers.

'And?' prompted her dad, too drowsy to use full sentences anymore.

'There are no confessions or anything, don't worry. It's an acronym.'

'Pardon?' replied Robert, whose eyes were now completely closed, as though he was conserving the last of his energy by concentrating on only one of his senses. 'I was listening, I promise.' He'd sunk so far down in his chair he was almost horizontal, but he shuffled upright and waited for Anna to continue.

'FIBS. It stands for Females in Business Scheme,' explained Anna, scanning the pages in her hand. 'Mum was setting up a mentoring programme.' Her eyes glistened, and in a reversal of roles, it was her turn to be proud of her mother. 'It's to support women in their professional careers,' Anna said, feeling her lips tremble. 'I guess she saw me struggle at some points, fighting my corner in some of the kitchens I worked in . . .'

Robert was awake now. 'She'd started *what*?'

Anna passed him the paperwork.

'Goodness me,' exclaimed Robert, raising his eyebrows.

'It's a cause she knew I felt strongly about,' said Anna, resting her head in her hands. 'She mustn't have had the chance to see it through to the end . . .' Anna searched her pockets for a tissue. Grief could jump out at her like a jack-in-a-box. 'Not the best name though, is it, we'll have to do something about that,' she added, thinking of the Grimfluence agency, or whatever it was called, and shuddering.

Robert passed her the papers back. He was on his feet now, a final stand against slumber.

'Maybe we could call it something Cumbrian . . .' Anna said. Thinking of the Lake District always stirred up her best ideas.

'Yes,' said Robert, yawning so widely Anna worried he might wobble backwards. 'Good plan.'

'It's Mum who's done all the hard work,' said Anna, wrapping her arms round the wallet and hugging it tightly to her. She knew in that moment that she would carry on what Marion had begun. 'This could have the potential to help so many people.' Anna leaned her chin on the hard, card edge of the file, curling her body round it protectively. 'Think of the power for *good*.'

'She was a very good person,' said Robert, never too tired to utter praise for his wife.

Good. The word rolled around Anna's head as she clasped the folder close to her heart for the rest of the way home. The project would be such a positive force, a scheme to support those just starting out in their industry, linking them up with people more experienced. Perhaps Rose could be *her* first mentee, Anna wondered, as she unlocked the door to her house. When at last she flopped into bed, she gave a sigh that had lived inside her since the day her mum died. But tonight she had finally said farewell to the lung-squeezing shame she had carried ever since. And in the few fleeting seconds it took for her to fall asleep, for the first time in what seemed like forever, she herself felt good.

15

'Barry as in the boy's name?' said Robert, doing his best to maintain a neutral face, but failing, like he'd been dared to take a bite out of a lemon and not make a fuss.

Anna shook her head. 'No. Barie as in "good".'

'Ah. In Cumbrian dialect,' replied her dad.

'Yes.' Anna nodded.

'Right.' Robert spluttered like he'd accidentally swallowed a pip. 'I think it'll probably make more sense when you show me the designs for it – the logo and everything,' he added diplomatically.

Anna felt deflated, like she was made of delaminated croissant dough. Her idea hadn't gone any better when she'd told Dani earlier in the day.

She'd spent the morning ensuring everything was set for Sally's return that evening and now, in the interim between the lunch and dinner services, she was sitting with her dad in his sun-gilded garden, discussing what to call the mentor scheme.

'Dani didn't like it either,' said Anna, recalling her colleague's reaction to the title 'Barie Business Mentorship Programme.'

Her pastry chef had wrinkled her nose before saying, 'No, I'm not a fan of that, to be honest.' For all the time Dani appeared to waste, she saved a lot of it by never beating around the bush. 'It would make more sense written down, but when you say it out loud, "barie" sounds like a lad's name.'

'I liked that double meaning,' countered Anna. 'I thought it underscored the point,' she explained. 'In a subtle way.'

'What do you mean?' Dani's expression was twisted like a cheese straw.

'Well, you've always gone by Dani, or Dan, haven't you,' said Anna. 'Never Danielle, in the kitchen.'

'Yeah, I suppose you're right.' Dani nodded. 'I've had jobs where it felt like being a woman went against me.' She frowned at the memory. 'But not here, boss,' she added. 'This is the best place I've ever worked by far.'

Anna's eyes had stung like she'd been chopping shallots.

'And whatever you call this mentor thing, it's a great idea. You've taught me *so* much. Totally shifted my focus as a chef. Opened up my eyes.' She'd mimed prising apart her eyelids with her fingers. 'Before I started here, there were so many things – right in front of me – that I never knew existed. Think of all the amazing foraging stuff you've shown me.'

Anna had smiled, allowing herself to accept the compliment because she knew Dani meant what she said – she only ever spoke straight from the heart.

'All those articles about you championing women, they're totally true. None of the head chefs I've worked under in the past – male or female – have been half as supportive as you.'

'Really?' Anna raised her eyebrows.

'Yes.'

Anna swallowed as her old nickname threatened to lurch into the room like a spectre.

'And for the record, that stupid "cold as an air-conditioning unit" stuff is *rubbish*, okay? You're dedicated to what you do, and you don't stand for any nonsense, because you know that we have to be a *team*, because if we're not then the whole thing goes to shit.'

Anna bit her lip; Dani spoke so emphatically that all she could do was stand still and take notice.

'What you've done is *bloody* impressive, boss. You've changed my life, for one. The staff here are *family* to me. And you've shown me a whole new world of ingredients – all that wild food out there' – she flung a hand towards Hesta's back door – 'with flavours that blow my mind.'

Anna was blinking rapidly now.

'Buttermere is a *better place* because of you. Think of all the happy faces there are in that restaurant at the end of every service.' Dani jabbed her finger in the direction of the dining room. 'Those people come to Hesta to celebrate their birthdays, engagements – or just being here in the Lake District, on their holidays or whatever. You put the essence of Cumbria on a plate for them, *and you should be very fucking proud.*'

Anna couldn't help but laugh at Dani's swearier remix of her mother's words.

'But I can't believe you never told me your mum was a chef too,' Dani finished, with a shake of her head.

A little while ago, Anna would have crumbled at a remark like that, but with her mother's letter still echoing in her mind, she felt bolstered. She pushed back her shoulders. 'Yes, she was. She ran this place once, before she . . .' Anna faltered. 'Back when I was in London. I guess I wanted to do things under my own steam, not hang on to her coat tails to get ahead.'

'I would have clung right on to them.' Dani cackled. 'But I know what you mean. You wanted to prove you could do it yourself, without any help.'

Anna had nodded. 'But that was before I realised that actually, everyone needs a bit of help at some point.'

Now, as she sat in the garden in the honey-gold last of the heatwave, she took a sip from her glass of elderberry cordial. The rich, red drink was like liquid rejuvenation. She turned to her dad on the bench beside her. 'Dani had the same reaction as you.'

'Right.' Robert seemed relieved.

'No one achieves anything completely by themselves,' mused Anna. She sucked in a deep breath of summer-afternoon air: honeysuckle and sweet pea.

'How about the Marion Carleton Mentor Scheme?' she suggested, trying it out on her tongue. She smiled at the sound of it. 'What do you think?' She looked at her dad, his face tipped skywards as if consulting his wife.

'I like it,' he said. 'Very much.'

Anna gave a nod. 'Mum started the whole thing, so it feels right.'

'And you're continuing it.' Her dad turned towards her. 'A joint effort.' His lips shivered despite the warmth of the afternoon. 'She's still alive in you and Matthew, you know,' he added, his voice catching in his throat. 'That's what she'd say.'

Anna put a hand on his arm. 'I know. And every time someone says her name, or enrols in her programme, it'll keep that amazing spirit of hers going.'

Robert tilted his face back to the sun and closed his eyes, and Anna sat next to him, in silence, letting the flutter and buzz of the August garden wrap them up in the present, preventing them from slipping back to the past.

16

The scorching torture of the hot spell had ebbed away into autumnal blusters, and the atmosphere in the kitchen was much more pleasant. Sally was back, safety-briefed and suitably sorry for not saying anything sooner, and there was a fresh-start feeling among Hesta's staff that this time of year seemed to inspire.

Outside the restaurant, September had swathed the valley in splendid auburn-bronze shades, and adorned branches with lustrous berries that Anna sought out like priceless jewels.

She left Hesta through the back door, wound her way between the hedgerows of the lane that led towards the farm, progressing at a caterpillar's pace as she collected blackberries and sloes as she went, delighting at the layers of beauty that could be found in Buttermere's bushes and borders. Blackberries decorated the scramble of brambles like black diamonds, and the purple-blue bloom of the sloes never failed to make her smile: they were ripe and ready to be turned into all sorts of treats.

The lambs that had arrived in the spring were now grazing the fields surrounding Fell View, no longer wobbling on new-born legs, but frolicking on the grassy fellside, grown enough to stray from their mothers' sides.

Anna paused her berry-picking to take in the end-of-summer scene, marvelling at the cycle of the seasons, the natural progression of the animal and plant worlds. *We're part of all this*, she thought to herself. It was an interlinked tapestry that took her breath away.

Then the revving sound of a quadbike tore through the afternoon, and a few seconds later Anna turned to see Will driving towards her from the village. She raised a hand to wave as he passed, but to her surprise he pulled up beside her.

'Presume you're coming to this "soft opening" thing?' he asked, dispensing with any form of greeting. His wind-wrinkled expression didn't indicate whether or not he was pleased.

'Yes,' said Anna, her intonation making it sound like a question.

He had so much soil on his skin, in stripes on his bare forearms and beneath his fingernails, it was as though he and the earth were one. 'I'll give you back your basket then. Still got it,' he said, managing to make it sound like she'd inconvenienced him, when in fact she'd gone out of her way to take him refreshments that day in the field.

'Right,' replied Anna. She wondered whether to risk wishing him and Rose well with the last of the preparations, or if that was like taking a lit match to a straw bale and expecting it not to flame. She decided against it; they were on reasonable terms at the moment, and surely that was better for everyone.

'Very good,' he said with a nod, and then, with a roar of the engine, he drove the quad off in the direction of the farm.

'I wish we could have got everything up and running before now,' said Rose, early the following morning when she was dropping off the milk and butter. 'We missed all that sunshine,' she added, scrunching up her face.

'I can eat ice cream in any weather,' said Dani with a shrug. 'Special talent.'

Anna pursed her lips at her, before turning to Rose. 'I think you've done a good job moving as quickly as you have,' she said. 'It's no mean feat setting up a new business.'

'I couldn't have done it without you,' said Rose with a smile. 'And Jackson's been a rock too . . .' she added, almost to herself. The slightest smile flickered across her lips.

'Ooh, do I detect a hint of romance?' said Dani, giving up any pretence of kneading her bread now she'd sniffed out some gossip.

A crimson blush flushed Rose's cheeks.

'Ooh, I'm *right*,' declared Dani, eyes alight.

'For goodness' sake, you're like a truffle pig,' said Anna. 'Give the girl a break.'

Dani reluctantly turned her attention back to her brioche.

'If there are any final bits I can help with, let me know, okay?' Anna said to Rose, unloading the last of the milk.

Rose picked up the empty crates. 'You've done more than enough, and I'm so grateful,' she said. 'I couldn't have asked for a better mentor.'

'Are you on the Barry's Business thing?' asked Dani, ears pricking up again.

Rose's brow crumpled with confusion.

'It's called the Marion Carleton Mentor Scheme,' said Anna to the first audience that wasn't her dad.

'Oh, I like that.' Dani gave a nod. 'After your mum?'

For once, Anna smiled at the mention of her. She drew in a deep lungful of air as she stood in the centre of Hesta's kitchen, at the heart of the building where her mum had once worked too. 'Yes.'

But she noticed that Rose had sunk down against the worktop, no longer holding the crates, but cradling her head in her hands instead.

Dani grimaced. 'What did I say?' she mouthed at Anna. 'Oh, *shit*,' she added when she realised. 'I'm so sorry,' she said aloud to Rose. 'I didn't think. I really didn't mean to—'

'It's not your fault,' said Rose, lifting her head and smiling determinedly. 'It just hits me sometimes, and I struggle to get my head round it . . .'

Anna nodded, but there were no words she could think of that would make the situation better. She knew that platitudes only clanged like banged pans, hollow and unhelpful. She understood what it was like to not have a mother, but she could grieve hers, whereas Rose was left with the acute ache of abandonment.

Dani managed to control her craving for details for once. She didn't know the ins and outs of what had happened, had only heard that Rose's mother Lilian had left the farm for a new life in Manchester a long time ago – when her daughter was only a little girl – yearning for the hustle and hurry of the city.

'I get so confused with myself about it all,' continued Rose. 'I'm angry with her for leaving us and starting again, but sometimes I wish she was here, and she could see everything I've been doing . . .'

131

Anna's chest squeezed.

Rose heaved out a sigh, as though physically expelling her emotions.

'Do you ever see her?' asked Dani, face creased with compassion rather than curiosity this time.

Anna opened her mouth to intervene, but Rose shook her head in answer to Dani's question.

'You don't have to tell us . . .' said Anna, but when Rose continued to talk, she felt touched that the girl felt comfortable enough to tell them her story. Maybe it was cathartic, getting it out of her system. She wondered whether Rose ever spoke to Will about how she felt; and found herself hoping she did but fearing she didn't.

'She tried coming back a few times to visit but it felt weird, the way she popped in and then all of a sudden was gone again,' Rose explained. 'I found it too difficult, the way she was all chatty, always full of compliments about the farm and for me, like she was a stranger, a tourist or something.' Rose paused, as if snagged in the past by the prickly recollection. 'So we eventually lost touch. She kind of faded out of my life.' Rose swallowed. 'It's like I don't have a mum.'

Anna felt a churning squirm of empathy in her stomach.

'Did you think about going with her?' asked Dani, brioche abandoned on the side.

'Dad said to, if I wanted to.' Rose pressed her lips together to stop them trembling at the memory. 'But this is where I belong. Buttermere's part of me. I don't want to be in some big city, that was Mum's dream not mine, and I think she could see that. She could tell I was happy here, among the hills and the fields. And what would have happened to Dad? I couldn't leave him.'

'He would want what's best for you,' Anna found herself saying – for all Will's faults, his gruff manner and resistance to change, she could see he loved his daughter with every cell in his body.

'I know,' Rose acknowledged with a small smile.

'So you haven't seen your mum since you were little?' asked Dani, mouth agape.

'Not much, no,' said Rose. 'When I was old enough to go and see her on my own, there never seemed to be a good time. We were trying so hard to keep on top of things at the farm – I couldn't just drop everything as soon as Mum was free. And she was busy as well. So eventually we sort of stopped seeing each other.'

Silence seemed to ricochet off the stark surfaces that surrounded them. Even Dani was lost for words.

'We used to speak on the phone a bit, but I guess I felt like baggage from a time before. Like by calling I was dragging her back here to somewhere she didn't want to be. And she didn't really ever ring me.'

'Maybe she thought she was doing the right thing, leaving you to it,' said Anna, more aware now than ever that people's intentions could be so different from the way their actions came across to those they cared about most.

'How could it possibly be the best thing for *me*?' retorted Rose, a flare of defiance making her voice high-pitched.

'She might have thought she didn't want to upset you by interrupting your life here,' replied Anna.

Rose sighed. 'Maybe you're right. I don't know. Anyway, I get a card from her at Christmas and on my birthday, and that's about it.'

Pretty much the same relationship she and Matthew had, realised Anna, picturing her brother in Salford, working at

Media City, immersed in a brightly lit hub of cosmopolitan activity. Only two and a half hours away by car, but the complete opposite of Buttermere. The elastic bond that connected her and Matthew had expanded and contracted across space and time throughout their lives, occasionally snapping back to the closeness they'd shared when they were younger, but nowadays stretched and slackened. She ought to make more of an effort to speak to him. Maybe even take a bit of time out and go to Manchester. Customers travelled to Hesta from all over the country and would think nothing of such a journey. But the distance between them was down to more than geography. Anna had fallen into the gaping hole their mum left behind, while Matthew seemed to be standing on the other side of it, out of reach.

The sound of Rose slapping her hands on her thighs made Anna glance up.

'Anyway, I'd better get back,' said the girl, grabbing the boxes. 'And let you carry on.'

Dani patted the ball of brioche dough, pretending she'd never broken off her bread-making.

'Right.' Anna gave a nod.

'See you on Sunday,' said Rose, her wide eyes searching Anna's face for confirmation.

'Yes,' said Anna.

'Absolutely,' said Dani. 'Ice cream, you scream!' she added in an attempt to lighten the mood.

We all scream, thought Anna, as she watched Rose walk to the door.

17

'Sorry I couldn't get here before now,' said Anna, when Robert answered the door. 'We had this one table that would not go.'

He already had his coat on, had probably been sitting in it, waiting, for the last half an hour, she thought as a prickle of guilt made her shiver. September had brought a chill in the air, and although it was only four o'clock, the light was beginning to fade behind the fells.

She gave him a hug, noticed he was wearing a shirt her mum had given him one Christmas, wondered whether that was so he'd feel as though she was coming with them too. She would have liked it, thought Anna, as a memory of the four of them eating towering ice-cream cones on a family holiday, years ago, flitted into her mind. She blinked, and the image was gone again.

Robert turned back from locking the door and she linked his arm as they started to walk along the lane.

'Well, that's a good sign, if your guests don't want to leave,' said Robert, looking up at the cloud-covered sky and taking a deep breath of cool afternoon air. Perhaps he hadn't been outside all day, wondered Anna, and a familiar twist of worry knotted her tummy.

'So what is it we're going to again?' he asked as the farm came into view round the corner.

'The soft opening of Wild Rose Ice Cream,' Anna announced, noticing rosehips decorating the hedgerows either side of them like little ruby baubles trembling with excitement in the breeze.

'Ah.' Robert nodded. 'You brought me a tub of it, a while back.'

'Yes.' Anna squeezed his arm. A carton of ice cream wasn't going to give him back his zest for life. She wasn't doing enough. But what more could she do? There was an amber flare of fairy lights flickering on up at the farm as twilight tried to gate-crash the party. Perhaps the answer lay ahead of them, she wondered, thinking back to the glimmer of a grin she'd seen on his face the night he'd stood in for Sally at the restaurant. Might the newly formed Wild Rose Ice Cream company provide an opportunity for him to feel more like himself again?

They turned up the track to Fell View, and Anna noticed a few figures further ahead of them, hunched against the blusters. She looked behind her and saw a stretched-out straggle of villagers. All together, they formed a kind of elongated snake making its way towards the farm.

'You came!' said Rose, as they reached the barn, but her smile slipped away like the disappearing daylight. 'Shame it's not really ice-cream conditions,' she added, glancing up at the billowing sky.

'Bet it still tastes just as delicious,' said Anna, jerking her head at the shining glass cabinet in front of them, stacked full of an assortment of intriguing flavours.

Rose beamed. 'Hopefully.'

'And in fact this is a nice fine day, for the Lake District,' said Robert with a chuckle.

Rose laughed. 'Suppose you're right. Here, come and get a cone,' she added, indicating the variety of ice creams and sorbets there were to choose from, with a sweep of her hand.

'Oh, well now, how to choose?' said Robert, reading the labels with all the flavours. 'I'll have to have seven scoops.'

Rose giggled with bubbling pride.

'I'll have a crab apple one, please,' said Robert.

'This is my dad,' said Anna.

'I'm Wild Rose,' said Rose, in return.

'Robert. Pleased to meet you,' he replied. 'And congratulations. I was lucky enough to try the very first batch, I think' – he turned to smile at Anna, and she felt warmth flood through her chest as though the sun had come back out – 'and it was sublime. I wish you all the best with it.'

'Oh, Anna's my inspiration,' said Rose, eyes bright beneath the fairy lights. 'She encouraged me from the start.'

Anna felt a hot prickle of self-consciousness needle her spine. She hoped Will wasn't near enough to overhear. She looked about, and couldn't see him, but noticed several other pairs of eyes swivelled in her direction. There were more people here than she'd thought. Rose had said it would be a low-key launch. She was eager to get up and running to catch the tail end of the summer season, but Anna had been under the impression it would be only a handful of villagers here to wish Fell View Farm well with its new venture. She could hear whispered murmurs swirling about her like a babbling beck threatening to bust its banks. She clutched her dad's arm tighter.

'You're the guest of honour,' Rose said with a grin. 'I've got a red ribbon . . .'

Oh god. No. Anna's cheeks were on fire.

Rose was holding out a pair of scissors. 'We'd love you to say a few words. I think everyone's here to see you, really.' She laughed, visibly thrilled at the turnout.

'Local celebrity,' said her dad, letting go of her arm as though he was weighing her down.

'No, honestly, this is your night,' said Anna to Rose, holding up her hands. The dusk air chilled the bare skin at the base of her neck.

'Come on, boss!' boomed a familiar voice from behind her, followed by a boisterous clap. Anna twisted round to see Dani putting her fingers in her mouth to whistle raucous encouragement. 'Give the crowd what they want!'

A semi-circle of faces, pale and partly illuminated by the glow of the barn, were all tilted to look at her, like a crescent moon of expectation.

Anna's heart pummelled her chest. This wasn't her place. She was more on display than the ice cream in the chiller cabinet. More of an attraction for onlookers. The main draw. This wasn't what she'd wanted at all. She'd been happy to help Rose with product development, offer some words of support. But this event wasn't about her. She didn't want it to be. She'd always hated public speaking – she wanted her food to do the talking instead.

Her dad was clutching his crab apple cone now, and the rest of the audience were eating their ice creams and sorbets with their attention on her, like they were munching on snacks at the cinema.

Suddenly her throat felt dry, as though she'd sampled a spoonful of a flavour named 'sawdust'.

Robert beamed at her, an anchor in the ocean of anticipation.

Anna summoned a smile in return; she thought of her mum, who'd started setting up her mentor scheme with women just like Rose in mind, and stood taller as she realised this was exactly the kind of scenario Marion must have envisaged: a community coming together to support one another. She cast her eyes round the barn at the faces as familiar to her as the fells surrounding Buttermere. This village had rallied round her and her dad when they'd needed it most, and now this was her chance to give something back. Maybe this *was* where she was meant to be after all.

'It is my very great honour to welcome you all here today,' Anna began, a grin breaking out on her lips like a surprise sunbeam bursting through cloud. 'To celebrate the first day that Wild Rose Ice Cream is officially open to us lucky public,' she continued. 'It's a hugely exciting venture, and Rose, we are all behind you.' She cast her eyes around the barn to search her out, but instead caught sight of Will standing at the back, wearing a scowl. Then Dani whooped from somewhere near the front, and Anna found the courage to carry on. 'We're all immensely proud of what you've achieved so far' – Anna gestured round the twinkling interior of the barn – 'and we wish you a future filled with success.' Her gaze finally alighted on Rose to the left of her, and she saw the girl's hope-soaked expression, her dreams for the fledgling business so loud and clear they could have been painted in speech bubbles above her head. 'I for one cannot wait to try *everything* in this cabinet,' Anna added, pointing at the selection of hand-crafted flavours on display. A murmur of agreement rippled round the barn. 'Wild Rose Ice Cream is a taste of Cumbria—'

'Cheaper than Hesta!' someone heckled from her left-hand side.

Anna swallowed, sought out her dad and focused on him instead. 'It's made with the highest quality ingredients, including milk from Fell View Farm's very own dairy herd,' she continued, 'and unusual, interesting flavours that you won't find in *any other* ice-cream shops.'

A hum of appreciation reverberated round the walls. 'It's organic, all natural, and contains the finest fruits, nuts, and plants picked locally here in beautiful Buttermere. This is what really sets Wild Rose apart,' said Anna, finding her stride as she spoke about the landscape that seemed to reach out and restore her whenever she faltered. 'It's a breath of fresh air. The flavours are all sourced from within a few miles of the farm, and I guarantee there'll be something you haven't had before.'

A collective 'ooh' echoed throughout the barn. 'So without further ado, I declare Wild Rose Ice Cream officially open,' she called, cutting the red ribbon adorning the great glass chiller cabinet beside her. 'Let's hear it for Rose!' she finished, flinging an arm in the air, as the silken strands separated and Wild Rose Ice Cream officially entered the world. A chorus of cheers erupted, filling the barn to its rafters.

'Speech from the founder!' someone shouted.

Anna saw Jackson ushering Rose forward, kissing her before she stepped out from the throng.

Dani had been right about the burgeoning romance, realised Anna, as she sank back from centre stage, her job done, and sought out her dad.

He squeezed her arm once she was by his side. 'Well done,' he whispered.

But she wasn't out of the spotlight yet.

'Anna has been an integral part of the whole process,' Rose was saying.

The gathered group angled its gaze once again towards her.

'She made me believe I could do this and has been the most wonderful mentor. So, thank you,' she added, lifting her arms in an appreciative clap and encouraging others to join in.

Anna's skin was clammy. Rose had already expressed her gratitude; she didn't need to do it again in front of everyone. 'It's been my pleasure,' she mumbled as applause encircled her.

'And Jackson, you've been an amazing help too,' Rose said and, with a rush of relief, Anna felt the attention of the room swivel towards him instead. It was like stepping into a patch of shade on a sweltering day. 'I couldn't ask for a more supportive boyfriend.'

Anna caught Dani, in the crowd, giving her an I-told-you-so wiggle of her eyebrows.

'And Dad,' said Rose.

Anna glanced up. Will was no longer glowering; now his daughter was front and centre he was gazing at her with unadulterated pride. He wiped his eyes briskly with a sleeve, as though he'd suddenly been struck by hay fever.

'I know you weren't totally on board with the idea at the start,' said Rose, and silence descended upon the room as though unseasonal snow had started to fall from the ceiling. 'But thank you for always being there for me.' Her words rang out into the communal hush. 'I know it'll take a lot of hard work, running two businesses, but you've had two jobs for most of my life – being both a mum and a dad when I needed you to be.' Rose's eyes shone beneath the strings of lights. 'And lastly, thank you to everyone here for turning out to wish us well and for fully getting behind us. They say it takes a village to raise a child, but it takes a very special place like Buttermere to make it feel like home.'

The clapping that followed seemed to make the beams above vibrate.

'Three cheers for Rose!' shouted Jackson, cupping one hand round his mouth and wrapping his other arm around her shoulders. 'Hip hip!'

'Hooray!' rumbled the entire barn in response.

'Right,' said Anna to her dad, once the noise had melted away to a lesser level of chatter. 'I think I'd better get to Hesta.' She checked her watch. 'Full restaurant tonight.'

'Surely you've got time for a quick ice cream before you go?' he replied. 'You haven't even had one. Take a cone with you, at least.' He turned to see the swarm of people surrounding the display cabinet, like butterflies fluttering round nectar. 'Ah. Well, we can safely say the weather hasn't put anyone off,' he said with a chuckle. 'I'll head back with you,' he said, waving to acknowledge someone Anna vaguely recognised on the far side of the room, possibly the postman, but she couldn't be sure as she was always already at work when he called.

'No, you stay,' said Anna, putting a hand on her dad's arm. 'There are loads of people you know here,' she added, now searching the crowd for Dani, unconvinced she'd be quite as inclined to leave the get-together. 'And please thank Rose for me, if you get chance.' She watched Rose trying to keep up with the queue of customers flocking round the ice-cream counter.

'I will,' he said, acknowledging one of Marion's friends, who was now making her way through the horde towards them, holding hands with her husband as though they were traversing an unchartered jungle.

'See you soon, okay?' said Anna, squeezing him goodbye. 'I can always call round later.'

'I'll be fine, I promise,' said Robert with a smile. 'Go and cook up a storm.'

She hugged him again, before he was entangled in conversation with the couple coming over to speak to him.

Anna craned her neck – there was Dani, an ice cream in each hand, over in the corner where there was a bit more space to concentrate on the taste, but away from the sparkly lights. Here shadows congregated, and it was only when she left the crush and got closer that she realised Jackson was there too standing beside her.

'Evening,' he said with a nod as she approached, his eyes narrow.

'Here she is,' said Dani. 'Told you I had to get my quota in before she said it was time to go,' she added, waggling her cone-clutching fists. 'I take it we've got to leave?' she said to Anna, twisting her wrist to look at her watch in a carefully calculated manoeuvre, before resuming with her alternate licks of each flavour.

'Yes,' replied Anna. 'I know we prepped as much as possible before but—'

'No rest for the wicked,' interrupted Jackson.

Anna tried to smile but she felt like someone had sprinkled chilli seeds on her skin.

'Nice to meet you,' said Dani, pausing to wish him goodbye.

'Likewise,' replied Jackson. 'I didn't catch your name?'

'Danielle,' said Dani with a grin in Anna's direction, and suddenly Jackson's spikiness didn't seem to matter so much. As they walked through the joyous mass of ice-cream-eating guests, making their way towards Hesta, Anna felt her self-consciousness fade with the last of the day. She'd made a difference to Rose, and to Dani, in some small way.

18

'Not sure I should have eaten both of those, actually,' said Dani, putting her hands on her stomach like she'd swapped places with Sally. 'It's macaroni cheese for the staff meal as well, isn't it?' she said with a wistful smile.

Anna gave her a sideways glance as they wove their way towards the restaurant.

'I'll have to take mine home and have it later,' murmured Dani, not needing a response to continue a conversation.

But her colleague's companionable chit-chat was a welcome contrast to the unexpected stress of the soft opening, thought Anna, as the ochre glow of Hesta's interior came into view round the corner. Through the glass-fronted doors, she could see Ovie already sitting at the reception desk, checking through the reservations for that evening, and a wave of contentment came over her. The kitchen was her comfort zone.

'So how was it?' asked Sally when she came in at the start of her shift.

'Uh-ma-zing,' said Dani, closing her eyes for a moment. 'I had a hazelnut butter ice cream *and* a hedgerow sorbet which had all sorts of berries in – sloes, rosehips – did you not fancy coming?' she asked, merging sentences the same way she blended ingredients.

'Wanted to put my feet up for a bit,' said Sally. 'You know, recharge before tonight.'

'Oh, of course.' Dani shook her head. 'Didn't think.'

'D'you want some of this, Sal?' interjected Anna, in the middle of dishing up the team dinner.

'Yes, please,' she replied. 'I'm starving! I seem to be so hungry at the moment.'

'Go on, I'll have some, actually,' said Dani, leaning forward to admire the molten-gold sauce and crispy breadcrumbed top of the pasta. 'Can't resist this,' she said.

'Ooh, look at that!' said Ovie, coming in through the swing doors from the restaurant. 'Smells *delicious.*' He took the plate Anna handed to him. 'How was the ice-cream event? I wanted to go but, you know, would have missed bath time and seeing the kids before bed . . .'

Anna squeezed a generous dollop of shop-bought ketchup on her supper, from the bottle she kept in the fridge for just these kinds of occasions. 'It was . . . *nice,*' she said. Nice. The compliment that was really a criticism.

Ovie raised his eyebrows.

'She didn't like being the centre of attention,' explained Dani, reaching for the tomato sauce.

'Ah,' said Ovie. 'I see.'

Anna scooped up macaroni with her fork. 'I wanted to show my face but—'

'She had to address the whole village, and cut a fancy ribbon – and you didn't even get any ice cream, did you?' Dani bit her lip in mourning of the missed opportunity.

'You had mine, though,' said Anna, and Dani smiled like she'd just been commended for a selfless act.

'It was lovely to see so many people there, and to wish Rose every success with it,' said Anna, scraping the last glossy globules of sauce from her plate. 'But I'd rather be in the background.'

Ovie nodded. 'You always have done.'

She smiled at him, never quite able to believe that he'd uprooted his life and followed her to the Lake District to be front of house at Hesta.

'But I'm afraid you have quite a lot of fans, and sometimes people want to see their hero in the flesh.' He shrugged.

Anna went to slot her plate in the dishwasher, as though by leaving the spot where she'd been standing, she'd avoid the tribute altogether. She glanced up at the clock, keen to shift the subject away from her fame. 'Anyway, service is about to start, so let's get a move on, shall we?' she said, and everyone snapped into action, except for Dani, who traipsed towards her section with the speed of a slow worm, and a moan about having eaten too much.

'Right, last dessert going out now,' announced Dani loudly later on, as if there wasn't only her and Anna left in the kitchen. 'I can't wait to lie down,' she added as she placed the final dish on the pass and shouted 'service' at the top of her voice. 'I don't even want to *look* at any ice cream.' She held up her palm to obscure the perfect quenelle that accompanied the pudding she'd just put down.

'You can go if you want, I can do the clean down,' said Anna, thinking clearing up on her own was preferable to hearing Dani complain her way through it.

'Are you sure?' replied her pastry chef, already untying her apron.

Anna nodded, in keen anticipation of the calm to come. She wanted to pin down the last few elements of the upcoming autumn menu, and a peaceful atmosphere was key.

'Okay, see you tomorrow then, boss,' said Dani, halfway to the door.

'Bye!' called Anna, starting to scrub the worktops, the recipes whirring in her mind the moment the kitchen fell quiet. She ran through the finished dishes: the winter squash and smoked mackerel starter was sorted, and so was the ribeye main with mushroom-salt rub . . .

Then, once every surface was spotless, she went through to the empty restaurant where the tables were all set for the following day. She printed off a copy of the draft menu and took a pen from the front desk, then dimmed the overhead lights down low and pulled out a chair next to the big dark window, a blank canvas for her creativity. The black lake seemed to lap at the glass and she felt closer to nature with the wild outdoors facing her. She gazed out at the wide night, let the stillness envelope her. Ideas began to float forth and soon enough she was scribbling down different flavour fusions and concepts she wanted to develop. Autumn was her favourite time of the year for foraging; the Lake District's open-air larder seemed to be fuller than ever, brimming with vibrant ingredients. *Hawthorn berries*, Anna thought, imagining the citrusy taste in jams and jellies. They were meant to be good for the heart, she mused, a memory of Dominik drifting into her head—

A noise from the kitchen made her back stiffen. She froze, and for several seconds every sense in her body seemed to be on high alert. She could have sworn it sounded like someone coming in through the back door. She waited for them – Dani probably – to call out, but, when no other noise came, she scolded herself for being so jumpy and breathed slowly to settle her thudding chest. *Must have been the wind.* But at this hour, even the breeze seemed to have gone to bed, as Buttermere's waters were mirror-smooth and unmoving beyond the window.

The bang of an intruder. Unmistakeably threatening, like the single beat of a war drum.

Anna stood up, eyes wide in the gloom of the unlit restaurant.

Then a clattering noise and a shrapnel-string of expletives – someone was most definitely in the kitchen.

And it certainly wasn't Dani, because the voice Anna had heard was male.

19

Someone had broken in; Anna was sure of it. *Well, I left the back door unlocked for them*, she thought, certain they would think Hesta was deserted at this time of night, with all the lights turned down so low and no sign of any staff still here. She swallowed. What on earth should she do? Any moment now they were bound to come through looking for the till – they had to be searching for cash on the premises, or anything they deemed valuable enough to steal. The computer, maybe. She glanced over at the reception desk. Ovie would have locked the front door beside it from the outside. The only exit was through the staffroom to the rear of the building. She turned towards the kitchen. She was going to be forced to confront whoever it was. Probably the same person who'd thrown the stone through the still-room window, she thought, with a sudden surge of indignation. Adrenaline raced through her body, and her skin tingled like she was right in the midst of the most intense shift she'd ever worked in her life. Her legs propelled her forward, her brain doing its best to predict possible scenes that might meet her on the other side of the double doors. A troublemaking teenager, most likely. She told herself it would be nothing, they'd be scared away as soon as she appeared. But fear coursed through her body as she reached the threshold between confrontation and cowardice. Perhaps she should crawl back to the front desk and call the police, that would be much more sensible, but volcanic curiosity bubbled beneath her skin. She wanted to know who the trespasser was. She inhaled a sharp lungful of air as she raised a hand to push her way through to the other side of the doors, her mind deafening her with danger warnings as she did so. Then she burst into the kitchen and came face to face with a man standing by her chef's knives in the silvery half-light.

'Jackson.' Anna's rib cage felt as though it might explode with the force of her thumping heart.

Jackson took a step towards as her, as though daring her to flinch.

'If you wanted to frighten me, you've succeeded,' she said.

'Good.' He spat, eyes like slits in a medieval helmet. 'Come to teach *you* a lesson for a change.'

Anna didn't speak for a moment; all too aware that she herself had recently sharpened the razor-like edges of the knives. She kept her eyes fixed on Jackson, refused to look at the glinting metal tips hanging from the magnetic strip merely a metre from her face. She weighed her options carefully like she was crafting a recipe, not potentially walking a line between life and death.

Jackson jabbed his finger in the air to make her jump, and she jolted backwards a step. He laughed, seemingly high on having control in a place like Hesta's kitchen, and, judging by his breath, more than a little alcohol.

Sandwiched between the swing doors and Jackson, Anna felt the creep of claustrophobia scratching at her skin. Her stomach roiled.

'Meant to be a *culinary wizard*, aren't you, Anna Carleton?' he said, words dripping with ridicule. 'Well, how are you going to *magic* yourself out of this, then?'

Anna's mouth was parched like her tongue was a piece of rice paper.

'Hello?' rang out a voice from the staffroom, making Jackson start just as much as Anna.

'What the fuck?' he mouthed at Anna, knocked off-balance by the fact she had conjured up a saviour.

Sally, thought Anna, picturing her KP's pregnant stomach and praying to god she didn't come anywhere near the kitchen.

'Everything all right, Sal?' she called through to the back, keeping eye contact with Jackson as she did. 'Forget something?'

'Yeah, left my phone charging, didn't I?' The click of a cable being yanked from a plug socket. 'Got it now. See you tomorrow!'

'Bye!' replied Anna, but the small burst of relief she felt as Sally left unscathed was swiftly extinguished by the suffocating silence she left behind.

'Where were we?' said Jackson.

'Look, just take whatever it is you're after,' said Anna with a shake of her head. 'Cash, equipment, I don't know—'

'I don't want any of this shit,' he retorted. 'You think that's why I'm here?'

'Well, you haven't really said . . .' replied Anna but the noise of Jackson sweeping the Pacojet to the floor drowned her out.

She watched as other appliances crashed onto the tiles with metallic clangs.

'So, you wanted to speak to me, then?' Anna asked, when Jackson seemed to think enough debris decorated the ground.

'Yep.' He flashed a disdainful grin. 'Finally got my chance. That Danielle said you'd be here. Couldn't have stopped her blathering on if I'd tried, but as it turns out, she was *very* helpful. Told me all sorts of stuff. Didn't even have to ask.'

Anna swallowed as she remembered seeing Jackson standing beside her at the party.

'Told me you often worked late,' he continued, sticking out the thumb of his left hand as he numbered off the facts she'd given him. 'Always the last one here, when no one else was around.' He looked about the empty kitchen with menacing emphasis. 'Shouldn't have hired an idiot for your sous chef, should you.'

Anna winced like cold water had been poured down her spine. 'Dani's not an—' she began, feeling compelled to defend her pastry chef, but then a realisation struck her. 'Hang on, how do you know the hierarchy?' she said, feeling like she'd suddenly been shaken awake.

'What?'

Her question seemed to have wrongfooted him; out of the corner of her eye, she saw his shoulders lower an inch.

'You know the second-in-command is called a sous chef,' said Anna steadily.

'So? You think *I'm* an idiot because I work up at the farm?' Jackson hissed, clenching his fists.

'You're the only one saying anyone's an idiot,' Anna shot back, before glimpsing the bone-white knuckles of his balled hands, and feeling regret needle the base of her neck. 'I think you're very intelligent, actually,' she said and, to her surprise, she found she meant it.

'Flattering me's not going to get you anywhere,' said Jackson, but she could see it had confused him.

'And Rose clearly thinks the world of you.'

'Leave her out of this. I've had enough of you taking all the credit, making out like it's you who's responsible for every little thing when she's done it all herself. She doesn't need you. You haven't got a clue about the real world.'

'Then tell me.'

'What?' Jackson's eyes were red-mad paper cuts in his pale-white face.

She waited for him to explain.

'You think you're so fucking special with your fancy restaurant. It's a different life up there,' he jabbed a finger in the direction of Fell View. 'So stay away.'

'I'm not the enemy, Jackson,' she murmured, as anger blazed in his gaze. 'I was trying to help.'

'What do you know about *anything* up at the farm? What makes you think you can mentor everyone else all the time?'

'I could help you, you know, if you let me.'

'Fuck off.'

'I don't think we're that dissimilar, in some ways.'

'Are you *joking*?'

'And I knew someone on the farm once, when I was about the same age as you—'

'I don't want your fucking life story, okay?'

'Well, then, tell me yours. I think there's more to you than meets the eye.'

'What's that supposed to mean?'

'I know what it's like to hurt too, you know.'

Jackson's eyes shone and he rubbed the fingers of his free hand furiously across his face.

Suddenly Anna could see a love-starved little boy standing there beside her in the body of a man, and she wondered whether his appetite was actually for attention, rather than violence. 'I think you're trying to punish me for pain you feel.'

'Don't you tell me what I'm doing – you're not an expert on *everything*, even if you think you are.'

'What exactly have I done to cause you so much grievance?' Anna glanced around at the trashed kitchen, thinking how needless destruction never gained anything in the long run.

'You stand for everything that's wrong with the world,' shouted Jackson.

'Please will you explain how that's the case?' replied Anna, palms outstretched, genuinely wanting to understand. Having that accusation levelled at her stung like being handed a fistful of nettles.

'Places like this,' shouted Jackson, prodding the air. 'They're the reason my parents were never around. Too busy eating at the latest restaurant, swanning off to wherever, to bother about *me*.'

Anna thought of her own mum and dad and how devoted to her and Matthew they'd been. She couldn't imagine what it was like to grow up without that kind of demonstrative affection, but it was clear Jackson's suffering was an inferno inside him that he didn't know how to quell.

'There was always something more exciting than being with me. Wining and dining in all the latest restaurants with their fancy friends. Left me alone, with some nanny that couldn't care less. I don't know why they had me in the first place, if they didn't want to *be* with me.'

'People are such complicated things,' said Anna.

'Well, it's quite fucking simple really. Kids want time, not stuff.'

'But you're not a child anymore. Your life can be your own. You don't have to be a product of their making.'

'I'm *nothing* like them,' Jackson retorted.

'No, but this is your way of railing against them, isn't it? Taking out your unhappiness by doing things like this.' She waved a hand at the scene of devastation that surrounded them. 'You're protesting against a place that you associate with your parents and their kind of lifestyle.'

Anna felt a pang of pity as she watched him sag like a batch of forgotten profiteroles left out on the side. She expected him to shout at her for presuming anything about him, but instead Jackson drooped against the metal cabinet next to him and covered his face with his work-calloused hands.

'It's an understandable, if not wholly reasonable, reaction,' Anna said. 'Is that why you labour up at the farm? Because it's the complete opposite to their world?' Anna was experiencing the same puzzle-completing sense of satisfaction she felt when a risky new recipe was coming together. The pieces were starting to fit before her eyes.

'Yeah,' answered Jackson, his fingers falling away as though the rage he'd felt had suddenly fled his limbs. 'Can't really get much more opposite.' He gave the smallest hint of a smile. 'I tried a few different things before I came here, but the Lake District is just something else.' He sighed. 'It's very special.'

'I agree,' said Anna, returning his smile, as a sliver of similarity shimmered between them.

'I wanted to be closer to nature. We're part of this landscape, but everyone seems to have forgotten that.'

Anna nodded. 'I know what you mean. But not *everyone* has.'

Jackson opened his mouth, but then closed it again, as if the fight in his belly had abated.

'And Dani's a *chef de partie*, by the way,' said Anna. 'She looks after the pastry section, but we all tend to muck in as a team, to be honest.'

'Can't see the great Anna Carleton doing the real dogsbody jobs somehow,' replied Jackson, still some last dregs of aggression left in him like left-over spatters of hot oil fizzing in an empty frying pan.

'Well, who do you think's going to clean all this up?' she shot back, hands on her hips.

Jackson seemed to simmer down again, slumping against the work surface.

Exhaustion washed over Anna now, and she started to feel a headache hammering at her skull.

'I'm sorry,' said Jackson, so softly Anna wondered whether she'd hallucinated it in her tired state.

'Rose would be so ashamed of me if she could see . . .' He started to sob, his broad shoulders bobbing as he heaved out his sadness. 'I don't deserve her.'

'No, not if you're going to carry on like this, *ruining* things rather than nurturing them.' Anna folded her arms. 'But she thinks the world of you, Jackson.' She remembered Rose speaking about him, right there in Hesta's kitchen, in the run up to the ice-cream shop opening, with such a tender look on her face. 'She said you'd been a rock . . .' As she repeated the words Rose had spoken, a thought unfurled in her fatigued mind. *A rock.* 'You threw the stone through the window, didn't you?' she said, the realisation hitting her like she'd been physically struck.

157

Jackson nodded, the heels of his hands pressed into his eye sockets as though to protect him from the repercussions of his actions. 'I'm so sorry. I shouldn't have done it. It just sort of happened. Hit a nerve. All the chinking glasses. Reminded me of my parents. I could see you all standing in the restaurant, drinking champagne, looking all smug . . .'

Anna gritted her teeth. The memory of her team gathered together for a moment of hard-earned celebration flitted into her head. 'Those people work day in, day out, just like you do, and they deserved that,' she said. 'You need to look beyond first appearances, Jackson. Learn not to simply *assume*.' She thought of all the wild ingredients she foraged among the fells and forests, and how important it was to study each one carefully, make sure a plant was really what it seemed. 'The staff here are passionate about what they do, and preserving the landscape, too, you know. They have as much appreciation for nature as you. Don't confuse a few customers like your parents with the chefs behind the scenes.'

Jackson slid to the floor and covered his head in a crash-landing position. The image of him in a sea of wreckage reminded Anna of the accident with the—

She slapped her hands over her mouth. 'Jesus Christ!' she exclaimed. 'The helicopter incident . . . did *you* have anything to do with that . . .?'

Jackson howled like a wounded dog, curling onto his side on the tiles. 'I swear I didn't mean for anyone to be harmed . . .'

'What did you think would happen?' Anna raked her fingers though her hair.

'I don't know,' he wailed.

'What did you do, for god's sake? Tamper with it in the field?'

'No. I chucked a rock . . .'

'Christ, Jackson. What did you expect?'

'I didn't mean for it to . . . I thought it would dint the paint . . . annoy the owner. Not cause *that*.'

'Must have been some stone.'

'It wasn't. It was only like a pebble, too small to use for the wall. But it hit the tail rotor . . .'

'*Jackson*,' breathed Anna.

'I wasn't even aiming for it . . . I just . . . I was angry at them for arriving like that and—'

'I can't believe what I'm actually hearing.'

Jackson wailed as regret punched him in the stomach. 'I never imagined they'd end up in hospital. I only wanted to . . . cause a bit of inconvenience . . . make them think twice about their choice of transport to a sustainable restaurant—'

'Punish them for being like your parents. Or so you presumed.'

Jackson emitted an affirmative moan. 'Oh god.'

'Bloody hell.' Anna rubbed her temples. 'That family could have been *killed*, Jackson.'

'I know, and I can't tell you how much that eats me alive every single day,' he said, voice hoarse with emotion. 'I can't believe it crashed. I would never do anything I thought would actually injure someone.' Jackson met her gaze with urgent eyes. 'You have to know that,' he begged, his tear-damp cheeks bright red with the effort of explaining himself.

Anna saw the truth burning from his body. 'I believe you,' she said, and he sank back against the stainless-steel cabinet.

20

She should call the police right this second, Anna thought, the horrifying realisation that Jackson was responsible for such a sequence of events circling in her brain. She put her hands on her pockets.

'Let me do it, please,' croaked Jackson, as though they'd managed to bond enough for him to read her thoughts. He looked up at her. 'I'll ring them myself,' he said, holding out his hand for her to pass him her mobile. He closed his eyes in surrender and keened like a maimed animal. 'Rose will break up with me when she hears . . .' he said with an anguished groan. 'And Will'll get rid of me.' He scrunched up his face.

Anna heard the utter despair in his tone, yet she knew the best thing she could do was not to offer empty comfort but try to do something practical.

Jackson splayed his fingers, waiting to feel the cold touch of the fate-sealing phone.

But Anna took his hand and pulled him to his feet instead.

'What are you doing?' he said. 'Let me sit there and wait for them to come, please.'

'You can help me clear this up first,' Anna replied.

Jackson shook his head. 'I think we're meant to leave everything . . . it's a . . . crime scene,' he said between sniffs. He wiped his eyes with his shirt sleeve and blinked as if he could hardly believe the damage he'd done.

'No. This is the start of a new chapter, Jackson.' Anna picked up a metal baking sheet from beside his feet and put it by the sink. 'You can wash anything salvageable,' she added with a jerk of her head towards the spray tap. 'Seeing as it's all been on the floor.' She raised her eyebrows at him.

Jackson swallowed. 'Are you serious?'

'Yes. Come on, chop chop, plenty more jobs after that.'

'I don't understand.'

'If you help get this kitchen straight, you'll have one less thing on your plate. I can't help you with the helicopter incident' – she saw Jackson wince like she'd pinched him – 'but I can wipe the slate clean from that point onwards.'

'Why would you do that?' said Jackson.

'Because I don't know what there is to be gained from making you feel worse than you already do now. I think all this' – she swept a hand through the air to encompass the mess before them – 'is a cry for attention. The actions of a desperately unhappy person.'

'Rose makes me happy,' said Jackson. The slight smile that appeared as he spoke her name dissolved again. 'She's the best thing in my life, and now I'm going to lose her.'

'Let's deal with one thing at a time. As wonderful as she is, Jackson, that acceptance of yourself, that *peace* you're searching for, is something she can't give you. That has to come from here.' Anna pressed her palm to the left side of her chest. 'I should know.'

21

'Where's the Pacojet?' asked Dani with a frown the following morning.

'Broken,' replied Anna. She'd had two hours' sleep and hadn't quite worked up to using full sentences yet.

'How?' said Dani, staring at the space where it normally stood on the work surface. 'I only used it yesterday. It did that damson sorbet perfectly.'

Anna wracked her barely awake brain for an explanation, but balancing the truth with what was best for Jackson's future was a difficult equation.

'What's happened?' said Dani, scrutinising her boss's face.

'Er . . . I . . .'

'What's going on?' Dani glanced round the kitchen. Clocked other equipment that was missing. 'Have you sold it? Wait a minute, have we got money problems? But we've been so busy lately—'

'No, that's not it.'

'What then?'

'I thought it was time for an upgrade—'

'Bollocks.' Dani cut in. She was scrutinising the floor for clues now, leaving no centimetre of the tiles unscoured. 'There's something you're not telling me,' she continued, with the tenacity of a sniffer dog.

Anna felt the itch of untruth irritating her throat. She coughed. 'Look . . .'

'What's this?' said Dani, bending down to pick up a shard of broken crockery. 'We didn't use these dishes yesterday. They're for the new autumn menu.'

Dani was wasted as a pastry chef, thought Anna. She should have followed her cousin's choice of career instead.

'Right, I'll tell you, but you mustn't say a word, Dan,' said Anna. 'I mean it. It's really important.'

'Why?' Dani folded her arms.

'Because everyone deserves a second chance,' Anna replied. 'Remember when you said the staff here were family to you and that coming to work at Hesta had—'

'Changed my life,' finished Dani. 'Yes.'

'Well, can you think back to how you felt before that?' asked Anna.

'Don't really want to, it was a pretty shit time, but yeah, I guess,' said Dani. 'I was stuck. Lost. Had no proper direction. Was just grinding away.' She blew out a breath. 'Probably about to burn out, if I'm honest. Fed up of working fourteen-hour days for someone who couldn't care less . . .'

'Right. And then?'

'I came to the Lakes, and started here, and you showed me how to forage, helped me find my style as a chef, took the time to teach me new techniques – wait, you know all this, boss. What is it you're trying to get at?'

'The point is, you were going down one route and you wanted to change that and go in a different direction.'

'Correct.'

'Well, there's someone else who needs a bit of help to do the same.'

'Hang on, are you replacing me?' asked Dani in disbelief.

'No! That's not it at all.' Anna sighed. She put her hands on her hips. 'There's no other way to say this . . . Jackson came to the restaurant last night. Intending to ransack the place. He broke some of the equipment.'

'Christ on a stick.' Dani cupped her hands round her mouth. 'The guy I was talking to at the ice-cream thing?'

Anna nodded.

'Holy shitballs,' Dani gasped. 'I told him you'd be here,' she said, through her fingers. 'It's my fault he knew where to find you. I was chatting to him about—'

Anna held up a hand. 'It would have happened anyway. It was only a matter of time.'

'What do you mean?'

'He's had it in for me for a while, for reasons we've now talked about – calmly – and I think we understand each other a lot better for it.'

'What are you, the fucking *thief whisperer*?' said Dani, eyes wide. 'He could have hurt you.'

'I think it was a call for help.'

Dani put her hands on her head. 'Are you crazy?'

Anna shook her head. 'He knows wrecking things isn't the answer, really. I think he was on a path of self-destruction more than anything.'

'Well, thank fuck the Pacojet's the victim here and not you,' said Dani, her arms falling to her sides in astonishment.

'He apologised.'

'I should think so.'

'And offered to call the police of his own accord.'

'Good.'

'This isn't gossip, Dan, okay?' said Anna. 'You gave me your word.'

Dani sighed. 'I promise I won't say anything. To anyone.' She puffed out her cheeks. 'But I will say this: you're a very special person, Anna Carleton.'

22

A loud knock on the back door meant Anna didn't have a chance to acknowledge Dani's compliment. For a moment, she wondered whether the rapping knuckles might belong to the police, and the subsequent shiver of shock she felt seemed to make her skin shrink around her flesh, but when she heard Will's gruff voice shout 'Good Morning', relief rushed through her.

'Got me today, not Rose, I'm afraid,' he said as he plonked the dairy delivery down on the countertop. 'She's busy doing ice-cream orders already.' He grinned. Pride shone from his face the same way the moon was lit by the sun.

'How did the rest of the evening go?' asked Anna.

'I didn't want to leave,' added Dani dreamily. 'That berry sorbet . . .' She licked her lips.

'Oh, it was *grand*,' said Will with a nod, but he was already disappearing back out to the van.

Dani raised her eyebrows at Anna. 'Busy man. Runs an ice-cream empire now, I heard.'

Anna laughed. 'Well, I'm pleased it's off to a good start, anyway.' She reached for a saucepan just as Will reappeared in the kitchen.

'This is for you,' he said, setting down her own wicker basket as though it was a gift he'd woven himself.

'Oh. Thanks,' replied Anna, feeling Dani's inquisitive gaze upon her.

'Righto. Take care.' Will raised a hand in a wave and then was gone.

'Why'd he have that, then?' asked Dani as soon as he'd left, going over to inspect the basket.

Anna felt a warmth flare across her face like she was standing by the switched-on hob mid-service. 'Um, I took him a bit of cake when he was silage-making. Ages ago. Back in summer—'

'OOOH!' interrupted Dani, distracted by the contents of the basket. 'Look what's inside!' she squealed, lifting out a tub of Wild Rose Ice Cream like it was a new-born baby. 'Meadowsweet,' she cooed, reading aloud from the label. 'Notes of almond and vanilla.' She sighed gleefully. 'I was dying to try that one.' She cradled the container, before lifting out another one. 'Ugh. Wild mint sorbet' – she stuck out her tongue – '*Toothpaste* flavour. Not bothered about that one.' She dug to the bottom of the basket like an intrepid excavator. 'Blackberry and crab apple,' she declared, tilting her head from left to right as she weighed her verdict. 'Can take it or leave it.' She lifted out the final tub. 'Yes! Some of that hedgerow one too!'

Anna came over to stand beside her.

'Oh, look, there's a note as well,' Dani said, plucking out a card tucked into the bottom of the basket. 'Addressed to you.' She handed it to her. 'Ah,' she said with a sigh. 'Does that mean all the ice cream's meant for—'

'You can share it,' said Anna as she took the envelope. 'Unless we have to give it to our customers because there isn't anything *else* for them to eat,' she added pointedly.

Dani began putting away the milk and butter. 'Bagsy not the Colgate flavour,' she called over her shoulder.

But Anna didn't hear; she was too absorbed in reading Will's handwritten words.

Dear Anna,

I know we haven't often seen eye to eye on things, but maybe that's because I've had mine closed for a very long time. Rose always tells me I'm set in my ways and it's true, I don't do well with change. I tend to associate it with bad things happening. For all my many faults, I have tried to be a good father to Rose and all I want in the world is for her to be happy. Seeing her in her element last night was something very special. I have you to thank for that. I'm sorry we got off on the wrong foot but, if you're willing, I'd like to start again. Hearing Rose speak so fondly of you in her speech melted my stubborn old heart. We are both very grateful for all you have done for us.

Regards,
William

Anna closed the card and looked at the picture on the front. She'd been so eager to see what he'd put inside, she hadn't even glanced at it. A photograph of Buttermere. The lake with Fleetwith Pike beyond, but, instead of being in the background, the mountain was the main focus of the shot. The image was moody and almost completely black-and-white, but there was a chink of light breaking through the clouds in the top-left corner that rendered it hopeful, rather than gloomy.

'What's it say?' asked Dani, looking over in her direction.

Anna pushed the note back into its envelope and flipped it over. 'It says "To *Anna*",' she enunciated loudly, before slipping it safely into the pocket of her apron.

When the last of the lunch guests had left, and everyone else was taking their afternoon break between shifts, Anna made herself a double espresso and sat down to run through the reservations for that evening. She yawned, feeling as though, if she closed her eyes even for a split-second, she'd fall asleep right then and there. She gazed out at the wind-rippled water beyond the glass and rested her weary body against the back of her chair. She took a sip of her drink as she tore her attention away from the window to read the printout in her hand. She scanned the notes and special requirements: four vegetarian diners, one guest that was allergic to shellfish, and a party of six celebrating a fiftieth birthday party. A mix of regulars, a lovely couple who lived in the village and – Anna almost spat out her mouthful of locally roasted coffee – Olivia Lawson on table nine.

23

'She's paying for the meal herself, apparently,' said Ovie with a shrug, when Anna asked him about the booking that evening. 'She asked to be put on the cancellation list a while ago, and then a table for two came up for tonight.'

Anna pursed her lips.

'Card details are all saved here on the system,' he added, angling the computer screen on the front desk so Anna could see for herself. 'Not sure why she thought she could have it all for free the first time,' he added with a sideways glance. 'I know they say your food is magic, Anna, but all this' – he wafted a suit-swathed wrist for emphasis – 'doesn't just *appear* out of nowhere.'

'Maybe she's used to that happening, being lavished with things,' said Anna.

'Probably, but at Hesta all guests are treated exactly the same,' he said with a nod, and straightened his already-straight tie. 'Each and every person that comes through those doors deserves to feel special,' he added with a glance at the gleaming glass-fronted entrance with its frosted logo of foraged foliage encircling the initial 'H'.

Anna smiled. Ovie's devotion to delivering the best possible customer experience was second to none, and she was extremely fortunate to have him heading up front of house.

'I hope she doesn't spend the whole time staring at her phone,' he said with a sigh. 'She wouldn't get the full experience and it would be such a shame.'

'Well, let's give her a chance to prove she can survive without it before we just assume,' said Anna.

'There's no point coming all the way to the Lakes if she's not going to actually *appreciate* it.'

'What the customer *thinks* is out of our hands, Ove,' replied Anna with a shake of her head. 'But what they *eat* is not, so I'd better get back to it,' she smiled.

'Have you seen this, boss?' asked Dani, thrusting her phone at Anna as soon as she was on the other side of the swing doors. 'Olivia Lawson's coming to Cumbria.' She tapped the screen at lightning speed to show a series of posts.

'Oh, yes, the *influencer*,' replied Anna, just to see Dani's eyebrows raise in surprise.

'D'you reckon she's coming *here*?' said Dani, retracting her arm to reanalyse her findings. 'Hesta's the best restaurant in the Lakes, after all.'

Anna opened her mouth to say there were plenty of other places that were just as good, but closed it again, touched by Dani's fervour.

'She *should* be, if she isn't,' Dani continued, the phone screen a few centimetres from her face. 'It's hard to tell exactly where she's off to, though, from her social media trail. I guess she can't be giving away her exact location' – she scrolled through a series of dishes pictured on Olivia's profile – 'For security reasons,' sounding as though she were Miss Lawson's official spokesperson.

'So, you're one of her four hundred thousand followers, then?' asked Anna.

'Yeah,' replied Dani without looking up. 'She does loads of food stuff. Reviews. Restaurant promotions. Look.' She tilted the phone to show Anna, as though sure that, if they were discussing something culinary, the conversation could technically still be classed as work.

'Lovely,' said Anna to the grid formation of perfect squares. The images were too small to see clearly, and she had a fully booked restaurant due within the next couple of hours that she was more concerned about.

'She's been to all sorts of places. High end as well as cheap eats. Have to check out the competition, don't we, boss?' said Dani. 'Keep an eye on what everyone else is doing.'

Anna shook her head. 'Or we can just focus on our own thing.'

But Dani wasn't listening. 'She's going out with that guy off the TV . . . you know, whatsischops.'

'Ah, yes,' said Anna, with no desire to know who he was or to encourage that strand of enquiry.

'A lot of the places she features are in Manchester, obviously, but she does go all over,' said Dani, zooming in on one post. 'She went to London a couple of days ago. To a pop-up called A Pitta Me. Best tzatziki outside of Greece, apparently.'

'Good to know. If we're ever in London. But right now, Dan, we're in the kitchen at Hesta, and I really need you to crack on.'

'She's just put up another reel,' squealed Dani.

'Right, okay. I've got an announcement,' said Anna, clanging a metal spoon against a saucepan. 'We're actually about to cook for the woman herself, so would you *please* do some prep?'

'WHAT?' Dani's head snapped up. 'Olivia Lawson's booked in *tonight*?'

'Yes.' Anna sighed.

'Why didn't you tell me?'

'I had a wild idea it might distract you.'

'Oh my god. I can't believe it. How did you find out?' asked Dani, finally reaching for a baking tray.

'There's a new sleuth in town,' replied Anna. 'So you'd better concentrate on your day job.'

Dani's eyes were wide.

'Only joking,' said Anna, standing by the stove. 'Her name's written in the reservations book.'

'She's here!' shouted Dani from her lookout station behind the double doors that led into the restaurant. 'She's soo glossy and gorgeous,' she gushed, peering through the little porthole window. 'I love what she's wearing. It's like a silky green jumpsuit,' she said over her shoulder. 'With a stole.'

Thank goodness Dani was responsible for puddings, not starters, thought Anna, as she listened to the running commentary from over by the pass. Contrary to her hopes, confirming that Olivia was indeed eating at Hesta that evening had led to an even slower pace of pastry-cheffing than had previously been achieved.

'I feel like a gremlin,' said Dani, glancing down at her clogs.

'Well, you're not, you're a *chef*,' called Anna to no avail.

'I haven't caught sight of the boyfriend yet,' said Dani, standing on tiptoes to try and get a better view. 'I can't fully see their table from this angle.'

'Sorry, should have had an open kitchen, shouldn't I,' said Anna.

'Ooh, Ovie's coming!' Dani announced, leaping away from the doors. 'Wonder what Olivia's having . . . she'd better leave room for one of my desserts . . . imagine if she posts about it!'

'Table nine's order,' Ovie said as he came in.

'Table nine, check on!' shouted Anna, taking the slip of paper he handed her. 'One goat's cheese and one hen of the woods, followed by one bream and one open lasagne.'

'What's she like?' asked Dani, putting a hand on Ovie's sleeve as he passed her.

'You know I don't like talking about the customers, Dani,' he said with a shake of his head. 'It's not . . . polite. But she seems a bit . . . upset. So, let's do our best to cheer her up, shall we, and serve her the best meal she's *ever* had.'

'Sent back from table nine,' said Ovie, sliding the untouched starter onto the pass.

'Is that Olivia's order?' asked Dani, coming over to see what was wrong.

Anna studied the plate beneath the spotlights. Perfectly pan-seared. Still hot; she could see the steam coming off it.

'What reason?' she asked, taking a spoon to sample it for herself: the butternut squash purée beneath the hen of the woods steak was smooth, and the wild mushroom sauce was full-bodied and flavoursome. The seasoning was spot on. Everything was as it should be.

'She thought it would be "chicken, not a mushroom",' quoted Ovie.

'Right.' Anna flinched involuntarily. Whenever something was returned to the kitchen, however rarely, it always felt like she'd failed – the customer was dissatisfied, even if it wasn't really her fault.

'But it clearly says it's not meat on the menu!' exclaimed Dani, with such outrage Anna could tell her fandom was being tested. 'There's a "V" symbol next to the description!' she added, looking like she might be about to give Olivia a V-sign of her own. 'And she hasn't even tried it! So how does she know she doesn't like it?' She turned her back on the porthole window and the glimpse of summer-grass silk visible beyond. 'I wouldn't have expected that from Olivia,' she said as if they were real-life friends. 'I thought she'd know her stuff. She's meant to be a food influencer. Why didn't she ask, if she didn't know what it was?'

'Maybe she didn't want to admit it. Easier to say it's not up to scratch,' said Ovie.

'Well, it's back here now, so let's try and sort it out. Would she like something else instead?' Anna asked Ovie, setting aside her dismay to try and solve the issue.

'No, she doesn't,' said Ovie.

'Nothing?' interrupted Dani. 'She's come for dinner and she's not going to eat anything?'

Anna reached for the rejected dish. 'Look, you can have it, Dan. I know how much you love hen of the woods,' she said, knowing there was only one way to stop Dani speaking.

'Definitely don't want it going to waste,' Dani replied, already starting to devour it.

'Okay, well, offer her a drink, or anything else she'd like,' Anna said to Ovie, subdued at the fact that, so far, Hesta clearly wasn't to Olivia's taste.

'I already have,' said Ovie, smiling at her supportively. 'Fingers crossed for the mains,' he added before disappearing back out to the restaurant.

'Unbelievable,' said Dani with her mouth full. 'Doesn't know what she's missing.'

'At least you know it's her and not you,' said Ovie as he put Olivia's discarded second course down on the stainless-steel shelf once again, totally intact.

'What's wrong this time?' said Anna, lifting up a golden layer of her handmade pasta with a fork to reveal the fragrant porcini filling.

'She said it's fallen apart.'

'It's an open lasagne!' said Dani. 'It's a deconstructed dish! This is fucking ridiculous.'

'That's all?' asked Anna with a glance at Ovie. 'She won't eat it because it doesn't look like a regular one?'

'How's she an influencer when she's *completely* closed off to anything different?' cut in Dani.

'She said it's too many mushrooms for one meal as well,' admitted Ovie.

'She's the one that bloody ordered them, isn't she?' said Dani, digging into the abandoned dish. 'I'm going to sprinkle them on her pudding if she's not careful.'

'She's not having one,' said Ovie. 'Just a chamomile tea.'

'Probably be too soothing for her,' said Dani. 'But that'll be your problem, as we don't do the hot drinks.'

'What about everyone else?' Anna asked Ovie, setting out a row of azure and turquoise glazed pottery plates for the party celebrating the fiftieth. 'Is the rest of the restaurant okay?'

'They're all really enjoying it,' said Ovie.

A peal of laughter followed by the jingle of glasses clinking post-toast filtered through to the kitchen as Ovie opened the doors to return to front of house.

'Oh, that table had better be careful,' said Dani, licking her spoon. 'Sounds like far too much fun for Olivia's liking.'

Anna had just sent out six different main courses for the birthday group when Ovie came back in with another message from Olivia.

'She wants a tour of the kitchen.'

'Now? In the middle of service?' said Dani, arranging cheese biscuits on a board.

'She can come in for a quick look, but it's a bit hectic,' said Anna, relieved she'd got the big party's mains out of the way.

'But she didn't even like any of the food, so why does she want to see where it was made?' said Dani.

'She says she wants something exclusive.' Ovie left off the latter half of Olivia's sentence: 'not something boring that anyone else can order.'

'Something off the upcoming autumn menu, maybe,' said Anna, trying to run through the new dishes they'd been working on in her head, while keeping track of what was due out next from the pass. 'How about a piece of that parkin you made?' she called to Dani.

'Won't it be too cakey for her?' came the reply.

'Ooh, it was delicious,' interjected Sally, coming over to hand Anna a clean pan. 'Made me feel so much better when you gave me some to try this morning – and I was really out of sorts.'

'Sounds like just the ticket, then,' said Ovie.

Anna turned to face him. 'It's the only thing I can think of that's ready to go. Freshly made today.'

'Perfect,' he replied, disappearing to deliver the news.

'She's getting rewarded with a free dessert for being difficult,' declared Dani.

'Well, I'd like her to leave happy, if possible,' said Anna.

'Sounds about as likely as me leaving a billionaire,' shot back Dani.

'And what's this?' asked Olivia, holding up the cube of gingerbread between her forefinger and thumb. An array of rings glittered as she examined it.

'Hogweed-seed parkin,' said Dani.

'Pardon?' said Olivia, wrinkling her noise as though the answer had been '*Poison*'.

'We hand forage the seeds of the common hogweed,' Dani started to explain, noticing how Olivia's lips puckered at the mention of the word 'common', but it was an important distinction. Giant hogweed was an entirely different beast—

'Why would you do that?' asked Olivia, with a shake of her head that made her gold earrings wink. 'Put random plant bits in the recipe.'

'Flour comes from a plant,' said Dani, under her breath.

'It's a wild spice, and it has a lovely bitter-floral flavour,' said Anna, holding out a container of the ground seeds. 'We toast them to really bring out the aromatics. Have a smell.'

Olivia looked at the contents like Anna had offered her a box of animal droppings. 'No, thanks. Not my thing.'

'Well, these notes of cardamom, orange peel and ginger really make a simple parkin sing,' persevered Anna, before her pastry chef could say anything acerbic.

178

Dani's sideways glance said *I bet she'd still be unimpressed if it literally burst into song.*

'Tastes like bonfire night,' concluded Anna, realising not a single crumb of the cake would be passing Olivia's lips.

'I'll take your word for it,' said their guest. 'Doesn't really look that sexy, though, does it?' she said, flicking a wrist at the finished traybake. 'Bit brown, to be honest. Wouldn't look good in a photo.'

That was the final straw for Dani. 'It's not plated up with all its accompaniments, is it?' she said, whisking the parkin out of sight. 'I don't think you'd like *anything* we gave you, would you? Even if it was a fucking jewel squid, hand-dived by mermaids, you'd find a reason to send it back.'

'No, I wouldn't,' said Olivia, jutting out her chin. 'That would get loads of likes on social media.'

24

'I'm sorry but she was being totally out of order,' said Dani, wiping down her section. 'She needed telling. Nothing we could have done would have pleased her, and I'd bet my last bean there's more to this than meets the eye. There's a bigger reason she was acting like a total—'

'Thank you, Dani,' said Anna, yearning for silence after the brain-splitting intensity of service. 'You can go home now. I'll sort the rest.'

She'd comped Olivia's entire bill, apologised profusely for any upset, and sent her home with a hamper of Anna Carleton products, including the last jar of spiced plum chutney. All she could do now was hope for the best.

'See you in the morning,' she said to Dani, trying to chivvy her out of the door. She wanted some space to decompress after the events of the evening.

But Dani wasn't for shifting.

'I'm determined to get to the bottom of it,' she said, phone in hand. 'It's not right we get the brunt of her bad mood.'

'You can't please everyone all of the time,' said Anna.

'But the customer is *not* always right,' retorted Dani.

'I know, but sometimes it's best simply to swallow it.'

'Disagree. We cooked our bloody guts out, for her to throw it back in our faces. Fair enough if there was a valid explanation. But she was clearly wrong way out from the start. We didn't have a chance.'

'There are bound to be difficult guests, you and I both know that,' said Anna. 'We've dealt with hundreds of them before, and we will do again. But you can't go around—'

'Dishing out home truths?' finished Dani. 'I don't see why not, if they *deserve* it.'

'Because it leaves a bad taste, Dan.'

'Doubt it, seeing as Olivia wasn't up for having any other taste in her mouth – she didn't eat a *thing*,' said Dani.

Anna sighed, defeated. Dani was defiant. And despite the fact she'd had to do some serious damage limitation, deep down Anna had to admit that part of her admired the fact Dani had called out Olivia's rude behaviour. She wished she'd stood up for herself more, especially in the past, when she was younger. Perhaps then things would have turned out differently with Dominik.

'I knew it!' declared Dani, yanking Anna out of her thoughts. 'There aren't any photos of thingamy on her Instagram anymore! They've all been deleted!' she said in the sing-song voice she used for breaking news. She tapped away on her phone for a few seconds, then looked at Anna, suddenly solemn, like a reporter glancing up from their notes to announce a national bulletin. 'Olivia Lawson and Freddie Beaumont have split up,' she stated, as if it were a headline. 'Only just announced. She hasn't made an official statement yet but there's no trace of him on any of her social media accounts.'

Anna felt the searing sting of heartache suddenly hollow her out, an unexpected aftershock so many years on.

'That's it,' said Dani, tearing her gaze away from her phone. 'That's why she was being such a complete—'

'You were right,' said Anna, folding her arms as if wrapping a makeshift bandage round her ruptured chest; she knew the empty echo of lost love all too well, and it never seemed to hurt any less, no matter how much time passed. No wonder Olivia was distraught; there was no bodily pain that compared.

'She's been dumped,' said Dani.

And that was where the similarity in her and Olivia's situations ended, thought Anna. For it had been her who had been the one to say goodbye to Dominik.

25

'She's still here,' declared Dani the next morning, as though Olivia was a poltergeist that haunted Hesta.

Anna didn't engage; they had a mountain of mise en place to do before lunchtime.

'She's posted a selfie from by the lake,' carried on Dani, never requiring any secondary input to continue a conversation. 'She's put "Better off in Buttermere" as the caption. Confirms I was right about the break-up.'

Anna had tried to push the previous evening from her mind, but a kernel of concern had planted itself in her stomach and, with every sentence Dani spoke, it seemed to expand.

'Any mention of the meal here?' she asked, the question spilling out before she could stop it.

Dani shook her head. 'No. Think we might have had a lucky escape. Maybe the change of scene really has sorted her out and she's woken up all refreshed and full of the joys of the world.'

'Let's hope so,' said Anna, as tendrils of doubt tightened round her tummy. She'd met too many onion-layered individuals with all their intricacies and idiosyncrasies, throughout her years in hospitality, to believe that would actually be the case. People were as unpredictable as the Cumbrian weather and as multifaceted as the landscape. Herself included. She knew how life shaped you into someone else over time. The heat and pressure of a succession of commercial kitchens had transformed her, the same way metamorphic rocks were created.

Beep beep beeeeeeeep. A tractor horn blasted from beyond the back door.

Probably Will, stuck behind a tourist trying their best to navigate the narrow lane, thought Anna.

Beeeeeeeep beeeeeeeeep beeeeeeeeep. Right outside the restaurant.

'Think someone might be trying to get your attention, boss,' said Dani, tucking her phone into her pocket as though the noise had pulled her back to the real world from the depths of the virtual one.

Anna made her way towards the din, reasonably unconcerned because, surely, she and Will had reconciled their differences. He'd given her that thank-you note, hadn't he? So why did she get the distinct impression his irate honking was directed at her, rather than a fellow driver—

Beeeeeeeeeeeeeeeeeeeeeeeeeeeeeeeeeeeeeeeeeeeeeeep.

'All right!' said Anna aloud, as she stepped beyond Hesta's back doors and walked towards the lane.

He'd pulled into the gateway at the side of the road and was clambering down from the cab. 'I need to speak to you,' he shouted, slamming the door and making the whole vehicle shake. 'About the *visitor* you had.'

The sky glowered above, the clouds threatening thunder as much as Will.

Oh god, he must know about Jackson, thought Anna. That had to be why he was here.

'Please, come in,' she said, gesturing for him to go into the back. The last thing she wanted was any of Hesta's guests getting an impromptu package of a meal plus a show.

Will didn't sit down, and the room seemed to shrink with his broad frame filling it.

'Look, I didn't tell you about our unexpected guest because I thought this would be how you'd respond,' began Anna, an image of Jackson, hunched and vulnerable on the kitchen floor, appearing in her head. What good would it have done to make him feel worse? Crush him down further? There had to be a balance between dishing out comeuppance and stamping on the final spark of hope someone had for a happier future.

'How could you possibly know how I'd react?' roared Will. 'You have no idea what effect this will have—'

'Well, I was right, wasn't I?' said Anna, gesturing at him standing in front of her. 'You're furious.'

'I'm not,' replied Will, his cheeks beetroot. 'I'm concerned about Rose getting hurt, but you wouldn't know that because you don't have all the facts—'

'You have to let her make her own decisions,' said Anna. 'I know what it's like to have an overbearing parent who thinks they're doing what's best for you.' She put her hands on her hips.

Will raked his fingers through his wind-wild hair. 'I just want to protect her – she's my absolute *life*.' He thumped his chest, an audible full-stop.

'That's clear to see,' said Anna more softly.

Will sank down on a chair and it creaked with the weight of his worry. 'I know it won't make sense to you, but I don't

185

want them to see each other.' He covered his eyes with earth-streaked hands.

'You can't stand in the way of that,' murmured Anna.

Then Dani's head peered round the door that led in from the kitchen.

Anna grimaced at her to go away, but she ignored it.

'Not that I've been earwigging,' Dani began, 'but are you both definitely on about the same thing?'

'What do you mean?' asked Anna with a frown.

Will's hands fell from his face.

'Well, I thought I'd better check, seeing as we've had a *few* surprise visitors recently.' Dani looked from one of them to the other. 'What with the whole Jackson incident and then Olivia Lawson turning up out of the blue.' She shrugged. 'Just making sure you're not talking at cross purposes,' she added, as Anna and Will both blinked back at her.

26

'I thought you were here about Jackson!' said Anna to Will, just as he said, 'I was talking about the bloody *influencer* and her mother who are in Buttermere thanks to you!'

They turned to stare at each other.

'*Jackson*?' repeated Will, and Anna saw a flash of fear cross his face as he pictured Rose's boyfriend. 'What's he done?'

Anna searched for a suitable lie but it felt like foraging for morels in the middle of Manchester: impossible. What could she say? Unlike the wild treasures that concealed themselves among the lakeside trees in lace-like swathes of leaf-cast shade, the truth always wanted to be found. 'Oh . . . I . . . erm . . . had a small run-in with him, that's all, but it's sorted now.'

Will narrowed his eyes.

'He came to . . . speak to me . . . one evening . . .'

'When?'

'After the launch for Wild Rose.'

'Why? About what?'

'Me mentoring Rose . . . mainly . . . he thought I was interfering . . . but we've ironed it all out.'

'Ah.' Will looked down at his wellies. 'I think I might have fuelled that point of view a bit. I'll speak to him. Explain that you've been very helpful—'

'No need . . . it's water under the bridge.' Anna clapped her hands together. 'But let me get this straight, you're angry because Olivia Lawson's here?' she said.

'Not angry—' corrected Will.

'But that's the issue, is it?' asked Anna. 'She's here and you think I'm responsible?'

Will nodded. 'I do have valid reasons for—'

Anna cut him off. 'Olivia was booked in for dinner last night, but I didn't *invite* her,' she explained.

'She wouldn't have come here if it wasn't for you, though,' retorted Will.

'I'm not the cause of *everything* you have a problem with,' countered Anna. 'I didn't particularly want her at Hesta, knowing the kind of coverage there could be on social media' – Dani swiftly ducked back out of the room – 'but she was meant to be visiting as a paying customer. There was nothing I could do about it. What would you like me to do? Run my reservations list past you in future?'

'No, of course not,' muttered Will.

'I didn't have any idea who Olivia Lawson even *was* until recently,' Anna carried on.

'And neither did Rose, but now she's going to the farm to review the ice cream.'

'So what? She's got a bit of clout on the Internet but it's not the be-all-and-end-all. Influencers' opinions certainly aren't something I obsess over.'

'No and it wasn't anything Rose was concerned with until she set up accounts for the ice-cream business.'

'Anything *new* isn't automatically bad,' said Anna. 'Contrary to what you might think.'

'That's not what I'm saying. You and Rose think I'm an old-fashioned stick in the mud,' said Will. 'You don't understand.' He gave an enormous sigh like he'd been punctured.

'Bringing the farm into the modern world is a good thing,' said Anna. 'Change can be positive. You're just used to it being the opposite . . .'

Will pinched the top of his nose.

Anna moved to put a hand on his shoulder. It couldn't have been easy raising Rose on his own.

'Farming is hard, but being a father is way more difficult,' he mumbled.

'Well, most importantly, Rose knows how much you love her,' said Anna, squeezing his arm. 'We all do.'

Will bowed his head. 'I hope so,' he mumbled, before stomping back over to the tractor and climbing into the cab.

27

'Did you hear him say Olivia's here with her mother?' asked Dani, the second Anna stepped into the kitchen. 'Must have subbed her in after the break-up with Freddie.' She stuck out her bottom lip to make a sad face. 'Ovie said his name was on the booking to begin with.'

Anna didn't reply; she already felt drained, though the working day had barely begun.

'So what else did Will say?' asked Dani, realising there were more recent events to be discussed.

'By your own admission, you could hear everything,' said Anna with a sideways glance at her pastry chef.

'No,' Dani shook her head. 'When I was over by the stove I missed a bit. The cooker hood's too noisy—'

'I'll get rid of it so you can listen in better,' deadpanned Anna from over by the fridge.

'Hey, if it wasn't for me, you'd both still be going round in circles,' said Dani with a pout.

She had a point, thought Anna, exhaling. 'He didn't seem to know about Jackson,' she admitted with a shrug. 'But was very wound up about this influencer going to Fell View. I guess it's so far out of his comfort zone.'

Dani was waggling a hand. 'I don't think that's all there is to it,' she said.

Anna shut the fridge door. 'What do you mean?'

'I think there's more to this than meets the eye.'

'Not everything is a detective drama, Dan,' said Anna, sliding the sheet of butter pats onto the side to soften before service. She was reminded of Fell View as she looked at them, and wondered if Will might be warming too as time went on.

'Aren't you always telling me to interrogate things?' continued Dani. 'Not take stuff at face value, double-check my first impressions?'

'Yes, when we're out foraging but—'

'This is no different. Look at what happened with Jackson. He was a false chanterelle and we should have known.'

Anna turned Dani's description over in her head. It was a fitting analogy, to be fair. False chanterelles were almost identical to true ones in appearance, but whereas real chanterelles had a symbiotic relationship with the tree roots and grew directly out of the ground, the false kind were unstable, not firmly attached to a solid base, and fed off debris on the forest floor. Instead of having a sweet, fruity flavour, false chanterelles had bitter-tasting flesh.

Maybe Dani had a point, mused Anna. But Jackson hadn't really intended to harm them, she was sure of it, and besides, they were talking about Will.

She reached for a ceramic dish, fragile and unique, from the shelf above her head. 'What are you saying?' she asked.

'I think all's not what it seems and there's something Will's keeping secret.'

191

Anna looked over at her. 'But why?'

'Maybe because he's scared that if he isn't careful –' she bowed her head at the brittle bowl Anna was holding – 'and he mishandles whatever it is he's hiding, Rose's heart will break into a million pieces.'

28

Anna felt as though she'd worked seventy-two hours straight by the time she'd finished the lunchtime shift. She flung her chef whites in the laundry sack and left the building, longing to be surrounded by Buttermere's sweeping scenery instead of the stainless-steel landscape of Hesta's kitchen. Her feet seemed to carry her of their own accord along the lane towards her dad's house, as though seeing Will so wrought with worry for his daughter that morning had given her a glimpse into how Robert had felt all those years ago.

She could still picture her dad's face, the panic shining in his eyes, when she'd shared the news about Dominik's proposal. A present for her eighteenth birthday, that had surprised her parents as well as Anna. Marion had been less concerned, probably assumed their young relationship would run out of steam at some stage, but Robert had been beside himself. And so what had begun as a special, celebratory day, became memorable for all the wrong reasons, as Anna, with tears streaking down her cheeks, had gone to the farm to hand back the ring.

Her dad hadn't been trying to obstruct the love between her and Dominik, though that's how it had seemed at the time. He'd just not wanted her to throw away her bright future in the big city for the first boy she'd fallen for. She'd forgiven her father a long time ago, known the situation must have appeared different from his perspective, but perhaps now, finally, she *understood*.

'Anna!' her dad said when he opened the door, delight illuminating his face in place of the September sunshine which had apparently clocked off at 4 p.m. too. 'Lovely to see you.'

'You too. Fancy a walk?' asked Anna, as the breeze ruffled the leaves on the trees like a cheerleader urging them on.

'Sure,' said Robert, reaching for his coat.

They'd only just begun their wander when they bumped into Rose picking blackberries from the jet-jewelled hedgerows.

'Hi!' she said, waving at them with her free hand; the other clutched a container laden with gemlike fruit. 'How are you both?'

'Very well, thank you,' said Robert. Always his response, regardless of whether it was really the case. Anna glanced at his smiling profile and felt glad she'd suggested the stroll. He was like a plant reviving in a ray of light, she realised; alone in his house he was starved of conversation, but out and about, he came back to life. 'How's the ice-cream venture going?' he asked Rose.

'Busy,' she replied, blowing a strand of hair away from her face. 'But good. Few bumps here and there, though – some customers a bit disappointed we don't have regular flavours.'

'Really?' asked Robert.

Rose nodded. 'But, as Anna says' – she grinned at her mentor – 'that's our USP. We're not like other places.'

'Precisely,' replied Anna, pinpricks of pride tingling her spine.

'Someone asked for vanilla yesterday,' continued Rose. 'Didn't even look at the chalk board, just ordered. I felt dreadful saying we didn't have any.'

'Did you suggest they try meadowsweet?' said Robert. 'It's got a lovely almondy-vanilla flavour, from what I remember.'

'Yes! That's exactly what I did!' Rose grinned. 'I gave them a taste, and they actually said they preferred it.'

'There you go then,' replied Robert.

'Fancy a job?' joked Rose, expecting Robert to laugh.

But he didn't. 'I do, actually,' he said, eyes gleaming like two glossy berries. 'I couldn't think of anything better.'

Rose raised her eyebrows. 'Really?'

'I'm being serious,' said Robert.

'I mean, it's pretty manic . . .'

'I'll manage,' said Robert. 'I'm sure I'll master it once I've been shown what to do.' He looked at Anna for reassurance, and she felt the somersault-sensation of them switching roles once again.

'You'd be great, Dad,' she said, hugging the arm he had linked in hers.

'I'm prepared to work hard,' said Robert, turning back to Rose. 'I know I'm possibly not the right image . . .'

Anna thought of Olivia the influencer, and wondered how her trip to the farm had gone . . .

Rose batted the air. 'I'm no Instagram model either,' she said kindly. 'I saw you chatting away to everyone at the launch, though – *that's* the right impression. Friendly and welcoming.'

Robert beamed. 'Well then, when can I start?'

'I'll have to see what we can afford – it'll only be part-time,' said Rose.

'That's perfect,' said Robert with a nod. 'And I can do weekends, or whenever really . . .'

Anna's stomach tensed. All those hours she spent at work equated to long solitary days for her dad that must seem like they stretched on forever.

'Great!' Rose shrugged as though she'd lifted a heavy backpack off her shoulders. 'We could definitely do with an extra pair of hands and if you're flexible, that's ideal.' She glanced down at her foraged haul. 'I can walk home with you, if you're going this way,' she said.

'So, I hear you had an influencer come and sample some of your wares?' said Anna as they sauntered along in the last of the afternoon's warmth. 'How did that go?'

'Dad didn't think it was a good idea, but I guess he just doesn't get it,' Rose said with a shake of her head.

'Social media has its upsides,' said Robert.

Anna glanced across at him.

'I joined a virtual book club a little while ago,' continued Robert. 'We're all over the country, but once a month I look forward to chatting to a group of people who used to be complete strangers but now feel like friends.' His brow crumpled. 'Incredible, when you think about it.'

'Gosh,' murmured Anna.

'Wish you'd tell Dad the online world isn't all bad,' said Rose, twisting her lips. 'This Olivia Lawson seemed lovely – very complimentary about the whole set-up and super grateful for the goodie bag we gave her.'

Anna raised her eyebrows. It didn't sound like the same person who'd graced the doors of Hesta less than a day earlier.

'Said I'd cheered her up massively, and ice cream was just what she needed,' continued Rose.

Comfort food to console her after a break-up perhaps? wondered Anna, as Dani's I-told-you-so expression swam into her mind.

'I keep checking to see if she's posted anything about us,' said Rose, pulling out her phone as she spoke, the pitch of her voice going up a notch. 'Nope. Not yet. Just photos of the lakes and mountains – must be such a novelty, coming from the city. Besides, there's *never* any signal round here. Perhaps she's waiting till she's back in Manchester. And she wouldn't want super fans following her about, either.'

'Maybe she's enjoying the last bit of her jaunt with her mum,' mused Anna, soothed by the recurring motion of her dad's footsteps beside her.

'Oh, I didn't know she'd come with anyone?' replied Rose. 'She was by herself – bit of a surprise really. I was expecting some sort of entourage, or at least an assistant, but she was very low key.'

They could see the farm now, hear the hum and moo of the milking parlour in full swing. Anna could just make out Jackson, dressed in overalls, cajoling a queue of black-and-white bovines into the building.

'I'd better go and help,' said Rose, catching sight of him too and starting to hurry along the lane. 'I'll get back to you about the job!' she shouted over her shoulder to Robert, and Jackson looked up at the sound of her voice. He gave Anna a grim wave when he spotted her.

Was he okay? she wondered. His features were too far away for her to read them reliably.

'Coming, babe!' Rose called to him with the carefree tone of someone unaware of the whole situation, and, even at this distance, Anna could see his face light up like a shaft of sunshine in the squalliest storm.

29

The blue-tinged, bird-fringed beginning of dusk was almost upon them when Anna and Robert turned back along the lane. The grey day had decided to close in early, and they clutched each other close as they retraced their steps to the village. Just as they reached the track that led to the farm again, a figure appeared in the yard. For a moment, Anna wondered who she'd prefer to encounter, Will or Jackson, but as they drew closer she could see it was neither. The man standing on the cobblestones was a police officer. A patrol car was parked outside the barn. She stopped still, strained to see the man make his way towards the farmhouse.

'What's going on there?' murmured Robert, turning to look at her.

'I don't know,' replied Anna, which was true. Who had rung and what had they said?

They watched as the three silhouettes of Will, Jackson and Rose emerged from the milking parlour into the fast-fading day, outlined by the harsh lights of the interior.

Anna couldn't watch. 'I've got to get back to work,' she mumbled. Her shift was starting soon. Sally and Dani would wonder where she was if they got in first.

Robert's forehead crinkled. 'Are you okay?'

She nodded.

'Are you sure? Is it something to do with what's going on over there?' her dad asked, as switched-on as the strip lights of the cow shed.

Anna glanced up at him. 'I'm fine, I promise,' she said, turning back to see the trio of shadows tailing the police constable as he trudged across the yard. *I'm just not sure they are.*

'I really hope they're all right up at the farm,' said Robert when they reached his doorstep, with a jerk of his head back in the direction from which they'd come. He bit his lip; the same way Anna did when worry overflowed her brain and wriggled into her body.

But she couldn't bring herself to say they'd be fine. Who knew what was happening there right at this moment? Every minute of each day, one person's dream was being born at the same time as someone else's died. The best and worst of life happening simultaneously. And then there was everyone else in between, blindly luxuriating in the ordinary, only aware of the blissful nature of the mundane once it existed merely as a memory.

'There's something you're not telling me,' said Robert. He put his hands on his hips. Another mannerism handed down to her.

Anna glanced at her watch and the seconds ticking by. 'I honestly have to go,' she mumbled, but its pale round face seemed to reprimand her, like the surprised-looking moon in miniature. *You should make more time for your dad* could have been carved on its dial.

'Then I'm going to be here, wondering what on earth's going on,' replied Robert. 'When you're a parent, you don't stop bothering when your offspring's grown up.'

As she looked back at him, Anna felt the watch hands rewind. Her silver-spun hair and wrinkle-rumpled skin might as well have been a dressing-up-box disguise as, underneath, she was still his child, his daughter.

'Jackson broke into the restaurant,' she said.

'What?' said Robert, shock blanching his cheeks.

'I was there, the back door was open—'

'Oh my goodness, you could have been—'

'But I wasn't.'

'And that's why the police are there?'

'I don't know for certain . . .'

Her sentence was muffled by the front of her dad's jumper as he pulled her into a hug.

'It's okay, Dad,' she said into the wool. 'I'm fine.'

'Did he harm you?' he asked, stepping back to look in her eyes.

The blades of her own chef's knives glinted in Anna's mind. 'No.'

'Thank god. Why did he want to—'

'A protest against the world,' said Anna, 'and all its injustices. I just happened to be the unfortunate target.'

Robert frowned. 'What have you done to deserve that?'

'Nothing, but I think he thought Hesta symbolised everything he was rebelling against. Growing up with money is no replacement for affection. I feel very sorry for him.'

Robert puffed out a breath. 'What did I do to deserve such a good-hearted daughter?' he asked, scratching the side of his head. 'This man comes blustering into your restaurant, giving you the fright of your life, I imagine, and you say you feel sorry for him.'

'He's had no support from anyone, a pair of absent parents . . .' Anna gazed at her own dad, saw the care creased into his features, and remembered how she'd once thought him *too* concerned about her. Blamed him for her losing Dominik, when in fact it had been her own decision. Then there was Jackson, stuck at the other end of the spectrum. 'He's a damaged soul, and he deserves a second chance.'

The sound of her mobile phone ringing made them both jump.

'That'll probably be Dani, wondering where I am,' said Anna, nodding to confirm it was her name on the screen as she clicked to answer the call. 'Hi, Dan, I'll be there in a minute. Just down the road at Dad's—'

Robert read the rapid movement of Anna's eyes and the open-mouthed silence that followed, in place of any further conversation her end. Something awful had occurred. Not someone wreaking havoc at Hesta again—

'Call an ambulance right now, Dan. I'm on my way,' he heard Anna say, before her daze-glazed eyes met his.

'I need to go. No time to explain,' she said to her dad as she stuffed her phone back in her pocket and began to race along the lane in the direction of the lake.

30

Please be okay, please be okay, please be okay, Anna prayed on repeat as she pounded along the path beside the water's edge. Where had Dani said? By the stream beyond where they picked ceps, but before the rock-cut tunnel that led further round the lake.

Her own breath deafened her as it thudded in her ears, her mind rushing as much as her limbs.

How was it possible? Here? She'd never heard of it happening in Buttermere before.

'Dani?' she yelled as their favoured foraging spots came into sight on her left-hand side.

No answer.

She ran along the bank, eyes flitting between the leaf-confettied forest floor and the next section of Buttermere's shore.

'Dani?' she shouted again, summoning as much volume as her pumping lungs would allow.

She lurched forward as her foot caught a camouflaged tree root but righted herself before she stumbled to the ground.

'Dani?' she tried again, stomach stitching from too little time spent swimming and the sudden unexpected exertion.

She stopped still on the track, tried to listen for any reply.

Nothing.

Just the chitter and chirp of birds and the rustle and ruffle of the wind-taunted water.

She leaned forward, put her hands on her knees.

Then a voice that didn't belong to her pastry chef and the face of a woman she'd never seen before. 'Are you Anna?' shrieked the woman, mascara rivers streaming from their blue-eyed source.

'Yes,' panted Anna. 'Where is—'

'She's here. This way. Oh god.'

Anna followed; throat cinnamon-stick dry.

Then there in front of her was Dani, phone clamped to her ear, hunched over a girl, beside a bubbling beck, its chatter and roil drowning out any other sounds.

Anna hurried over to them, mind trying to piece together the fragments of information before her.

The slumped figure of Olivia who, only a few hours earlier, had been up at Fell View Farm.

Anna crouched down, saw the lesions on the girl's skin and gasped.

Burn marks. Livid red blisters covering her hands and arms.

As soon as she laid eyes on her, Anna knew what had happened. She winced as she watched Olivia writhe on the ground.

The woman squatted beside her and instinctively reached out to comfort the girl, but every inch of the influencer's fingers was swollen with sores.

The unfamiliar woman retracted her hand and gulped back a desperate sob. 'What do we do?' she said, turning her makeup-streaked face towards Anna.

'Have you got any water?' Anna asked, and with fumbling fingers the woman began rummaging in a pink-leather ruck-sack designed for shop-lined streets not hill-flanked lakes.

'Yes, here.' The woman handed her an unopened bottle of Evian.

Anna unscrewed the top and tipped the contents over Olivia's swollen sores.

The girl screamed in pain as the water washed her wounds.

The woman leaned forward, clearly feeling Olivia's hurt as keenly as if it were her own, her powerlessness compounding it, making her cry out, and as Anna glanced round to explain her actions, she knew in that moment she was looking at Olivia's mother.

'It's important to rinse the skin as quickly as you can . . .' murmured Anna, looking from her to Olivia. 'The faster you clean it off, the less possible damage it can do . . .'

'Oh god,' wailed Olivia's mother.

Dani put down her phone. 'An ambulance is on its way,' she announced, before addressing Anna. 'I wondered at first if we could get her to hospital ourselves but it's so severe . . .' she said in a low tone. 'I've never seen anything like it. I was worried she might go into shock . . .'

'Jesus,' whispered the girl's mother.

'You did the right thing,' said Anna to Dani with a nod. 'We need to get her medical attention ASAP,' she said in a hushed voice. 'Could we make it to the road, do you reckon? That way they'll reach her quicker.' She turned to Olivia. 'Can you walk?' she asked.

Olivia swallowed, shaking now at the sight of the eruptions on her body. 'I think so.'

Anna and Dani bent to pull her up from underneath her arms.

'Argh!!!' screamed Olivia. A bird screeched high above them like an echo.

'They'll have to come here,' said her mother. 'You're hurting her!'

Dani and Anna settled Olivia back down to the ground.

The girl reached a hand towards her face and it was Anna's turn to cry out.

'Don't touch your eyes!' she warned, her gaze on the savage welts making the girl's hands swell. 'What else did they say on the phone?' she asked Dani urgently. 'Any other instructions?'

'We need to keep her covered up,' replied Dani, starting to take off her jacket. 'Stop any of her skin being exposed further. She *has* to stay out of the light.'

'There isn't even any sun in the Lake District!' cried Olivia's mother, staring in horror at her daughter's disfigured forearms. 'That can't be causing *this* surely. Please can *someone* explain what's happening? I can't bear it!' She put her palms on her head in panic.

'Giant hogweed,' replied Anna and Dani in unison, the same grave respect for the wild dangers of the great outdoors tolling in their voices.

'What?' cried Olivia. 'But you gave me that cake when I came to the restaurant!' Her features were contorted with hot pain and confusion. 'I remember you saying it had hogweed seeds in it!'

'Is that true?' demanded her mother.

Dani shook her head as she laid her coat gently over Olivia's body like a hairdresser's cape, taking care not to make contact with her fire-red flesh. 'I tried to explain to you when you were in the kitchen,' she said to the girl. 'Common hogweed is completely different from the giant type.'

'And that's what's done this?' replied Olivia's mother. 'A *plant*?'

'I'm afraid so,' replied Anna. 'A chemical reaction takes place, removes the skin's protection from the sun.'

'You've got to know your stuff before you go about picking things willy-nilly,' said Dani with a cautioning look at Olivia. 'Why were you touching it anyway?' she asked, eyes narrowed.

'Making social media content,' said Olivia defiantly. 'I think you'll find it's my *job*.'

Dani raised her eyebrows. 'You're a food influencer. Why were you featuring something that's toxic as hell?'

'I didn't know that, did I?' retorted Olivia. 'It just looked like a bunch of leaves!'

'It's not her fault it's unsafe round here,' said her mother, hugging her leather bomber tighter round her, as though she'd found herself on a foreign and frightening planet.

'Everything in the world's a hazard if you're not *careful*,' said Dani sagely. 'If giant hogweed's undisturbed, it's no threat. It's the sap in the stem and the leaves that's dangerous and causes the photosensitivity. You shouldn't handle things you have no idea about. Did you pick it on purpose?'

Olivia blinked back at her.

'Where was it, anyway?' Anna asked her. 'Somewhere near here?'

'I can't remember, can I?' snapped Olivia. 'I didn't go searching for it! Scars aren't the kind of souvenir I usually go looking for on holiday!'

'We only want to make sure the same thing doesn't happen to anyone else,' reasoned Anna. 'No one's saying you did anything wrong.'

Shame momentarily flamed across Olivia's face. But then she jutted out her chin. 'I grabbed a handful of what I thought was harmless greenery. It must have been this morning. When I was filming a reel.'

'What sort of reel?' enquired Dani.

'For Instagram.'

Dani tilted her head to one side, waiting for Olivia to carry on.

'A review, all right?' the girl admitted.

'For Hesta?' probed Dani.

Olivia's cheeks were bright rhubarb. 'Maybe. Stop quizzing me!'

'So, a *bad* one?' pressed Dani, visibly tempted to take back her jacket.

Olivia huffed out a breath. 'A story about my visit, that's all. I'm allowed to post whatever I like! It's *my* account!'

Anna thought of the restaurant, about to open its doors for the evening service despite there not being a single chef present. She sighed. Sally would be wondering what was going on. Ovie would be beside himself. Yet here both she and Dani were, setting all that aside to help someone who was blatantly prepared to try and tear down all they'd built.

'Boss, we should get back,' said Dani, getting to her feet.

Anna's head snapped up.

'We've done all we can.' Dani shrugged. 'The ambulance'll be here soon. The experts'll take it from here.'

'What? Wait! Don't go!' squealed Olivia, clinging on to Dani's coat, still draped over her shoulders, in protest.

'Please. Stay with us!' said her mother.

'They know your location,' said Dani. 'There's nothing more for us to do.'

'Don't leave,' pleaded Olivia's mother.

'I'm sorry!' sobbed her daughter. 'I'm sorry, okay? Please stay!'

'We've got customers to cook for,' replied Dani. 'Appreciative ones,' she added under her breath. 'We'll point the paramedics this way if we see them,' she said, setting off along the path back in the direction of the village.

Anna got to her feet, opened her mouth to tell Dani she'd hang back and catch her up once the ambulance arrived—

'Nooo! Don't go!' Olivia bellowed after Dani before Anna could speak. 'Look, I'm saying I'm sorry and I won't post it, all right? I promise!'

Dani looked back at her. 'So, it *was* something nasty, then?' she said.

'Yes! I'll delete it from my phone, though!' said Olivia. 'I swear! I won't share it!'

Dani pursed her lips.

Anna bent down beside the girl. 'We're not going anywhere,' she soothed. 'Don't worry.'

'Thank you,' said Olivia's mother. 'Thank you.'

Anna gave her a nod of acknowledgement.

'It's no excuse, but . . . it's been a . . . stressful time for Olivia,' her mother explained. 'She's not feeling herself . . .'

Olivia began to bawl in big hysterical gulps. 'My boyfriend . . . broke up . . . with me,' she sobbed.

'He was meant to be coming with her to the restaurant,' said her mother.

Dani returned, arms folded, mainly to hear that she'd been right. 'I knew it,' she said. 'That's why you were in the wrong

208

frame of mind from the start,' she added, pointing at Olivia, 'and wouldn't have liked *anything* we served you.'

'I know,' Olivia admitted, hanging her head, her shoulders now heaving. She absentmindedly wiped away a tear, before realising what she'd done. 'I touched my face!' she shrieked, starting to hyperventilate. 'I rubbed my eye!'

'I told you not to do that!' shouted Dani. 'You could go blind!'

'Oh god!' cried the girl's mother.

'Is there any more water?' said Anna, turning to her.

Olivia's mother shook her head. 'No. What do we do? What do we do?'

And then there was a twig-snapping rush of green-and-yellow uniform as two paramedics hurried towards them through the trees.

31

'I thought me and Ovie were going to have to cook the whole menu between us!' declared Sally when Anna and Dani finally arrived at Hesta. 'Three tables are already seated and we've given them each two baskets of bread and all the nibbly bits we could find.'

'I said there'd been an unforeseeable emergency,' said Ovie. 'And that we would do our very best to make everyone comfortable during the slight delay.'

'Well done, both,' said Anna as she tied on her apron, prioritising getting on with service over explaining where she and Dani had been.

Her pastry chef thought differently. 'It was that influencer who was in last night!' she announced to the others. 'I found her when I was out foraging this afternoon, in the forest by the lake, in a right mess. Giant hogweed burns.'

'Jesus,' said Sally, sucking air through her teeth.

'That sounds horrific,' said Ovie with a shudder.

'I've never seen anything like it,' continued Dani. 'Wouldn't wish it on anyone, however awful they are—'

'Hopefully she's all right,' cut in Anna. 'For now, shall we get on?' She clasped her hands together. 'Let's give these diners a meal to remember for the *right* reasons.'

'Yes, Chef!' chorused the rest of the staff, as Anna reached for the first check of the evening.

It was only when she bundled her whites into the laundry bag at the end of the night that she recalled the card Will had written her and remembered seeing the police car at the farm earlier in the afternoon. She dug out the apron she'd been wearing the previous day, found the crumpled envelope forgotten inside its pocket and hoped the fact it was all screwed up wasn't a sign.

But when the landline phone rang out at that moment, reverberating around the deserted restaurant, repeatedly requesting her reply, she worried that perhaps it was.

'What a mad week, boss,' said Dani, reaching for her coat the following night.

A flashback of Olivia's boil-bubbled flesh flew through Anna's head at the sight of Dani's jacket.

'D'you think she'll be all right?' asked Dani, as though she could read Anna's mind. 'I looked online and there are some absolute horror stories out there – skin grafts and all sorts . . .'

Anna shook her head to dispel the images from her sleep-desperate brain. 'I don't know. I hope so. However awful she is, she certainly doesn't deserve *that*.'

'Agreed,' said Dani. 'Can't help wondering what she was actually *doing*, though, can you?'

'I don't have the same incurable curiosity as you,' replied Anna. 'But thank goodness you did go to investigate.'

'If only madam influencer was as grateful,' said Dani, shooting her a sideways glance. 'Right, I'm heading off. I'm cream crackered.'

Anna nodded. 'See you in the morning.'

'You're going soon, too, aren't you?' checked Dani, adopting the same stern expression she'd used to extract Olivia's promise not to post unfounded comments about the restaurant.

'Yes,' said Anna, as an enormous yawn was born from her mouth.

But a bang on the back door soon woke them both up.

'Jesus,' said Dani, jumping at the sound of the unexpected knock. 'Somehow I doubt that's Olivia with a bouquet of flowers to say thank you . . .'

Anna straightened herself. She had a pretty good idea who it would be, after the phone call the previous night.

But before she could answer, Dani barged past her to see.

'Don't you dare come in here!' Anna heard Dani yell into the darkness.

Her pastry chef's body was blocking the door, arms braced against the frame.

Anna strained to look over Dani's shoulder. 'It's okay – I said it was fine—'

'You've caused enough mayhem – go home!' Dani shouted.

'I only want to speak to Anna – I'll stay out here.' Anna heard Jackson's voice, drained of his usual fight, feeble.

'It's all right, Dan,' said Anna softly, and her pastry chef reluctantly moved aside.

She didn't see Jackson for a second or so, but as Anna blinked into the night, let her eyes adjust from the brightly lit kitchen to the squid-ink black sky, his shadow appeared, leaning against Hesta's stone wall for support.

'I'm sorry . . . I didn't know who else to call . . . where else to go.' His voice cracked. 'I was lodging in the farmhouse but . . .' He slid down to the ground as though he'd dissolved into despair.

'Come on,' said Anna, extending a hand to pull him to his feet. He was shivering, despite the fact he was used to being outdoors in all weathers.

'I'm staying then,' said Dani with a sigh. 'Not risking a repeat of what happened last time you paid a visit,' she added, glaring at Jackson.

'There's no need,' said Anna. 'Honestly.'

'It's fine, I'll go. I should never have come,' said Jackson, standing now. He turned and began to walk towards the lane, hands jammed in his pockets. He'd already melted into the night when Anna called after him. 'Jackson!'

She ducked back inside for her coat. 'Please can you lock up?' she said to Dani.

'Why are you following him when he decimated our kitchen?' Dani replied from the doorway.

'Because he doesn't think anyone gives a damn about him,' said Anna as she passed her, 'and that's a dangerous road to go down.'

'You can't save everyone!' shouted Dani into the darkness as Anna disappeared after him.

'No, but I can try my best,' said Anna, looking back at her pastry chef illuminated in Hesta's white-gold glow. 'You've all saved me.'

Buttermere was deserted, and the billowing clouds were blocking any light from the moon. Which way had he gone? wondered Anna, turning to look left and then right down the lane. She picked a direction at random, but could see no sign of Jackson. Perhaps he'd gone the other way? She switched on the torch function on her phone, and her vision stretched a few more metres along the tarmac. 'Jackson?' she called along the late-night lane. Then she spotted a car tucked into the side of the road. No one parked in front of that gate for fear of Will finding them obstructing the access to his field. She peered inside the driver's-side window and could see Jackson with his head resting on the steering wheel, his arms folded in a comfortless skin-and-bone pillow.

She thought about tapping on the glass but instead went round to the passenger door, squeezing past dusk-dampened fronds of foliage to catch sight of his face turned away from the world.

His eyelids opened at the flicker of torchlight and the click of the handle.

Anna clambered into the seat beside him but said nothing, waiting for him to speak if he wanted to. Sometimes you just needed someone there next to you, making the universe seem a little bit smaller – she knew that.

'You don't have to be here,' said Jackson with a sniff, dragging himself upright.

'I kind of do now,' said Anna, thinking back to his phone call the day before, sinking back against the cushioned fabric as fatigue flooded over her. 'Seeing as you're bailed to my address.'

'You didn't have to say yes.'

'No, but I did.'

Jackson stared straight ahead out of the windscreen, as though scared that if he turned to look at her she might disappear like a midnight apparition, and he'd once again be alone. 'Why do you care when I've done nothing to deserve it?' he murmured.

Anna gazed out at the blank rectangle of darkness beyond the dashboard, a clean black chalkboard of unwritten beginnings.

'Because I think, somewhere inside, you have potential. You're more than this angry person you portray most of the time.'

'I'm not some kind of project, someone for you to mentor to make you feel *superior.*'

His words needled her, as though the seat beneath her was upholstered with thorns.

'That's not what I meant. So, you think I'm here for *my* benefit.' Anna gave a humourless laugh. 'You were the one that called *me*, I'd like to remind you.' She laid her fingers on the doorhandle.

'I don't know *why* . . . I shouldn't have done. Go on then, leave like everyone else.' Jackson closed his eyes.

Anna turned to wish him goodnight. But there would be severe consequences if he broke the conditions he'd been given. She couldn't bring herself to walk away, when she too, had been there at rock bottom. She caught sight of the rucksack in the footwell behind him, and the heap of belongings that had been hurled into the back. Were he and Rose now broken up? Had he been sacked by Will? He said he'd been living up at the farm . . . There was no way she could let him jeopardise any chance of a future by spending the rest of the night *here*, by the side of the road, with only a thin sheet of steel separating him from the stars above.

'Are you going to sleep in your car, then?' she said, turning to face him. Her breath clouded slightly as she spoke and she tugged up the zip of her coat.

'No, I'm about to go and check into my luxury accommodation,' Jackson replied without opening his eyes. 'The butler's ringing when it's ready.'

Anna suppressed a sigh.

'I'll be fine. I'm used to being cold.' He shuffled down in his seat, making a show of settling in for the night.

'Right, well, I'm going to get back home now. It's been a long day,' said Anna. She opened the door and the September air smuggled itself in. 'The spare room is yours if you want it. It's a bit full of stuff but I imagine it's a damn sight better than being in a police cell.'

Jackson frowned at her. 'Why did you say yes? I pretty much destroyed the kitchen at your restaurant and now you've agreed I can stay at your *house*. That doesn't make any sense.' He shook his head. 'Why would you trust me to be in your home when I've given you absolutely no reason to? Are you nuts?'

An image of Dani, wide-eyed with disbelief, floated through Anna's mind.

'Maybe, but perhaps you could prove that wrong and resist trashing the place for a night?' she replied.

Jackson's eyes shone in the interior light. 'I promise you won't know I've ever been. I just need to work out what to do with myself going forward . . .'

'Chop chop, then,' said Anna, before he could slip into gloom again like a cloud-drowned moon. She shut the car door behind her and began striding off down the lane in the direction of home.

Jackson sat there for a second in the ensuing silence, letting Anna's kindness seep into his skull. She was giving him somewhere to rest his head, after everything he'd done and all the horrible things he'd said. He'd never be able to pay back her generosity. But he could try and be the person she believed he could be. Strive to be better. Show her that her faith in him had not been a mistake. He turned to grab his backpack off the seat behind and then flung open the driver's door as though it was the entrance to a brand-new realm.

32

Anna was halfway along the landing, early the next morning, when the sight of the shut spare-room door reminded her she had a guest. She'd either been so exhausted that she'd slept right through any smashing up of its contents, or Jackson had indeed gone straight to bed and given himself a rest.

Now, the house was quiet apart from the usual sounds of her pre-work routine: the whir and gurgle of the coffee machine and her chuntered grumbles about the un-done chores continually mounting up. She opened and closed her empty-bellied fridge, a self-reproachful ritual she hoped would spur her on to actually do a shop. But she was never home. Any food would be left to shrivel and wilt, and would eventually go to waste, a mulch reminder that her only real residence was Hesta. She hardly spent any time outside its walls and even less inside these four here.

She yanked open an ice-encrusted freezer drawer, found some sliced white bread so old she feared even the toaster would spit it back out. But there was nothing else to offer

Jackson for breakfast. She sighed. She had to go soon. What was she supposed to do if he still hadn't appeared? She hadn't said what time she'd need to leave, she realised, wrinkling her nose at the frost-covered loaf. She shoved the freezer closed with a thump, wondering if the noise would carry to the room above. Perhaps he wasn't even in the house anymore, had absconded, deciding it was more hospitable in police custody after all . . .

Anna sipped her throat-scorching coffee as she watched the seconds on the clock tick by. She could call Dani; tell her she'd be in late. But her pastry chef had dealt with enough recently. She'd already left her to lock up by herself the previous night. No, she needed to go. Couldn't wait till Jackson rose. She took one of the letters from the scattered pile of unopened post on the kitchen table and scribbled a note on its blank-faced back.

Good morning, Jackson, she began.

She paused. What now? Tell him to make himself at home? But that was a terrifying thought; she might return to find a razed heap of rubble . . . She tapped her pen against the milk-white paper.

Sorry I don't have much in, she continued.

Why was she apologising to him? She'd invited him into her sanctuary, possibly against her better judgement, regardless of the state of it.

Help yourself to what there is.

Black coffee and barely edible bread.

Have a shower if you like. There's a clean towel in the airing cupboard. I hope.

I'll be back about four. Here's a spare key for the front door.

She'd written the last line before she'd really thought about it. This wasn't like leaving one of her staff in charge of the restaurant. With his track record, she oughtn't to trust Jackson with her *kettle*. Yet putting her confidence in him was a risk she'd subconsciously weighed, and her decision was made.

Then she heard stirring from the bedroom above, the trodden-wood whimper of footsteps on floorboards and the yawn of the bathroom door. She imagined Jackson expecting to wake up at the farm, then finding himself here, amongst stacks of old editions of *The Caterer* and storage boxes filled with obsolete equipment. She wished she'd got round to clearing all the junk out, didn't want him to look around and feel as redundant as her mother's past-tense pressure cooker. *He needs a purpose*, she thought, as she put down her coffee cup.

She dug her second set of keys out of the desk in the hall, and was about to put them next to the note on the table when Jackson came down the stairs, sleep rumpled and sheepish, his hands stuffed in the pockets of his hoodie.

'Morning,' said Anna.

But before Jackson could open his mouth, there was a rap on the door, and a ring of the bell. A summoning twice-over.

Something doubly urgent.

Oh god.

They both walked towards the shadow standing on the other side of the blurred glass.

A uniformed officer on the step.

The woman confirmed Jackson's name, came into the living room.

Anna couldn't remember the last time she'd sat down in here; it made the situation feel even more formal.

Jackson's feet seemed to give way before his body reached the sofa.

Anna took the seat beside him. They'd face this together.

The police constable took the armchair. Started speaking. Saying something about Air Accident Investigation . . .

Anna's heart was beating so wildly it was hard to hear the woman's words.

Jackson bent forward, held his head in his hands.

Anna put a palm on his back.

'Reckless . . . Crash . . . Criminal . . .' said the police constable.

Anna was struggling to compute the sentences she was saying. She looked across at Jackson, clammy fingers clamped to his cheeks in disbelief.

Then the PC stood, news dispatched, just another morning for her, but one Jackson and Anna would never be able to forget.

33

Jackson wept, his body trembling like yarrow in the breeze, head bowed, too heavy to hold any higher. Anna wrapped her arms round him, cradled his crying face the way she imagined she would a son. There were no words she could say: everything seemed insufficient in the circumstances.

She didn't know how long they stayed like that for. Both unmoving, each entangled in a thicket of their own thoughts. But eventually Jackson unfurled himself and drew in a deep breath, stretching like a sweet pea in sunlight.

'Thank you for standing by me . . . even when . . .'

Anna squeezed his shoulder. 'It's okay . . . It's going to be okay . . .'

They both stared at the indent in the chair where the police constable had been sitting, the only proof of what had just happened.

Beyond the window, the hill-filled horizon looked like a painterly impression of freedom.

'I had so much, all along,' said Jackson. 'I see that now. But only when—'

'You're all right,' murmured Anna, following his line of sight to the far off fields of Fell View Farm. 'It's all right . . .'

'I'd made a life here in Buttermere. Found Rose.'

Anna knew what it was like to lose a love, only to realise in retrospect you'd done it all wrong.

Jackson turned to look at her. 'I have to tell her what the police said. Otherwise she might hear it from someone else and think I didn't—'

'She knows you do. But definitely tell her,' said Anna, wondering why it was so easy to encourage others to follow their hearts, when it was so hard to do it yourself.

'She might not want to see me.'

'You can only ask,' said Anna. 'Invite her here, if you like. I'll be at work, so you can talk. With no distractions.'

'Thank you.' Jackson's eyes glistened; he swiped at them with his cuff. 'I don't know what I'd have done if I didn't have—'

'Well, you did, and you do. Don't mention it.' Anna slapped her hands on her thighs, then stood up. She walked over to the window and opened it wide, welcoming in the dawn-decorated day.

'You're alive!' exclaimed Dani when she came into the kitchen later that morning, to find Anna in the middle of a stock inventory. But her relief was replaced with outrage before Anna had finished checking the restaurant supplies.

'I rang my cousin right after you left,' she continued. 'I was worried out of my mind!'

Anna wondered whether the woman who'd come to see Jackson earlier was Dani's relation. Her delivery of information had been just as direct, but at a blessedly lower volume.

'She told me the situation. What *he* did.'

'He had nowhere else to go, Dan. What was I supposed to do?'

'Holy fuckballs, you didn't let him *stay* at yours? He was arrested, Anna.'

'Yes, I'm aware, but it actually isn't as simple as that—'

'It seems very fucking straightforward to me. Leave him be.'

'Well, he's no longer on bail so—'

'Thank god. He belongs in jail.'

'What he did was reckless and stupid. He knows that. But he didn't cause the helicopter crash.'

'What?'

'The police checked with air accident investigation. It was pilot error. It's all in their report.'

Dani was wide-eyed.

'That rock Jackson threw didn't bring the aircraft down,' Anna continued. 'He just thought it did. He handed himself in because he was convinced he was responsible, even though it was simply coincidence.'

Dani was speechless, a rare occurrence.

'He's learned his lesson,' continued Anna. 'Had a huge shock and got a fine for criminal damage and a caution. He'll have to be on best behaviour for the next couple of years.'

'Good.' Dani pursed her lips. 'But if I ever see him again, I'll give him a piece of my mind.'

Anna nodded, then turned back to her stocklist. 'Right now, though, could you give *me* a hand?'

Rain was cascading from the sky as though the cloud-crowded mountains themselves were crying tears of relief on Jackson's behalf. Anna wondered whether he'd managed to speak to Rose as she walked towards her father's house, huddled under a huge black Hesta-branded umbrella. She hoped so.

The sound of the water droplets hitting the domed canopy above her dipped head masked the thunder-rumble of Will's tractor coming along the lane.

She looked up when she heard the cab-door slam with such force she could have sworn the fields surrounding them shook.

'Where is he?' Will demanded, water streaming down his face. 'I've seen his car parked back there. I know he's somewhere.' The slants of rain were pelting him sideways as though attempting to throw him off course as he came striding towards Anna along the road, the Cumbrian weather trying its best to extinguish his wrath before he reached her.

'Jackson's got his punishment, I can promise you,' she shouted over the downpour.

'Good. I hope he's locked up long enough for Rose to forget about him!'

The rain seemed to surge more heavily in protest.

Did she know he'd been released? wondered Anna. Had she and Jackson spoken?

'He's not going to prison,' she replied. 'It isn't a crime to steal your daughter's heart.'

Will rubbed rain-soaked hands across his face. 'Tell him to *stay away* from her.'

'That's not my business,' replied Anna.

'Oh really? Because it seems like everything else is!' Will yelled back.

'What is it exactly I'm guilty of now?' said Anna.

224

The rain eased as though eager to hear Will's response. 'Why do you always have to get involved?'

'What would you rather, I stay in my own little world, like you?' Anna shot back.

Will swept water off his coat sleeve, as though trying to wash away her comment.

Anna's indignation was dampened the second the sentence slipped out of her mouth; she knew how much he cared for Rose, that all he wanted was for her to be okay. 'Look, I've no idea what it's like to be a parent . . . but I do know how it feels to be a daughter. You can't protect her from everything. She has to make her own choices. Decide the course of her own life.'

'So, if you were me, you'd let her see someone convicted of causing a crash?' Will pushed sodden hair out of his eyes.

'He's not to blame for the helicopter coming down. It was an accident.'

'And you believe that, do you?' he said, body vibrating, raindrops glancing off his shoulders. 'Got *you* under his spell as well, has he?'

'That's not what *he* says, Will. That's the *police* line.'

'*What?*'

'The outcome of the official investigation. He's been cleared.'

'Well, he's still forbidden from the farm.' Will turned and clambered back into the tractor cab. 'I'm not going to sit back and watch him be reckless with Rose's heart.'

'If you do that, you'll only drive a wedge between you and your daughter,' said Anna, grabbing hold of the door. 'Jackson's been judged in the eyes of the law, brought to justice. Don't penalise Rose just for falling in love.'

He wrenched the door off her and slammed it shut, but the rain continued to hammer on the roof as though trying to drum some sense into him.

'Goodness me, what's happened to you?' said Robert when he saw her standing outside his house, clothes stuck to her skin, her umbrella defenceless against the deluge. She so desperately wanted a hug, but spared him a drenching. Instead, she shrugged off her coat, carried it through to dry by the fire; its welcoming crackle already calling her from the hall.

But her dad didn't follow, reappeared a few moments later with a folded woollen jumper that had belonged to Marion. Magenta-coloured. As bright and cheerful as her mother had been.

Anna remembered her wearing it. Could still feel the softness of it against her skin as her mum pulled her in for a cuddle as a girl. She closed her eyes as she tugged it over her head, its warm embrace a cashmere shield against the harsh world.

'I bumped into Will,' she said.

'Oh right.' Her dad raised his eyebrows as he handed her a tea-filled cup. 'What was that going on at the farm the other day, then . . .?'

Anna sighed, took a sip of her drink like it was liquid comfort.

'Were you right, was it to do with that Jackson fellow?'

'Yes. But don't worry, he won't be putting a foot wrong from now on.'

'Good, I'm glad to hear it.' Her dad gave a nod. 'So, you pressed charges? For the break-in?'

Anna shook her head.

Robert frowned. 'What do you mean, then?'

She took a breath, tried to form a sentence that might explain, but her brain was flagging despite the fact she still had the second half of her shift to go.

'Oh,' said Robert, as though she'd spoken. 'I think I know what you might be going to say.'

It was Anna's turn to frown. How could he possibly know her thoughts when she didn't have them straight herself?

'But I'm not going to interfere . . .' He trailed off, but they both felt the gut punch of inference, the clutch and claw of the past.

Robert leaned forward to stoke the fire, trying to make the room more homely, but to his dismay, all he seemed to have done was stir up his daughter's emotions.

'I don't think you do know, actually,' Anna said, sitting up straight as though she'd been prodded with the poker.

'I'm sorry . . .'

Was his apology for now or back then?

'All I meant is . . . I don't want there to be a risk he could do it again.' Robert reached slowly for his tea, as though Anna was a lioness primed to bite.

'There's always a *risk* attached to everything in life. You have to decide yourself whether it's one you want to take.'

Robert took a gulp of his drink. Decided to stay quiet, hardly dared move.

But this seemed to provoke Anna even more. 'What did you think I was going to say, then? Stick up for Jackson?'

'Nothing . . .' Robert murmured. 'Forget I said anything.'

They both knew she couldn't do that. She might have forgiven what he'd said all those years ago about Dominik, but she hadn't managed to erase it from her mind.

'Look, Anna, I know I've made mistakes . . .'

227

She knew what he was talking about without him having to mention his name.

'It's fine. It was my choice ultimately . . .' murmured Anna. Hindsight so often wasn't twenty-twenty like they said it was, sometimes it was a confusing kaleidoscope of what-could-have-been.

'I shouldn't have tried to dissuade you . . .'

'Dad. Don't.'

'No, it's important. We need to have this discussion. It's long overdue.' Robert set his drink down on the table. Clasped his hands together. 'I was misguided, perhaps, but I promise I meant well. I wasn't against Dominik, I just didn't want you to curb your dreams—'

'You didn't think he had anything to offer.'

'I couldn't help thinking how *I* felt when I met your mother. Didn't want that to cause tension between the two of you . . .'

'But you and mum were—'

'She was this incredibly talented chef, and I was just a local lad,' continued her dad.

He'd worked for a small press in Keswick that published Lake District guidebooks for walkers, climbers and cyclists, then later looked after the kids once they'd come along, while Marion brought home the bacon. 'She could have travelled the world, gone anywhere and done anything. But she was stuck here, because of me.'

'She wasn't. She loved you.'

'And I loved her.'

'Then what more could anyone want?' Anna's face was fire-hot and flame red. Her insides burned with upturned memories muddled with regret. 'It doesn't matter now. I

228

ended it with Dominik . . . ages ago now . . . and I'm responsible for my own actions.'

'I need you to understand that I wanted the best for you.'

'I know, Dad,' she said, subsiding into the sofa. And she *did* know. But it had always been simpler to cling to the excuse that, if things had been different and she'd stayed in Buttermere, she'd have been here at the end of her mother's life.

She pushed herself up off the cushions, went to hug her dad. 'I love you. I only wish I'd been here to tell Mum too.'

'She knew,' replied Robert, clutching Marion's cashmere jumper close, as though she was here as well, wrapped up in the middle of them both.

'What was it you thought I was going to say before?' Anna asked again as she pulled away.

'I wondered whether you were going to offer to mentor Jackson.' Her dad lifted the teapot, poured them each another cup without looking up.

Anna gazed at him as he tipped in milk. 'It's not what I was going to say . . .'

'Oh, thank goodness.'

'. . . but it's a really good idea.'

'Oh no. Really?'

'I know Mum set it up for women, but why stop there? He's a prime candidate . . . crying out for attention . . . lacking guidance and goals, a structure . . . You're absolutely right.'

'Oh, Anna—'

'He could really benefit from—'

'But what about you? Isn't it too much on top of everything else? Just because you're carrying on the programme, doesn't mean you can mentor everyone yourself.'

'No, but I think Jackson and I have some sort of . . . bond.'

'Doesn't sound like it if he broke into—'

'*Since* then, I mean. I think he might see me as a sort of parent figure.' She scratched her head.

Robert sat back down on the sofa.

'He rang *me* when he was released from the police station. Why would he do that after what happened at Hesta?'

Robert shook his head. 'Maybe he feels he can trust you, but *he* isn't my concern—'

'He hasn't had the support I've had,' she said, eyeing him over the top of her tea.

Robert gave a cautious smile.

'He's estranged from his mum and dad. Hasn't got a safety net, family he can fall back on,' continued Anna.

Robert felt a bloom of relief unfold inside him; he'd tried his hardest to be a good father, and Anna's words warmed him more than the amber-embered hearth.

'Well, be careful,' he murmured, as he stooped to put another log on the fire.

Anna nodded.

'I'll say no more on the subject . . .'

'What about you, anyway?' Anna asked, remembering how full of life he'd been, like a flame-born phoenix, when he'd spoken to Rose about a part-time job up at the farm. She hoped the opportunity hadn't disintegrated to cinders with everything else that had gone on.

Her dad's eyes shone. 'I don't know whether I'll hear any more, but I rather liked the idea of working at the ice-cream place.' He gazed into the fizz and flare of the fire. 'It was a nice thought while it lasted.'

'I think Rose was keen too,' said Anna. 'I'm sure she meant what she said. But it's understandable she's not had much chance to do anything further about it . . .'

'Yes, of course. And I doubt there's been much call for ice cream in this weather . . .'

Anna lapsed into thought-filled silence. Pictured Rose and Will up at Fell View, now with an entire farm as well as a fledgling venture to run between the two of them. Maybe they had bitten off more than they could chew . . .

Because of you, said a nettling voice in her head. Doubt clouded her mind. Had she been misguided, meddled in Rose and Will's business when she'd only meant to help?

And was this how her dad had once felt?

'If you see her, tell her I'm still interested,' said Robert, cutting into her thoughts. He tilted the teapot, watched the last dregs dribble out as though he was witnessing his final spring of hope suddenly run dry.

'I will,' said Anna. 'I'm sure she'll need an extra pair of hands now more than ever . . .' She trailed off; she wasn't truly certain of *anything.*

Robert was watching the wood gradually change into ash in the grate.

'What is it? There's something else, I can tell,' said Anna.

'I just . . . I'm glad you know . . . that I'm always here for you.' Robert's cheeks flushed in the flickering firelight.

'Of course I do, Dad. You always have been.' Anna put down her cup.

'I've never meant to . . . poke my nose in.'

Anna nodded. 'I know.' Being confronted with Jackson and his situation made her see her childhood relationship with her dad afresh. He'd always been steadfast, full of affection, and any firmness was born of concern. If it wasn't for him, she'd have felt as route-less and lost as if she was up Fleetwith Pike at midnight without a map.

34

'Have you seen this?' said Dani when Anna arrived ready for the evening shift. She shoved her phone screen in her boss's face, so close all Anna could see was a vivid blur of brightly coloured video.

'If it's something on social media, then no, probably not,' she answered, scrubbing her hands in the wash basin.

'You need to,' said Dani, following Anna to the dustbin with her scrunched-up paper towel.

'Dan, I need to crack on with—'

Her pastry chef had increased the volume on the clip; Anna recognised that voice. *Olivia?* She turned to frown at the reel Dani was replaying on a loop – and possibly had been since the end of the lunchtime service.

Yes, that was definitely her, their influencer guest.

'All recovered from her little rendezvous with the local flora?' asked Anna, switching her attention to the remaining mise-en-place tasks.

'You're not *watching*,' said Dani.

Anna bit back a retort that *she* wasn't *working*.

'You need to see it, boss.'

Dani followed her over to the fridge now.

Anna finally relented and peered at the pixels in front of her.

It was Olivia talking to the camera.

'. . . so treat everyone and everything around you with respect,' she was saying, the ring stacks on her fingers flashing as she gesticulated at her followers, failing to distract from the still-livid lesions that snaked across her skin.

'. . . I've been stung in the past by people who weren't what they'd first seemed . . .'

'Reference to her ex-boyfriend, there,' chipped in Dani.

'And dismissed others for silly, superficial reasons . . . like what they wore . . . without getting to know what was inside.' She touched her collection of gold-chain and charm necklaces.

Anna glanced at Dani. 'Has she had some sort of epiphany after her encounter with the—'

'Shh,' said Dani, jabbing a nail at the screen. 'You need to listen to this bit.'

'I've learned that kindness is more important than anything . . .' continued Olivia. 'Not what you look like or which fancy places you've been to . . .'

Anna was momentarily distracted by the numbers increasing in the corner of the screen; likes and comments multiplying by the second.

'We need to be more considerate of each other. And I'm going to try and be a good example.'

'It's still a bit *me, me, me,* but we can't expect a miracle, and I honestly think she means this next part,' said Dani.

'So, recently, on my trip to the Lake District, I got very badly hurt . . .'

Here she held up her hands and arms for her viewers to see more clearly.

Anna winced at the scars the hogweed had carved.

'As you can see, it's not pretty.' Olivia wrinkled her sun-freckled nose. 'But it could have been really, *really* bad. I owe the fact I'm here speaking to you guys now, and not still stuck in hospital, to two amazing people. Shout out to Anna and Danielle from Hesta restaurant!'

'Spoiler alert, she doesn't admit she'd met us the night before and really wasn't very nice,' interjected Dani.

Olivia's lips quivered as she recollected the event, and Anna felt her stomach squeeze as she watched the memory travel from the influencer's brain to her mouth.

'And thanks to their quick thinking . . . I was saved from even nastier injuries.'

'God, they're severe burns,' said Anna.

Dani nodded. 'Hell of a reminder of her trip here.'

'I can't thank the incredible people at Hesta restaurant enough,' continued Olivia, her words quavering. 'For coming to the rescue and taking care of me when I needed it most.' She looked like she'd been about to admit something else but stopped herself. 'I'll honestly be forever grateful,' she finished.

Dani clicked off the screen. 'What do you think of that, then?'

'I'm glad she's all right. Still looks painful,' replied Anna.

'Yeah, it'll take a while to heal properly, that.' Dani shuddered. 'Seemed for a second like she was going to say how horrid she'd been, but maybe that would have been a step too far.' She was about to put her phone away when it lit up again with a notification. 'Hang on, she's sent me a direct message.'

'Really?' said Anna. Her mobile was in the staffroom – where it ought it be. 'What does it say?'

Dani frowned as she digested what Olivia had written. Then angled her phone towards Anna so she could read the message for herself.

Hi Danielle,

Just wanted to say a big thank you from me and Mum for calling the ambulance and staying with us till it came. They said at the hospital that my injuries would have been a lot worse if you hadn't washed off the plant sap. I would have had to have a skin graft for sure.

I'm sorry for how I was when I came to the restaurant. You were right, I was in a bad place and took it out on you all. I shouldn't have lashed out like that. It wasn't fair and I see that now.

Meeting you and Anna made me realise the impact words and actions can have on others. Deep, hey! I want to use my influence for the better from now on. Be a platform for good.

I need to clear my conscience first of all. I picked the hogweed because I was going to post a bad review for your restaurant after you told me a few hard truths in the kitchen that night. I wanted to make out how easy foraging was. Make fun of Hesta to get back at you. So I filmed a story down by the lake and pretended I had a clue what I was on about. That's how I'd got in that

state when you found me in the woods. And you still helped me after I'd been shit to you. I didn't deserve it. You have very good hearts both of you. I'll message Anna too. I hope to come back and visit again some time – in a better mood, I promise. I want to appreciate everything properly, and give it the respect it deserves. See, new me!
I hope you will forgive me,
Love,
Olivia xx

'What a confession,' said Anna from over Dani's shoulder.

'Yeah. She'd have looked like a fucking fool if she'd posted about foraging, made out she knew her stuff, then ended up in hospital. No wonder she's grateful I stopped her.'

Anna nodded. Couldn't help going through to glance at her phone too – and sure enough Olivia had typed – copied and pasted – the same apology to her as well. Along with a screenshot.

A photograph of a booking page. With the distinctive initial entwined with wild herbs at the top, as unmistakeable as her own face in a mirror.

A confirmation page from Hesta's website.

True to her word, Olivia was going to return.

Maybe this time, she'd actually try the food.

An owl hooted from its hidden hollow high above Anna's head as she made her way home between the shivering hedgerows. No sprinkled twinkle of velvet-set stars tonight. Even the moon was tucked beneath its cloud duvet. Autumn was well and truly in the air. Alone beneath the endless sky was when her mind often turned to Dominik. She looked up into the night. Was he sleeping somewhere, under the same patchwork quilt of darkness and light? She wondered if he'd recognise her now, her hair silvered by time, face creased like Crinkle Crags. Was there a core of her that had stayed the same, or did people change so much as the seasons sped by that there was nothing of the girl she'd been that still remained?

The clouds drifted, revealed a glittering solitaire that stole her breath. Was that Venus? she wondered as she stared at it. But it disappeared again, buried beneath a blanket of blackness as though it had never been there.

She was almost back at her house before she remembered Jackson. What if he'd changed the locks, sold everything she had? she wondered for a fleeting second. Was she being completely crazy? Her dad and Dani, the two people who probably cared most, clearly thought so.

She turned her key in the door, let out a breath she hadn't realised she'd been holding as she stepped into the hall. 'Hello?' she called as she slipped off her shoes. The lights were on in the living room, the yellow glow of home making her heave a sleep-starved sigh, but no one replied. 'Jackson?' she shouted up the stairs.

A creeping prickle pinched her neck.

Then she saw a shape on the landing, looming in the gloom. 'Jackson?' she said again.

'She didn't come,' he croaked, crumbling to the carpet. 'Rose didn't come.' He sat on the top step of the stairs, a sledger on a slippery slope of sadness.

Anna shed her coat like a skin, swapping her efficient, unflappable head-chef persona for the vulnerable version of herself that returning home so often revealed.

Usually, she'd wind down for an hour or so after her shift, watch a cookery programme, cram her brain with flavours from far off places, anything to escape her own mind before bed, stop worries and what-ifs expanding like weeds left to wild. But not tonight: the path to sleep was – quite literally – blocked by Jackson sitting in bits by her bathroom door.

She wasn't sure what to do. In the kitchen at Hesta, she almost always had the answer. But here in her house, it never really felt like home, with its unlived-in living room and undined-at dining table. Without her family of staff surrounding her, and the sound of cutlery-clinking customers chattering excitedly, she felt like she was floundering. This soulless domestic setting only served to highlight what was missing. She thought back to when she'd made Will the elderflower sponge cake at the start of summer, brought a spark of life to this little cottage kitchen. Was that really the last time she'd made anything for anyone outside the restaurant? She summoned her last shred of energy and shouted up to Jackson.

'Have you eaten?'

He shook his head.

'Let me see what I've got . . .' Anna began opening and closing cupboards, wondering what she could whisk up. 'I'm afraid it's not going to be anything elaborate,' she called over her shoulder, grimacing at the bareness that stared back at her.

'Honestly, I'm not hungry,' said Jackson from the stairs. 'Thanks, though,' he added, a garnish of gratitude.

She wanted him to know that someone cared, and the only way she knew how to do that was through food.

'You can't go to bed on an empty stomach,' she shouted.

'Why, when I have to with a broken heart?' came his reply.

'So, you tried talking to Rose?' she asked, going to stand in the hall, hands on her hips.

Jackson nodded. 'I sent her a message asking if we could meet. Said it was better if we spoke in person – I couldn't explain everything in a text – and she just said she couldn't leave the farm.'

'I guess there's only her and Will,' replied Anna.

'I could be working!' said Jackson, fists grasping his hair. 'Helping her with stuff!'

'Give her time. She's a lot on if she's running the ice-cream shop and—'

'I hate thinking she's struggling. There was always so much to do before—'

'She knows where you are.'

'But she thinks I'm—'

'We don't know what she's thinking. And we won't till you two talk,' said Anna, standing in the shaft of light from the sitting room, a golden sliver that illuminated the kitchen doorway.

'Come on, have something,' she said, looking up at him from the foot of the stairs. 'I can make you cacio e pepe?'

Jackson screwed up his face. 'What's that supposed to mean?'

'I'll show you,' said Anna. 'In fact, you can make it. Take your mind off things.'

'I'm not a chef.'

'No, but I am. We'll do it together.'

'I've had enough lessons recently,' mumbled Jackson.

'If you've never had it, I think you should try it.'

'Actually, I've had so much Catchy Peppy lately it's getting a bit samey.'

Anna raised her eyebrows. 'It's very easy—'

'Yeah, for you, maybe.'

'And you won't *believe* how delicious.'

'What is it, then?' Jackson asked, his eyes flitting towards the kitchen.

'Come down and see.'

Still, he didn't move.

'Okay, it's pasta,' conceded Anna, turning to go into the kitchen.

'Oh. Is that all?' Jackson called after her.

She heard him plod down the stairs.

'Told you it was simple. Three ingredients and done.'

Jackson squinted in the bright light.

'It's spaghetti with cheese and pepper.'

Jackson clamped his lips together as though in protest.

'You can grate some parmesan,' instructed Anna, filling the kettle. 'Should really be pecorino romano but I don't have any in.'

'Hate it when I run out of pecky rhino,' replied Jackson, taking the grater she handed him.

Anna laughed. 'About eighty grams of that,' she added, sliding a set of weighing scales towards him. 'And afterwards you can crush the peppercorns.'

Jackson looked up. 'I thought this was a joint effort?'

'I'm toasting them,' said Anna, putting a pan on the hob.

'Bit more complex than I was led to believe,' he mumbled, watching the number on the scales closely as snowlike shards of parmesan settled in the dish.

'Roughly two teaspoons of the peppercorns,' said Anna, as she scattered them in the pan.

'I feel like I'm on a cookery show,' said Jackson, straightening up now his weighing was done.

'Wrap the cheese up properly, it's good practice – wax paper's in here.' Anna yanked open a drawer with her free hand. 'Reusable and fully environmentally friendly, before you say anything. Don't want any protests . . .'

Jackson gave her a small smile. 'Good to know.'

'Right, tell me when you're ready for your next job,' continued Anna, before his thoughts could slide back in time.

'Not sure this is as relaxing as you said . . .' Jackson put the wedge of parmesan back in the fridge.

'I said it might distract you,' corrected Anna. 'Can you smell that?' she asked, as the spicy-sharp fragrance wafted from the pan. 'Black gold, that is,' she added with a grin.

'Not sure I'm a fan,' said Jackson, pulling a face as he peered over the pan, watched the little peppercorns bouncing about in the bottom like dreams that didn't yet know they'd be crushed.

'*Patience*,' said Anna. 'Don't judge a dish before it's finished.'

Jackson nodded, fell silent for a moment as though contemplating her words.

'Right, there you go, pestle and mortar,' said Anna, placing the pepper-grinding tools in front of him, then bending to put two plates in the warming drawer. She hadn't been planning to have any, but when was the last time she'd had company? Cooked a proper meal? Not just catered for one? The clock on the oven said midnight, but for the first time, her kitchen felt *awake*.

'I've only got dried spaghetti,' she said, taking an unopened packet from the back of the cupboard.

'Oh, I only eat homemade,' shot back Jackson, with a shake of his head.

Anna chuckled. 'I'll make a chef of you yet – you've already got the humour.'

She expected him to be ready with a biting retort, but Jackson beamed back at her instead.

'Next, cheese and pepper in here for the sauce,' said Anna, placing a stainless-steel bowl on the work surface.

'Yes, Chef!' replied Jackson with a jokey salute.

'See – you know exactly what you're doing,' said Anna with a grin. Her cottage had the buzz of a professional kitchen, but without the pressure of paying guests, the need to uphold a reputation . . .

'Right, put a bit of the pasta water in that dish,' she said to Jackson.

'Seriously? That can't be the recipe.'

'Well, it is,' Anna insisted, handing him a large metal ladle.

'If you say so.' Jackson stirred the mixture, staring into the dish with a distinct air of doubt.

'I'll drain the pasta,' said Anna, carrying a colander over to the sink.

'I know how it feels,' quipped Jackson.

'Have you got a paste yet?' asked Anna.

'Yeah.' Jackson gurned. 'Perfect for wallpaper.'

Anna came to look over his shoulder. 'Spot on. Exactly the right consistency.'

'Really?' said Jackson, forgetting his reticence for a second.

'Yep,' said Anna, tipping in the pasta. 'Stir it now.'

Jackson took the pan handle and Anna passed him a pair of tongs.

'Then I'll teach you how to twizzle it onto the plate. Technical term.'

Jackson laughed. 'Is that it?' he asked, glancing up. 'I'm still not convinced.'

'Wait until you taste it,' said Anna, taking the tongs and twirling a tangle of homemade magic into a Hesta-worthy twist.

'Wow, that does actually look amazing,' murmured Jackson as the aroma of the melted parmesan and pepper-coated spaghetti reached him.

Anna flung open the cutlery drawer, glanced at the neat rows of never-normally-used knives and forks and felt a flurry of satisfaction as she reached for a handful. She swept the tabletop debris to one side. When had she last sat here? Eaten anything other than a hurried sandwich or bowl of cereal standing up by the sink? 'Go on, try it,' she said to Jackson.

'That's *unreal*,' he said, eyes wide with wonder as he devoured the dish.

'Good.' Anna smiled as she curled spaghetti round her own fork, forever in awe of the power of a plate of food.

35

Jackson came downstairs the next morning just as the first dawn of October was breaking beyond the Buttermere hills.

'I wasn't expecting anyone so I haven't got a lot of food in, I'm afraid . . .' said Anna when he appeared in the kitchen, as though she quite often entertained. She shuffled the pile of post she'd shunted to the far end of the table the previous evening, distracting herself from acknowledging just how spare the guest room usually was.

'I should have grabbed some bits yesterday . . . sorry,' replied Jackson, looking as out of place as the moon that still hung in the sky despite the emerging day.

'You okay?' said Anna.

Jackson nodded. 'Yeah.' He fidgeted in the doorway, and Anna wondered what thoughts were percolating through his brain.

'Milkless coffee?' she held up a mug.

He shook his head. 'I'm okay, thanks,' he said, as though convincing himself. 'I was wondering if I . . .'

'You don't have to rush off, you can stay till you've found your feet,' said Anna. 'It's just more of a B than a B&B.' She smiled.

'I can pay my way,' muttered Jackson. 'I've got savings.'

'That's not what I meant,' replied Anna, batting the air.

'I thought maybe I could come with you to Hesta,' he said, the words bursting out of him as though they'd been brewing since he'd gone to bed.

'Sorry?' said Anna.

'I could help. I'll do anything.' He tilted his head to one side.

Anna stumbled to make sense of what he was saying. 'You want to work at the restaurant?'

Jackson nodded. 'Pay you back.'

Anna blinked at him.

'For letting me stay . . . and for everything else. Make it up . . .' He shifted his sock-clad feet, suddenly self-conscious. 'Or are you really wanting rid of me right now?'

'No,' said Anna. 'It's not that. Stay as long as you need.' She wondered how long he'd want to spend waking up in an unlikely haven of heaped hospitality magazines and surplus kitchen supplies. 'I just . . . you know a lot's gone on at the restaurant . . .' she noticed Jackson swallow, the fact he'd hindered rather than helped recently not lost on him, 'and I need to show my staff I'm there with them.' She meshed her fingers together, miming a well-gelling team.

'I can chip in. I promise.' Jackson's gaze rested on the set of keys. 'You've trusted me to be here, so why not Hesta? You can show me what to do. I'll learn, like last night.'

'I don't have time to train you—'

'I'm a fast learner.'

Anna's eyes flicked over to the clock. There was too much to catch up on. She felt as though she was constantly skating on a winter-frozen lake, conscious that everything could come crashing down in one split-second.

'Show me the basics,' he pleaded.

'Jackson, you can't just walk into a kitchen and be a chef. It takes years to learn the ropes.'

His scrumpled hair, grown long like summer grass, fell over his eyes as though shielding him from a response he didn't want to accept. 'What am I going to do instead?' he said. 'I've no job to go to. No girlfriend. I can't just sit here. I'll go *mad*. I'm made to be busy.'

Anna understood; she was the same.

'I need to concentrate, Jackson. I've a business to run. The new menu's meant to start today—'

'Please, I'll do anything. Let me come with you. I don't want to be on my own.'

She looked at the ceiling, noticed a cobweb in the corner. The spider's intricate work of spun silk not for show, for *survival.*

'Okay.' She sighed. Folded her arms as though underlining the decision before she could take it back. 'You can come, but it's hard graft, I'll warn you now . . .'

'I can handle it.'

'It'll be peeling and chopping, at most. Nothing glamorous.'

'It's not showbiz up at the farm. I want to make things right . . . Please, give me a chance to.'

Anna nodded. She knew the feeling of needing to achieve something, prove you were alive. 'Okay, come on, then. Shoes on. No time to lose if I've got to show you everything. And I have to warn you, I think you'll have a job on your hands winning over some of the team.' She thought of Dani's fiercely protective streak.

As they stepped out of the front door, Jackson took a deep breath like he was inhaling a lungful of hope. Buttermere was waking up around them, and the birds were singing so loudly it felt like nature's chorus heralding their arrival at Hesta. But as grateful as Jackson was to be accompanying Anna, he felt inside-out with loss.

'What do I do about Rose?' he blurted out as they started walking along the lane.

Anna watched their feet taking mirrored steps, side by side, giving the illusion they were on the same journey, though their paths were years apart. 'I'm not sure I'm the best person to ask for relationship advice,' she said. The birds trilled from the trees, their early morning music seemingly louder, stopping her from slipping back to the past.

'Give her some time,' said Anna.

Jackson blew out his cheeks. 'The look on her face, man, when I told her.'

Anna squeezed his shoulder. 'Was that before you called the police?'

Jackson nodded. 'I wanted to tell her first. All of it. But the way she looked at me . . . Like she believed I was someone else completely, and she'd just seen me for who I *really* was.'

'No,' said Anna with a shake of her head. 'I think it's the other way around.'

Jackson smoothed down his hair. 'She knows me better than anyone ever has . . . but even if I tell her that the crash wasn't my fault, I don't think that'll make a difference now.' He groaned like he'd been winded.

'Give her time. Focus on you for now. That's all you can do.'

He raked both hands over his face. 'I love her.'

'I know,' said Anna.

Jackson wiped his sleeve across his eyes. 'She's the best thing I ever had, and I've fucked it up.'

Anna felt a sharp twist in her gut; she knew what that was like too. She searched for the keys to the restaurant in her jacket pocket as they rounded the bend, and clasped them tightly as Hesta came into sight.

'What the actual eff is he doing here?' said Dani to Anna in place of 'good morning' when they got there. She was scowling so much her eyes were almost closed, as though she couldn't even bear to look at Jackson.

'He's going to be a commis for us, Dan,' replied Anna.

'And I'm going to set up a sister restaurant on Mars,' Dani shot back. She turned to Jackson. 'Have you *any* idea of the amount of—'

Anna put her hands up.

'I've come to help,' murmured Jackson.

'Ha!' snorted Dani. 'Then the best thing you could do is *leave.*'

'Dan,' reprimanded Anna.

'I can be your assistant,' said Jackson to Dani. 'Dogsbody, whatever. Just tell me what to do.'

Dani jutted out her chin.

'I promise I pick things up quickly,' said Jackson.

'Yeah, and then smash them on the floor,' finished Dani. She looked at Anna. 'We've only just got the new Pacojet—'

'We're turning over a new leaf today, Dan,' said Anna. 'We've all needed to do that at one point or another.'

'You do know the last time he was here was to ruin the place—'

'Yes, and I'm going to teach him how to use everything the right way,' said Anna.

'Look, if you don't want me here after this morning, I'll go,' said Jackson to Dani. 'Properly, I mean. I'll leave Buttermere. Nothing's keeping me here.'

Dani glared back at him. 'Deal.'

Anna stared at him open-mouthed.

It was only when he was apron-clad and chef-clogged, and Dani was busy briefing him – pointedly – about hazards such as dangerous kitchen equipment, that Anna realised either Rose or Will would be coming with the delivery from the farm. What would happen when they saw Jackson here?

'Pot wash, storage, prep area . . .' Dani was indicating the different zones now, completing his tour. 'And my section's back there,' she finished, gesturing over her shoulder with a jerk of her thumb.

'Jackson'll be with me,' said Anna. 'But first, *breakfast*,' she announced, before slicing three thick slabs of sourdough, drizzling them with a quick flick of an upended bottle and then slapping them under the grill.

Jackson watched the bread turn golden-topped within seconds.

'Cumbrian cooking oil,' Anna explained, pouring a glistening globule on a teaspoon for him to taste. 'Only one there is. From a little farm in the Eden Valley,' she added. 'Try that.'

'Nice,' said Jackson, licking his lips. 'Little bit nutty.'

'How Dani would describe me,' Anna quipped as she sprinkled a pinch of sea salt over each crisp-crusted slice.

Unable to resist a hunk of hot toast, Dani reached over to take one. 'Okay, maybe you can stay if we get *this* every morning,' she said to Jackson.

* * *

'You've done a good job there,' said Anna a little while later, leaning over to look at the diced beetroot in front of Jackson.

'Thanks.' He grinned, gazing at the little ruby cubes as though they were real jewels.

'Pastry cases are all prepped,' called Dani.

'Perfect,' said Anna, picturing the finished beetroot, trout and rosehip tartlets in her head. A starter on Hesta's new autumn menu, to be served to customers for the very first time that afternoon. A flutter of nervousness butterflied in her belly as she mentally ran through the rest of the dishes—

But a knock on the back door interrupted the hum of productivity buzzing about the kitchen.

Anna's stomach tensed as Jackson turned to look at her, his mouth twisted, gloved hands stained guilt-red by the root vegetable.

Would it be Will or Rose with the order from the farm? she wondered when there was no sound from the back room other than the staggering shuffle of someone carrying heavy crates.

Jackson's brow shimmered beneath the ceiling lights.

Anna went through to the staffroom to help with the delivery, hoping to diffuse any drama before it exploded into her kitchen, threatened the dishes that were about to debut—

'Dad?' she said, eyebrows raised, as she caught sight of Robert standing there, face floating above the neat rows of Fell View milk cartons he was holding. 'What are you doing here?'

'Rose called me,' he said, as Anna took the box from him, his cheeks streaked pink like a surprise sunrise. 'And asked if I could start immediately.'

Anna noticed the sparkle in his eyes as he spoke.

250

'I offered to bring this down for her, so she could carry on with the ice cream, but I'm not here to interrupt, don't worry.' He was already making his way towards the door again. 'I'll just grab the other box, then I'll be off.'

She followed him outside.

'She's going to train me today – how to use the till, all sorts – then I'll start properly tomorrow.' He was beaming at her, hair blowing in the breeze like a skylark mid-song.

'You'll be brilliant, Dad,' she said, thinking that she ought to have done more. He was moving differently, she noticed, walking straighter, his limbs lighter, like he was being supported by the breeze, cheered on by the trees.

'I'm really looking forward to it. Bit nervous, but excited.'

She smiled at him.

'Hopefully the weather holds a bit longer. Forecast is dreadful for the next few weeks.' He glanced up at the churning clouds as though begging them not to break.

'People always want ice cream,' said Anna. It was her turn to look up now. She wished her mum could see him. Both of them. She'd give anything.

'I hope so,' he murmured. 'Right, I'd better leave you to it.' He gave a sigh that said he was pleased to be busy for once, and with something of his own.

'I'll come and see you when I can,' Anna called after him, feeling a gut-knot twist of love for him as he left. She pictured him chatting as he handed crammed-full cones to customers across the counter, glad he wasn't still squirrelled away in his cottage. She stayed to wave goodbye, watched till he vanished round the curve of the lane, then went back inside.

'Did she not even want to see me?' asked Jackson when Anna returned. 'Or was it Will?' He swallowed.

'Neither, actually.' Anna shook her head.

'So, I've been replaced just like that.' Jackson clicked his fingers.

'No. It was my dad. Does Rose even know you're here?' she asked, opening the fridge.

'I guess not.' Jackson's shoulders dropped.

'There you go, then. Come on, give me a hand with these, please,' she added, jerking her head at the Fell View Farm order.

Jackson picked up a container of milk like it was an artefact from another life. 'Second shelf from the bottom,' instructed Anna. 'Quick as you can. We need to get started on the celeriac purée.'

'What's that for?' said Jackson, looking up, distracted from his desolation.

'Goes with the halibut main,' replied Anna.

'Like posh mashed potato?' he said.

'Exactly.' Anna rooted out a celeriac to show him, its gnarled, rough surface disguising the sweetness underneath. 'You've got to peel off the thick skin, which is hard work but worth it,' she said, thinking how the same principle often applied to people.

36

They awoke to yet another storm-soaked sky, rain thrashing the windows and the wind howling its wild warning that winter was on its way.

'I'm worried about Rose,' said Jackson when Anna came downstairs to find him sitting at the table cradling a coffee in the half-light of early morning. 'It's not stopped,' he said, as slants of liquid silver blurred the glass.

'Have you heard anything from her?' asked Anna, eyes still sleep-small, voice hoarse.

He shook his head. 'It's been two weeks.' A fortnight of miserable weather to match his mood, like mother nature was mourning with him.

'I know it feels like forever, but—'

'I really miss her.'

'I know you do.' She put a hand on his shoulder.

'I don't want to pester, so I haven't texted again. But I can't help wondering if she's all right.' The windowpane shuddered with the force of the downpour.

Anna rubbed her temple. Her dad had said ice-cream sales were low. Armageddon-like gales meant tourists hadn't travelled, and locals had hunkered down to wait out the worst of it like hibernating animals.

'Have you spoken to her?' Jackson asked, turning towards her, his face moon-white like it was still night.

'No.' She'd been so busy inducting Jackson into the Hesta team and trying to perfect the new dishes on the restaurant's menu, she'd barely even seen her dad. 'I was planning to go up to the farm but . . .'

A blustery gust battered the cottage, answering for her.

'I can drive up this afternoon, if you like?' she offered, feet starting to turn to ice on the cold floor tiles.

'Really? You don't need to mention me, I only want to know she's okay.' His eyes were watering like the storm had sneaked inside him too.

Anna nodded. 'I'll go after lunch. Dad's meant to be working, so I'll pop and see him and check everything's all right.'

'Thank you,' said Jackson, taking out his phone to check for any messages from Rose, then sliding it onto the table when only the time stared back at him. Stay in the here and now, the clock seemed to silently scream.

Anna caught sight of the picture he had as a screensaver: Rose sitting on top of a hay bale in the summer sunshine, sweeping her hair away from her face as Jackson took the photograph.

Then the image faded to black.

'Want one of these?' Anna asked Jackson, as the lunchtime service came to a close, offering him a misshapen chocolate that hadn't made the cut to be a coffee-accompanying petit four and had somehow escaped Dani's clutches. He took it and smiled his thanks at her, putting the wild-mint-flavoured treat on his tongue as though craving something sweet to counteract the world's bitterness.

'I'll just carry on here, if that's okay?' he said. 'Prep for dinner. Do the pink fir apples for the feta salad and the other bits you showed me.'

Dani, already in her coat, raised her eyebrows at Anna. Less than two weeks ago, the gesture would have meant *you can't seriously be going to let him do that* but today it seemed to signal *why not?* There'd be less work to get through on her return later that afternoon, for one thing, but if Anna wasn't mistaken, she thought she'd seen a fragile bond forming between the two of them in the last few days – as brittle and beautiful as Dani's signature spun sugar, but *there*.

Anna frowned at Jackson. 'I don't want you to wear yourself out,' she said. 'You need a break in between shifts. D'you want me to drop you back home before I—'

He shook his head. 'I'd rather keep my mind occupied.'

She nodded at him. 'I understand. But have a bit of a rest, at least. Sit down for a while. Have a coffee or something.'

He smiled as her words wrapped round him, cloaking him in care.

'Thank you,' he said, picking up a beetroot to gently rinse it under the tap.

'I won't be long, I'll come straight back,' said Anna, looking at him standing by the sink, holding the red roots in his hand like it was his own ripped-out heart he was trying to prevent from bleeding.

Outside, the rain-grey day greeted her with a grizzle, the wind grabbed at her umbrella, tugged her hair and clothes.

She was reminded of the picture of Rose on Jackson's phone, and wondered how she and Will were faring up at the farm.

She left her car in the empty yard; the field that had been set aside hopefully for overflow parking for the ice-cream parlour was a squelchy spare square, a great grassy expanse absent of any guests.

There was no sign of either Will or his daughter. A Wild Rose-logoed banner flapped from the side of the barn. The fairy lights swung like the storm's skipping rope. Anything man-made was a plaything; only the unmoveable mountains were immune.

'Hello?' called Anna as she walked towards the building, saw the display cabinets stocked with untouched tubs of ice cream, and beyond, the huddles of chairs and tables set out in expectant clusters.

'Anna?' said a voice from behind her.

Rose.

Anna turned, saw her standing there, ponytail pulled back from her pale face, and was struck by the contrast between Jackson's picture and the person before her.

'Your dad's not here,' said Rose. 'There's no one about so it didn't make any sense for him to turn out.'

Anna nodded. The rain was aiming at them in diagonal arrows now, trying to reach them even inside the barn.

'He's been brilliant, but obviously, it's not the best time to be taking someone on . . .'

Anna felt like she'd been knocked sideways in the squall. Was it going to be the end of his new-found role before it had really begun?

'It'll pass at some point,' she said, looking up at the sunless sky.

256

'There's another week of this at least,' replied Rose, glancing at a gap in the roof where water had found a way in.

Anna looked at the girl, watched her mentally add the job to her to-do list. 'Is there anything I can—' she started to say.

Rose shook her head. 'No, look, I'd better get back. Milking time.' She jammed her hands in her pockets. 'Don't want to leave Dad doing it on his own.'

Anna followed her out of the barn. 'Erm, you know Jackson—'

'I don't want to talk about him.' Rose's cheeks were damp with drizzle and disappointment. 'I should have known it would never work out . . .' She wiped her eyes with wet hands, mingled her tears with the rain. 'There's no point being close to people – everyone always ends up leaving in the end.'

'I don't think he wanted to go . . .'

Rose turned to face her, lips shaking. 'Do you know what he did?' she asked.

Anna nodded. 'Yes, he was—'

'At best, a liar and at worst—'

'He's not. He might be a lot of things, but he wasn't responsible for the helicopter crash,' cut in Anna.

'Ha! Is that what he told you?' Rose's ponytail swung as she marched towards the cow shed. 'Don't believe a word he says. I doubt anything that came out of his mouth was true.'

'It's what the *police* said.'

'What?' Rose stopped and Anna caught her up. Could see the goosebumps prickling the girl's neck.

'He's been an idiot at times,' said Anna. 'But he isn't to blame for that, at least. I thought you should know.'

Rose squinted at her as the weather buffeted them both.

'Maybe talk to him,' suggested Anna.

'I don't have time for that—'

'Well, just don't leave things unsaid. If there's anything left, anything you want to tell him—'

A thunder-gurgle of a sob burst from Rose's mouth. 'I can't. Dad won't—'

'It doesn't matter what he thinks.'

'Yes, it does!' cried Rose. 'He's the only one who's ever been there for me – no matter what.'

'You have to make your own mind up about Jackson so you don't always wonder what if.' Anna met her gaze. 'Believe me, you don't want that. To be haunted by what might have been.'

'What do you mean?' asked Rose.

'I know what it's like to say goodbye to the person you love and then live to regret it.' Speaking the sentence out loud stung her skin as though she was standing in the icy outdoors unclothed.

They heard a shout from the milking shed. 'Rose?'

Will appeared in the yard, overalled and frown-faced. 'Anna,' he said curtly when he saw her, giving her a nod.

'Jackson didn't cause the helicopter to come down,' blurted out Rose to her dad.

Anna noticed his shoulders tense.

'I'll have no more talk of him on this farm,' he said. 'He's bad news, that boy. Not to be trusted.'

'Well, he's working at Hesta right now, apprenticing,' said Anna, glancing at Rose, glad to have at least told her that information. Now, it was up to her what she did with it. 'He owned up to what he thought he'd done. That's got to count for something.'

'It's *nothing* to do with you,' shot back Will.

'No, you're right, I just . . .' she trailed off, turned to leave.

Rose's shining eyes swivelled towards her. 'What?'

'Don't make the same mistake I did, that's all.' Anna held her hands up. 'I'll go. I just came to see if there was anything I could do when—'

'It was you who got us into this mess with the ice-cream parlour in the first place?' finished Will. 'Filling Rose's head with highfalutin rubbish. Foraged *this* and wild *that*,' he snapped.

Anna's eyes widened with surprise.

'It was my idea to start the ice-cream business, Dad,' murmured Rose.

'Yeah, and if it had flavours people actually wanted then maybe it would have worked.'

Rose flinched like she'd been jabbed with a cattle prod. 'It's the different ingredients that mean people come here, rather than somewhere else,' she said. 'Olivia Lawson travelled all the way from *Manchester*.'

'Did she ever post anything about Wild Rose?' asked Anna, thinking of the thank-you she and Dani had received and her pledge to use her platform for championing others. 'In return for all the ice cream and everything?'

'I haven't had a chance to check,' replied Rose. 'But I don't think so.'

'See, waste of time,' said Will.

'Well, I might mention it to her,' said Anna to Rose. 'If you think that would help drum up a bit more buzz. She's actually meant to be coming back to Buttermere—'

'She's not welcome here,' interjected Will.

'If you ban *everyone* from the farm then you really *won't* have a business,' said Anna, folding her arms. She turned to face Rose. 'I think the reason she forgot to promote Wild

259

Rose in any way was that she wound up in hospital with giant hogweed burns after her last visit.'

'*Ouch,*' said Rose. 'I've read about that in the foraging books. Sounds *horrible.*'

'Is she all right?' asked Will, surprising them both. 'And her mother? Was she with her?' he added, stepping forwards.

Rose raised her eyebrows at his sudden shift in interest.

'Yes.' Anna nodded. 'She's fine. Shaken up, and suitably warned about the dangers of disrespecting the countryside, but okay.'

'And Lily?' asked Will, as both Anna and Rose turned to look at him.

'Wait, how do you know her name?' asked Rose, as even the torrenting rain couldn't disguise the blanched expression on her father's face.

'That's Mum's name,' she murmured, rivulets of rain running down her waterproofs as though rushing away from the scene.

The revelation seemed to swirl around them in a muddling mist.

Will raked a hand through his hair, looked at the ground as he wrangled with what to say next.

Anna stood still, unsure what to do. She could feel the truth trying to push its way out, like a plant about to burst from the sodden earth.

Will rubbed his palms over his eyes.

'Dad?' said Rose. 'Is there something you need to tell me?' Water droplets trembled on the cuff of her coat.

Lily and Rose, realised Anna, the two flowers intertwining in her head. *Oh my god.*

Will shot her a look; panic painted all over his face.

260

Rose glanced from her dad to Anna, as though on a summit top without a compass.

'Olivia is your half-sister,' said Will.

Rose jolted backwards, hit by an invisible lightning bolt. 'What?' she said.

'She's your mother's other daughter,' he explained, blowing out a breath of relief at having released the long-kept fact – but it was served with a chaser of terror. 'I'm so sorry . . .'

Rose had her fingers cupped over her nose and mouth.

He stepped forward, stretched out a hand, but Rose stumbled backwards away from his reach.

Anna bowed her head; she shouldn't even be there. She turned to leave, heard a melancholic mooing emerge from the milking shed as she made her way back across the farmyard.

'Did you see her?' asked Jackson, the moment Anna arrived back at Hesta, dripping wet and dishevelled.

'You look like a drowned badger,' announced Dani from the kitchen doorway.

Anna nodded at them both in reply. 'Give me a minute to get changed,' she said from the staffroom, glad to have a moment to herself to try and work out what to say to Jackson.

'How was she?' he asked as soon as she was dressed in her whites again.

Anna sighed. It wasn't her place to tell anyone about Rose's secret sibling.

'I did these, by the way,' he added, indicating a pyramid of potatoes, a pile of perfectly cubed beetroot, and a celeriac stack ready to be puréed, like he was striking a deal with heaps of precious stones.

261

'Well done,' said Anna, surveying his efforts. 'Let's get that celeriac in some lemon water. Stop it discolouring,' she said, handing him a big stainless-steel bowl.

He looked at her, eyes huge, waiting for her to uphold her end of the bargain. 'And what about Rose?'

Anna adjusted her apron. 'I said she should talk to you.'

'Do you think she will?' he said with a tilt of his head.

'I don't know. I hope so. I said to make sure she listens to her own heart, and no one else.'

Jackson nodded. 'If it's done, it's done,' he said solemnly to the ceramic floor. 'I just wanted her to know the truth.'

Why hadn't Will thought the same? wondered Anna as she gazed at the grey tiles too. Tessellated, all in order. Everything in the kitchen had a purpose and a reason, but it wasn't always the same in the outside world.

37

'How long on the apple and caramel puds for table four, Dan?' shouted Anna from the pass.

'Five minutes – just come out of the oven,' she yelled back as a blast of sweet, syrup-scented heat reached the rest of the kitchen.

The baked-cake aroma seemed to call Jackson over. A self-saucing dessert had sounded like sorcery, but as he went to look at the ramekins cooling on the side, he could see that, just as Dani had said, the cake mixture at the bottom had now risen to the top.

'There'll be a sticky caramel sauce underneath now,' explained Dani. 'Great job on the apples, by the way,' she added, as though the compliment had bubbled up just as unexpectedly as the batter.

'Thanks,' replied Jackson, still staring at the apple slivers decorating the tops of the circular dishes; delicate fans of fruit that he'd spent most of the afternoon slicing. And now, gazing at the finished result in front of him, he found himself thinking it was *worth* it. He almost laughed. Wished he would be able to see the wonder on each customer's face as they cut into the liquid-centred treats. He could hardly believe he'd contributed to the creations on the countertop. He'd never even made so much as a cupcake as a child; no one had seemed to have either the inclination or the time to show him how. But here at Hesta, he felt utterly in awe of the alchemy he was witnessing first-hand; the way the most ordinary ingredients could be converted into *art*.

'I've baked an extra one,' said Dani, beside him.

Jackson could see there were four dishes instead of three on the rack. Had he done something wrong? 'Oh, is there a problem?' he asked as he surveyed the identical apple arcs before him, each uniform in their flawlessness, and frowned.

'For you to try,' said Dani, sliding one to the side, saving it for him. She smiled. 'You need to know what your hard work tastes like.'

Jackson grinned. 'Thanks. They do look incredible.'

'How long on those desserts, Dan?' called Anna again.

'Thirty seconds, Chef!' replied Dani, carrying the tray of puddings over to the pass.

Jackson followed to watch the plating-up process, fascinated by the precise presentation, the final flourishes that elevated the cake to a Hesta-level course, a fitting finale to a memorable meal.

'Pay close attention,' said Anna, glancing at him. 'Then you can do the ice cream next time.'

'Really?' muttered Jackson, flattered by the confidence she had in him, but feeling a follow-up thrill of fear. What if he screwed it up?

'And tomorrow, I'll show you how to use the Pacojet properly,' said Dani with an arch of her eyebrow, before she slipped her baking sheet in the sink beside Sally and went back to her section.

'That's what you use to make the ice cream, right?' Jackson asked Anna, his stomach starting to churn, not with anticipation for the following day's learning but at the reminder of Rose, toiling up at the farm, trying to make things work without a team like this surrounding her.

'Yes,' replied Anna, as Jackson leaned forward, tried to concentrate on her technique. She held the metal cylinder of ice cream in one hand and then dipped a silver spoon in a steel jug with her other. 'There's hot water in there,' she said, tapping the side of the container with her spoon and shaking off any excess. 'This is how to get a completely smooth-sided scoop,' she explained, gliding the warm implement through the soft swirl of miso-flavoured snow.

She made it look so simple, thought Jackson, watching her sculpt three seamless oval shapes in seconds. A trio of matching quenelles, ephemeral ellipses that had taken hours to create and, in a moment, would be melting on the tongues of the customers on table four, already turning into a memory.

But he was starting to see the point of it all now. Realise the joy that could be sparked by preparing a plate of food for someone. The sense of care that could be conveyed. He thought of the cheese and pepper spaghetti Anna had cooked for him, knew he wouldn't forget it, despite the fact it couldn't have been much easier to make. He recalled the fiery feeling of pride that had swelled inside him the first time Anna said, 'well done'. The satisfaction he'd felt each instance since. The excitement of unlimited flavour combinations, the sense of achievement when a dish turned out exactly as planned. The endless possibilities—

'Service!' Anna shouted beside him, sprinkling a pinch of pine-needle powder on the ice cream that accompanied the puddings, a puff of jade-coloured fairy dust to signal they were finished. Then one of the front-of-house staff whisked them away into the restaurant, and Jackson waited by the swing doors in case he could catch an exclamation of wonder or an earwigged word of praise. But table four was too far away for him to hear anything.

Only Anna knew who the desserts were destined for. Two of the group had indeed visited before. The third had been given the unenviable invitation to spend the evening alongside them, but Ovie didn't recognise that person; all three were booked under the same name. Lawson. The unknown man was probably a new boyfriend of Olivia's – but Anna wasn't remotely bothered and she had purposefully kept the reservations list out of Dani's sight to avoid her being distracted mid-service. She'd seated the guests in the furthest part of the dining room, positioned right in front of the panorama of Buttermere, a breathtaking stretch of silver bullion spread out before them, so if all else failed, they'd hopefully be pleased with the view at least.

'Jackson,' called Dani, and he strode over to the pastry section, expecting to be given another task. But she pushed the remaining caramel pudding towards him. 'Needs to be warm otherwise it's not the same,' she explained.

Jackson dug into the little bowl; took a mouthful of the toffee-apple taste of a childhood he'd never had. 'Oh my god,' he mumbled.

'Good, right?' said Dani.

Jackson nodded, scooping more sauce from the ramekin.

'*Like a culinary cuddle*,' said Dani, pretending to read a newspaper column while affecting the tone of an imaginary critic.

Jackson laughed.

'Okay, everyone,' called Anna, cutting into their companionable chatter. 'Check on for the party of six on table eight.'

Jackson put down the half-eaten dish.

Dani eyed it on the side, then tore her attention away and turned back to her boss.

Anna was holding up a printed order slip, poised to read the list of starters and mains aloud.

But then the door separating the spit and sear of Hesta's kitchen from the serene surrounds of the restaurant itself swung open.

Anna didn't look up from the little piece of paper in her grasp, just saw the dark-suited figure of Ovie in the corner of her vision. He stood to the side, waiting for her to finish, hanging back so he didn't interrupt.

She reeled off the next set of dishes to be cooked, clipped the slip of paper above the pass, and then turned to speak to him.

But it wasn't her Maître D at all. Or anyone from front of house.

The man standing before her was her brother.

Matthew.

'Anna,' he said with a grin, as though it was usual for him to drop in.

You've chosen now to come and say hi? she wanted to shout at him. They hadn't seen each other for *ages*, and this was the moment he'd decided to call on her – when she was at *work. Can't you see I'm busy?* screamed the stress-reddened whites of her eyes.

Ovie appeared behind him; lips clamped together in a silent apology to Anna for not having stopped Matthew from walking through the door in the middle of service.

Her gaze went from her brother to her head waiter and back again. A confusing concoction of emotions was crashing through her body. *Why on earth have you come tonight, after all this time?* His news-presenter's smile had at least snuffed out the spark of panic that something was wrong with their father. But he couldn't be here on business; no one else from BBC North West was booked in as far as she was aware. Why had he strolled into her kitchen, on a full-to-bursting Friday evening, after so many years, without even sending her a message to let her know?

'Hello, Matthew,' she answered matter-of-factly; this was real life, not a TV set in Media City, and she couldn't simply drop everything to speak to him. Yet she still felt a heart-flip of happiness at the fact he was actually *here*, at Hesta. Contradictions collided inside her as she looked at him. He was family; they shared DNA, a dad, and myriad minuscule memories of their mum that were treasured by only the two of them.

'Good to see you,' he said with a nod.

'You too,' she replied, among the steam and starched whites that surrounded her – and she meant it. His features were as familiar as her own, even after so long. It was disorientating seeing him in the flesh; nowadays she only glimpsed a fleeting flash of him if she managed to catch the headlines in between shifts. When was the last time they'd been face to face in person?

In the aftermath of their mum's death, her and Matthew's sadness had been shared yet separate, their journeys diverging more with every passing month as he'd moved to Manchester just as she'd returned home to Buttermere.

They'd hardly spoken since she died – the occasional text or call here and there but no soul-exhuming discussions.

Talking of her had been too upsetting, and everything else had seemed inconsequential. So gradually, they'd slipped out of the habit of being in touch much at all.

They knew jigsaw pieces of each other's lives – Matthew presumably had a partner, he always did, but they tended not to discuss relationships, not since he'd said what he had to Dominik all those years ago, told him to let Anna go.

Somewhere along the way his daughter had been born. It had been rocky with the girl's mother, Anna knew that much, but she'd been so wrapped up in her own work, trying her best to get Hesta somewhere, trying to do her mum proud. Anna had seen baby pictures, sent money on special occasions when the little girl was small, even met her once, ages ago, but it was hard to be close when each of their schedules was so hectic, when the distance seemed to have widened over time, and by now her niece must be grown.

Anna felt hot self-doubt singe her skin. Should she have sacrificed her healing, her own long-held hopes, to stop their brother–sister bond almost severing? But surely it was a two-way process. Matthew had seemed to need to physically distance himself from the past to forge his future, and she understood that. She'd thrown herself into setting up the restaurant. Coped by working all hours to make Hesta what it was in the present.

And Matthew had made it plain he preferred the city to the Lakes. *That's where the action is*, he'd always said.

But how could anyone say that once they'd seen each of the seasons here in all their splendour? wondered Anna. Witnessed a million everyday miracles happening among the hills and hedgerows, watched nature's life cycle unfold in front of their very eyes.

Marion had been the rope of motherly love that had bound her and her brother together more than blood alone could. Anna thought of the letter her mum had written, the part where she'd mentioned a picture of her and Matthew playing as kids. They'd had the same fell-climb-filled childhood, spent Marion's days off outdoors, explored the abounding fields, lakes, and waterfalls. The two of them had had an identical upbringing, unlike Olivia and Rose, but then turned out so completely different.

'It's all been a bit last minute this visit,' Matthew said now, smiling at Anna the same way he had done to win round their parents when they were young. 'But seeing as I've hardly taken any holiday so far this year . . .'

You're not the only one, thought Anna.

'I just thought why not?' He gave her his broadcaster's beam again.

Was that the best reason he could think of for being here? she mused, realising she was the only person on the planet resistant to his charms. She could sense Dani on the edge of her vision, staring at Matthew with the glazed gaze people developed in the presence of someone so recognisable.

Thank goodness most of the diners had been served by now and he hadn't strolled in at the start of the night.

'The meal was amazing,' he said, and she found herself softening. 'Really impressive.'

'Thank you.' Anna looked around, included the other staff in his praise. 'Are you sticking around at all?' she asked, glancing at the clock on the wall. *9.10 p.m. Mostly puddings from now on.*

He looked at his watch. 'We've got a taxi booked to the Lodore Falls Hotel at ten,' he said.

She nodded. 'Okay. Well, I can't really leave here until—'

'Me and Jackson should be all right after the big party's mains are out of the way,' said Dani, and Anna's chest squeezed at her thoughtfulness.

'Thanks,' she said, turning to smile at her over her shoulder.

'See how you go . . .' said Matthew. 'Don't want to interrupt.'

Anna's stomach tensed as she sensed her brother was about to slip away again, without her having any idea of when he'd next be back.

'Who are you here with?' she asked, prolonging the conversation despite herself; she didn't want to be the one to say goodbye.

'Lil and Livvy,' he replied, and a smile crinkled his eyes.

Lil and Livvy. Why did it feel like she had new puzzle pieces all of a sudden, that she couldn't seem to fit together? She frowned. 'Lil as in . . .?' Her brain was mid-shift on the second service of the day at the end of a long week. The world outside Hesta seemed a galaxy away.

'Lilian,' said Matthew. 'You remember her, right?' He looked at Anna as though *she* was the one behaving bafflingly.

'We've never met. You haven't brought her home.'

As soon as she said it, she realised Buttermere *wasn't* his home anymore. Time evaporated quicker than the liquid nitrogen they'd used when she worked in London years ago.

'Well, we got back together – a little while ago now,' explained Matthew. 'Decided to settle down a bit now I'm in my fifties.' A laugh laced with an underlying lack of confidence no one else would be able to hear.

'You look great,' said Anna, touching his arm. 'And that's wonderful,' she added.

'I'm trying to do things differently . . . now I'm older. Be a better dad. Like the one we had.'

Anna nodded. Felt a strange surge of pride as she looked at Matthew, now a grey-haired man. Still her brother but not the baggage-free boy she'd larked about with on the shore of Buttermere.

'Are you going to see Dad while you're here?' she said, suppressing the urge to say he could have invited him along.

Matthew stuttered, sensing her sisterly scold. 'Er . . . yeah, I just thought, you know, Livvy booked it and I'm trying to rebuild that bond . . .'

Livvy booked it . . .

'Oh my god, you're here with *Olivia Lawson*?' Anna said.

Matthew nodded. 'My daughter, yes.'

'Christ on a kebab,' exclaimed Dani from behind Anna, almost dropping her tray of trout tartlets before she'd safely delivered them to the pass.

Anna shot her a look, before turning back to her brother. 'So, wait a minute, you're saying Olivia's mother is—'

'Lilian Lawson. My girlfriend. Well, partner, probably, at my age.' He laughed again.

Anna fiddled with the cord of her apron.

'Are you all right?' said Matthew. 'You look a bit—'

'Yeah, I'm fine, just feels weird I didn't know.'

'I try and keep them out of the public eye as much as possible.'

But bringing them home to visit family was different, surely? thought Anna. It wasn't an excuse for never coming back. Though, he must need to be in the news studio every night, and it was as much up to her to make the effort to go to Manchester as it was to him to come here.

'It can be a cruel world. Especially on social media,' continued Matthew.

'But Olivia's an influencer. She loves the limelight,' replied Anna.

'Yeah, we've had that argument,' said Matthew, raising his eyebrows and reminding her even more of their father. 'I've tried to dissuade her. Explain the downsides. But she has to make up her own mind.'

Anna nodded.

'And it's not that I didn't want her to know you and Dad. I did. It's just . . . difficult. Lilian's always been a bit reluctant to leave the city.' He glanced back through the porthole window.

A picture of Rose and Will standing in the mud-puddled yard at Fell View Farm swam into Anna's head.

'Table eight's starters are ready to go, boss,' said Dani beside her, and Anna's eyes flitted to the pass.

'Anyway, I'll catch you afterwards maybe?' Matthew said, one hand on the door that led back into the restaurant.

Anna met his eye, felt the sibling tie between them tug as he turned to leave, frayed yet firm. 'Yes,' she said, and smiled.

Anna could feel the other diners' attention swivelling towards her as she pulled up a chair to join her brother's table.

Buttermere had evanesced into darkness, the lake no longer visible beyond the blackened glass, and its absence made her feel even more obvious. The hot stare of forty pairs of eyes on her back felt like she herself was a dish being served up on the pass. Even semi-cocooned by the soft fabric of her chair, she felt awkward, had never really been at ease on this side of the swing doors during service.

But she was grateful for the chance to sit down after a long shift, and for the opportunity to see her brother again, as surreal as the situation was.

Ovie came to stand next to her, a guardian angel with a sixth sense. 'Can I get you anything?' he said, as though the four of them were a regular group of customers.

Anna felt her shoulders relax a little.

'We're fine,' said Matthew, glancing at his watch which winked beneath the half-dimmed lights. 'Cab's coming in quarter of an hour.'

'Just a water then, for me, please,' said Anna, smiling her thanks and trying not to feel disappointed that her time with Matthew seemed to be diminishing as rapidly as if someone was dismantling their table item by item.

'So, *you're* my aunty!' squealed Olivia all of a sudden, cutting into Anna's thoughts, forcing her mind to stay in the moment. 'I have a famous chef in my family!'

Ovie set down a tumbler in front of Anna, and she reached for an ice-tinkling sip. 'Yes,' she said to Olivia. 'You're my niece, but I'm not so sure about the second part.' She smiled, took another gulp from her glass. 'You didn't know that, the last time you were here?' she asked, as an image popped into her brain: Olivia picking up the parkin cake like it was a piece of—

'No.' Olivia shook her head.

'Me neither,' said Anna, a sigh escaping her lips.

'Why's Dad never said I've got a celeb for an aunt?'

'He's the celebrity . . .'

'I'm sorry for how I was, though,' muttered Olivia. 'Again,' she added, throwing her arms round her aunt and hugging her tightly, bracelets jangling in Anna's still-ringing ears. But after the nonstop pressure and noise of back-of-house, the unexpected affection was a salve.

Olivia pulled back to show Anna her arms, red scars still visible, stark reminders to be kind.

'I'm glad to see that's much better,' said Anna with a nod of her head.

'Will you take me foraging properly?' asked Olivia from underneath her fringe. 'It's just I've got this idea . . . I want to rebrand.'

Matthew leaned forward. 'Anna actually runs a programme,' he said, and a warmth spread across her skin at the fact he knew about it. 'Dad told me,' he said.

Olivia's eyes lit up.

'Not a TV programme . . .' Anna clarified.

'No, the Marion Carleton Mentor Scheme,' said Matthew, 'after Mum.'

And then there their mother was again, pulling them closer once more, unseen but alive, turning their table for four into five.

38

'I knew you were Matthew's sister when we came last time,' said Lilian, 'and I thought about saying hello but I knew you'd be busy, and I didn't know what to say, and to be honest, Livvy was so upset, it was just after a completely out-of-the-blue break-up' – she directed a sympathetic pout at her daughter – 'and I just wanted her to be okay.'

Anna nodded. She'd been in the kitchen, oblivious to Lilian's presence.

Lilian looked like she was about to say something else, but stopped.

Matthew took her hand.

Lilian closed her eyes momentarily. 'I'm sorry, though, I should have made contact . . . I just find it really hard being here . . .'

'At Hesta?' Anna rubbed her temple.

'No, in Buttermere.' Lilian shuffled as though her cushioned seat was covered in the prickles of a porcupine. She turned to Matthew. 'I think maybe it's time everyone knew the truth.'

'What's that supposed to mean?' asked Olivia, eyelashes beating like two distressed butterflies.

Anna saw Matthew and Lilian share a look. Had felt that kind of wordless communication herself once.

'Oh my god, what's happening?' asked Olivia, gripping her napkin in both hands.

The crushed ice in Anna's drink chilled the back of her throat.

'I thought I was doing the right thing, keeping things separate when we were in Manchester,' confessed Lilian. 'But now you seem to have made this connection with the Lakes—'

'Separate? What are you saying?' said Olivia, a look of horror halloweening her face.

Matthew took her hand now, too.

'What is it? Please, spit it out!' said Olivia, pulling away.

Anna swallowed, her clammy palms making her cold glass cloud.

'You have a half-sister,' declared Lilian. 'Called Rose.'

'*What?*' shrieked Olivia, pressing her glitter-ringed fingers to her cheeks, just as the headlights of the taxi blazed through the glass doors, bringing the dinner to a close.

Anna blew out a breath as she went back into the kitchen, blinked as her eyes readjusted to the bright lighting – but for once it was quieter in there than out in the restaurant. Containers of ingredients only needed for the first courses had been packed away, squeeze bottles of sauces for the starters and mains were back in the fridge, and some of the countertops had already been scrubbed down. She was impressed. Leaving the team in charge might be something she could do more often. But where was everyone? Anna scanned the shining surfaces as she walked past each of the

277

stations. Then she noticed a stack of pots and pans in the sink. Surely Sally wouldn't have left those there till the morning? But maybe she'd needed a break. Perhaps they all had. Anna turned towards the rear door, deciding to join them out the back for a bit of fresh air and a debrief: they'd done a brilliant job this week. Jackson included. But as she strode in the direction of the staffroom, she spotted a spillage on the floor by the spray tap, a pool of soapless liquid glimmering on the tiles, and sighed. Splashed over the side in the middle of service most likely, but she'd said so many times that spillages must be cleaned up immediately. Emphasised how dangerous it was. She didn't want anyone slipping and falling and coming to harm. She fetched the mop. Sometimes it was faster to do things yourself but, as much as she didn't want to dampen the success of a smoothly handled Friday night, it was something she'd have to mention—

'Anna!' Dani's voice from behind her.

She spun round, saw her pastry chef's bleached expression, her fists balled in fright. 'What is it? she said, possible scenarios swamping her brain. Her heart rate rose as Dani struggled for words.

'It's Sally . . . she . . .' Dani clutched her own stomach in sympathy. 'And Jackson's gone . . .'

Oh no. Sweat stuck the collar of Anna's jacket to her neck. Had she put Sally at risk by bringing Jackson into Hesta's kitchen? Had some sort of altercation broken out when she'd been through in the restaurant with her brother—

'Did you . . . see the . . . on the floor?' Dani asked, not usually one to have a problem speaking but stuttering now.

Anna thought of the puddle, pictured the spray tap. What had happened? Had a playful splash spiralled into a fight?

'The baby . . .' said Dani.

'Tell me what's going on!' pleaded Anna. Her KP was almost eight months' pregnant, for Christ's sake. 'Where are Jackson and Sally now?' she demanded.

'On the way to the hospital,' said Dani, hands on her head. 'The baby's come too soon.'

'So Jackson is . . . he hasn't . . .' said Anna, trailing off, feeling a stab of guilt for doubting him.

'He's with her,' replied Dani. 'Offered to drive her there. Said his car was at yours and ran back to get it. Her waters broke when she was washing up.' Dani's speech was back, sentences rushing out of her as though to illustrate the speed with which everything had happened. 'What do we do now?' she said to Anna, so used to turning to her head chef for instruction.

Anna shook her head. 'I honestly don't know.'

A knock on the back door made them both start.

'Oh god, he can't have broken down, can he?' said Dani, running out to see.

But it was Rose standing on the doorstep, tousled and dirt-streaked in the darkness. 'I'll stay out here,' she said, glancing down at her wellington boots. 'But I wondered if I could speak to Jackson. Thought he might be finishing soon.'

'He's not here,' said Anna. 'He's . . .' She looked at Dani.

Rose's eyes were two black pearls in an ocean of night. 'Has he gone?' she asked, voice cracking. 'Left Buttermere, I mean?'

Anna shook her head. 'No, he's—'

'Gone with Sally,' finished Dani.

'Sally?' said Rose.

'Our KP,' clarified Dani. 'She's—'

'Oh, right,' replied Rose, cutting her off, taking a step back from the building. 'I see. No worries. It doesn't matter.' She sniffed, eyes gleaming. Then turned and started walking away.

'Wait!' Anna called after her. They hadn't made things clear . . .

But it was too late. Rose had disappeared as suddenly as if she'd been consumed by the gaping mouth of the moon.

Anna said goodnight to Dani, not sure she could deal with endless deliberation about whether or not Sally and her child would be all right. She hoped to god they would be, but there was nothing that could be done other than to await an update. She glanced again at her phone screen. Was sure Jackson would let her know any news. But as she wound her way home along the lane, the idea of waiting at the cottage alone, with only her own mind for company, seemed about as appealing as spending the night in a mausoleum. She pulled out her phone again. Half ten. Hovered her thumb over the 'call' icon. Then clicked to ring her dad. If he'd gone to bed and didn't answer, then that was fine. She'd stay here, keep herself busy—

He answered almost straightaway, a trace of laughter still on his tongue. 'Anna, hi.'

She hadn't expected him to pick up, but he sounded *happy*, and suddenly she felt pleased she'd heard the lightness in his tone; it had been a long time.

But then she sensed the aftertaste of concern hit him. 'Is everything all right? Are you okay?'

'Yes, yes,' she said. 'I'm fine.'

'Oh, thank goodness. You had me worried for a second.'

'Sorry . . . um . . . I wasn't sure you'd still be awake . . .'

'Book club night,' he said, and a hint of a grin returned. 'Couldn't believe what time it was when we logged off – we started at half seven,' he said.

She smiled. Even the sound of his voice seemed to soothe her.

'But how come you're calling? Everything definitely okay?' he asked again.

'Yeah, I've just finished work. I wondered if . . . I could come round.'

'Now?'

'It's probably too late, isn't it . . .'

'No, not at all. Fire's lit, and I even opened a bottle of wine.'

She sighed as she pictured the scene.

'See you in a minute,' he said on the other end of the line. 'I'll go and get you a glass.'

And Anna found herself quickening her pace in anticipation of the hug that would greet her.

She didn't really want the wine, but holding the cut-glass goblet always made her feel closer to her mum, made her think of Christmas lunches and birthday dinners when happy memories had been minted with merry toasts.

'It's nice to see you,' said her dad, settling into the chair opposite her. 'Sometimes feels a bit strange switching off the computer and coming back to the real world.'

'That's how I feel when I leave Hesta,' replied Anna as she sat down on the sofa. 'So how was book club?' she asked, mind craving escape from the madness of her own evening.

'Good, thanks,' replied her dad. 'Some of us who live a bit closer to each other are even planning to meet up for a meal. My idea.' He raised his eyebrows at her, as though he couldn't quite believe his boldness.

'That's brilliant.' She smiled back at him as she took a sip of her garnet-tinted drink.

'One of them suggested I take up wild swimming too.' Chatter was streaming out of him like a beck after rain, full again.

'And are you going to?' Anna asked.

'Might do. Is that crazy?' her dad replied.

Anna shook her head. 'I used to do it quite a lot. Should really do it more. If you want to, we could go together.'

'Really?'

'Why not?' she said. It would be something they could do outside these walls, the two of them. Something new. Maybe he'd wanted their home to be a memorial to Marion in a way, but tonight, for the first time, Anna could see signs of *life* as well as loss: the book on the coffee table, the ice-cream menu from the farm on the sideboard. Starting a new chapter didn't always mean leaving the rest of the story behind, she realised.

'We could go first thing in the morning, before work . . . If you're keen, we could give it a whirl tomorrow? The lake's only a stone's throw,' she said.

'Okay.' Her dad nodded. 'If the weather's better.' But then the light in his eyes seemed to dull as he leaned back in his chair. 'I'm not sure they're going to be keeping me on at Fell View much longer.'

Anna put down her glass.

'There's not enough business at the moment.' He sighed.

'But in spring and summer surely there will be?' said Anna, though it was like telling a diner at Hesta that their meal would arrive in the next few months. 'There must be something we can do . . .' she added, needing time to think about it when her brain wasn't quite so kitchen-frazzled.

'Anyway,' said Robert, 'tell me about your day. Anything exciting happen?'

Anna reached for her glass again, wondered where to start. She glanced skyward as she took another sip of wine, prayed Sally and her baby would be all right. She didn't want to tempt fate by talking about it, even touched her foot to the wooden table leg to be on the safe side, though she wasn't the slightest bit superstitious. *Hope makes you do ridiculous things.*

She didn't know whether to mention Matthew, if his visit was meant to be a surprise. But her brother was the passing comet that could put the light back in her father's eyes.

'Well, I tell you who I did see,' said Anna.

'Ooh, a celebrity?' replied her dad, tapping a finger on his chin.

'Better than that.'

'Who?'

'My brother.'

'In Buttermere?'

'At the restaurant.'

'Tonight?'

Anna nodded.

'Goodness me.' Robert sat forward to pour them each a top-up, as though the fact Matthew had been close by was cause enough to celebrate. 'There I was, thinking I'd missed him on the telly at ten o'clock, and he was actually here!'

Anna smiled.

'How is he?' asked her dad.

Like the northern lights, Anna wanted to say. *You spend ages hoping to see them and then they show up when you least expect it.*

'He seemed well – I only saw him very briefly.' She took a gulp of her wine. Wondered whether her dad knew more than she had done . . . 'He was with Lilian.'

Robert's brow wrinkled with the effort of wracking his wine-marinated mind. 'Olivia's mother,' he said, slapping his knee. 'Are she and Matthew an item again, then?' he asked.

'Yes, I think so.' Anna swirled the wine in her glass, made a mini Merlot whirlpool. Wondered whether, if she spun the liquid hard enough, she could rewind time, make a vortex that could transport her back for a second chance, too.

Her dad nodded slowly, sipped his drink. 'I haven't seen Olivia since she was little,' he said with a sigh. 'I know Matthew had a lot on. I didn't want to be a burden. There never seemed to be a good time to invite myself. And then she was grown up. What will she be now?' he pursed his lips. 'Twenty-four?'

'I guess so.' Anna felt the skin on her neck needle at the fact she didn't know.

'I have an *adult* granddaughter,' said Robert, raising his eyebrows in surprise, like he was on a rollercoaster named Speed of Time. 'That's probably the last time I went in the lake, you know; that day we took her down to the water's edge to paddle.' He drained his drink. 'She must have been about the same age as you are in that photograph Mum took of you and your brother on the shore.'

Anna remembered standing barefoot on the sun-dappled pebbles that day, before she'd had to say goodbye and go to work at Hesta. Her niece had been young, but at the time it had seemed like Matthew had waited forever to bring her back to meet Anna and her dad. Lilian hadn't come. Anna knew why now . . .

Should I have joined the dots sooner? she wondered. Lilian's reticence to visit Buttermere had probably caused tension between her and Matthew, might have contributed to their split.

'What is it?' asked Robert with a frown.

'Oh, nothing,' replied Anna, the lie stinging her lips as it left her mouth.

'That's not true,' said her dad, emboldened by the alcohol.

Anna swallowed; cooking up falsehoods wasn't her skill. Did her dad know that Olivia and Rose were related?

'I think I might have an inkling,' murmured her dad, bowing his head out of respect for the situation. 'Rose said something to me.'

'What, at work?'

He nodded. 'It's been unbelievably quiet up there. We carried on making ice cream, just in case, though I don't know why we thought there might be a sudden influx of people – they'd have to be serious rain enthusiasts.' He gave a laugh, trying to lighten the mood, but it was as transparent as a gauze of drizzle. She could see straight through it, tell he was upset his role might be petering out before it had properly begun.

'I didn't let Rose pay me,' he continued. 'I couldn't take the money. I was there for the company, the conversations with customers, but there have hardly been any lately.'

'Meant to be a bit better tomorrow,' said Anna, pulling out her phone, showing him the forecast for the following day.

'That's good. Dry for once. I'm meant to be going in for nine, but plenty of time for a swim before then.' He smiled.

The rain rattled the windowpanes as though to remind them both it was still there, hadn't gone anywhere yet.

'I've been doing my best in the circumstances,' her dad continued. 'Offering home delivery on litre tubs for the freezer, handing out flyers, but there's only so much you can do.'

Or was there always something more? wondered Anna, an idea forming at the back of her brain. There must be a glimmer of goodness to come out of this maelstrom . . .

'I think Rose is really going through the wringer at the moment,' said her dad.

Anna felt the truth vibrate in her bones like a rumble of thunder.

'What did she say to you?'

'She'd fallen out with her dad about something. I could tell they weren't speaking. She'd normally go and help with the milking, but she didn't that day.'

Anna's heart went out to Rose as she remembered the bombshell of betrayal that had been unleashed in the yard.

'I was getting on with what we were doing – making greengage and almond ice cream, as it happened—'

'Mmm,' said Anna reflexively.

'I didn't realise the time because Rose was still there and I was engrossed in the process.'

Even though Anna knew the story was about to turn sour, she smiled at the passion in her dad's voice when he spoke about the ice-cream parlour.

'And she spilled it all out to me,' said Robert. 'Maybe she thought you'd told me.'

Anna shook her head. Loyalty was a badge she wore alongside Hesta's emblem on her chef whites. 'So, what did you say?'

'Well, I just listened to begin with, but then I wondered whether I could give an insight into how it feels to be a father.'

'Oh, Dad,' said Anna, tilting her head to one side. They had certainly had their differences of opinion in the past, and it was only really now that she could fully appreciate his perspective. She wished it hadn't taken her so long.

'Will had known about Olivia, apparently,' said Robert.

Anna pressed her fingers to her lips. 'The whole time?'

Her dad nodded. 'Only that she existed, no more than that, but he hadn't had the heart to tell Rose, and that's why she was angry.'

'Anyone would feel the same,' said Anna.

'It'll take her a bit of time to get used to it,' said Robert. 'But maybe there'll be an upside to all this.'

'I hope so,' said Anna. Rose had been encouraging Will to modernise his thinking when it came to the farm, and now she was going to have to take her own advice and adapt to a whole new world herself.

39

Anna was in a deep dream-drenched sleep when the sound of the front door unlocking roused her. She reached for her phone, squinted at the screen: 6.30 a.m. *Jackson. Oh god. Sally.* The sudden memory of what had happened the previous evening jolted her awake. She hauled herself out from underneath the duvet, wrapped her dressing-gown round her instead, an alternative layer of cushioning against whatever was coming next, and went downstairs.

Jackson was curled up in the armchair, bathed in moonbeams from the window, watching the silvery light outside gild the night.

Anna stood in the doorway, saw the molten mercury streak of tears on his cheek.

Oh, please, no.

She sank down on the sofa and waited for him to speak. Worst-case scenarios cobwebbed her mind. The belt of her bathrobe bit into her stomach as she bent over, put her head in her hands.

'Sally's okay,' Jackson said eventually, voice hoarse with exhaustion.

Oh, thank god. 'And the baby?' asked Anna, glancing up.

'He's . . .' started Jackson, before letting out a long sigh in the half-dark and covering his face with his hands.

'What?' Anna raked her fingers through her bed-ruffled hair. *Please let him be okay.*

Jackson looked up, wiped his eyes with his palms. 'He's a beautiful little boy.'

'Oh, thank goodness,' said Anna, flopping back against the cushions. 'So, they're both all right?'

'Yes,' Jackson said with a sniff.

'Then why are you upset?' she asked softly.

Another sob escaped his chest. 'I'm not . . . I'm just . . . relieved.' He sighed.

She nodded. 'You did a good job. And well done for acting so quickly.'

'It pretty much happened as soon as you left,' he replied, deflecting the compliment as if he was unused to praise. 'When we got to the hospital, the baby was already coming.' A tremor in his tone like an aftershock. 'We got there just in time.'

We again, Anna noticed. He was already part of the team, a member of the Hesta family, she thought with a smile.

'Sally's mum was on her way when I left,' Jackson added, care creased into his forehead, and for the first time Anna saw the person Rose had fallen in love with.

A yawn twisted his lips and he pushed himself up out of the chair. 'I'm going to try and get some kip.'

'Okay. Obviously have a day off today,' said Anna, 'that goes without saying.'

Jackson shook his head. 'No, I'll be fine in a few hours' time,' he called from the hallway.

But before she could argue, she remembered she had something to tell him. 'Rose came to see you. After service.'

'Did she?' he said, coming back into the room, all trace of tiredness gone.

Anna nodded. 'I think there might have been a misunderstanding, though.'

'How do you mean?'

'Dani said you'd left with someone called Sally—'

But Anna didn't have chance to explain any more, Jackson was already out of the door.

Anna lay back down on the sofa, let her thoughts flit freely like nocturnal moths. She'd dreamed of Dominik again. Her head had been filled with him before Jackson came home. They'd been standing beneath a giant horse chestnut tree on a copper-coloured October day. She'd held out a burnished brown conker, watched it gleam in the autumn sunshine. But he'd been looking at her instead. *Kasztan*, he'd said, as he kissed her under the dream-painted sky.

He used to say that, beneath her spiky shell, she was beautiful, remembered Anna. That part was real at least.

She watched the first light begin to bleed beyond the fells, on the blue-grey brink of a brand-new day.

And then her phone buzzed beside her.

`Still on for swimming? Dad x`

She sat upright. Had forgotten all about that. It was past seven now, and the morning birdsong was a choir of encouragement.

She typed out her reply, said she'd meet him at his so they could walk down to the lake together, and leaped off the sofa to seize the first fine day they'd had in ages.

40

'I felt stupid for not realising who Olivia was sooner,' Anna admitted as they walked along the path that led to the water.

'But how could you have done?' said her dad alongside her. 'We don't tend to see things unless we're looking for them. I was the same. No idea.'

'Yeah, I wasn't expecting it, I guess,' she said as they wove their way between the vivid rain-gorged verges. It was the same with foraging, she thought. There was so much there, right in front of your eyes, that most people would miss.

'Olivia has her mother's maiden name for a start,' said Robert with a shrug.

Anna nodded. Her focus had been on cooking for a famous taste-maker sent by the Grinfluence Agency, the first time she'd seen Olivia Lawson as a grown woman, and then she had been concentrating on helping her after her vicious encounter with the giant hogweed that day in the woods. No wonder she hadn't twigged.

'Have you spoken to Matthew?' she asked, biting her thumbnail.

Her dad nodded. 'I had to tell him I knew Olivia and Rose were sisters. I thought he might need me. Or at least like to know I was there if he wanted to talk.'

'I never know when's the right time to ring . . .' Anna mumbled; it sounded like an excuse, even to her ears, but it was the truth.

'Oh, I probably call at the most inconvenient moments,' said her dad. 'But I would give anything to be able to talk to your mum, just once more.'

Anna wished she'd hugged Matthew tightly when she'd seen him at the restaurant, told him how much she missed him.

'He thought he was protecting you too, you know, by keeping a bit of distance,' said her dad.

'What do you mean?' said Anna.

'He didn't want to make a big thing about the connection between you two. Worried that journalists might treat you differently if they made the link. Wanted you to know all the articles and reviews – all the praise – was genuine, nothing to do with him being famous.'

'I had no idea,' said Anna. 'Why didn't he tell me?'

Robert shrugged. 'Maybe he found it hard to bring up . . .'

'I don't feel part of his world at all sometimes,' admitted Anna.

'So much of him is on show, I think he keeps the rest of his life under wraps,' said her dad. 'Is scared of it being splashed over the papers.'

That was understandable, conceded Anna, wondering at the contrast between her brother and his daughter, who seemed to crave being in the spotlight.

'Did you know Olivia is—'

'An *influencer*!' finished Robert proudly, as though it was another word for world leader. 'Yes. Matthew told me a while ago.'

Anna felt like a warm scarf had been pulled from her neck on a cold night. Why hadn't Matthew confided in *her* at all? Had she spent so long immersed in the restaurant, trying to distract herself from her own pain, that she hadn't been there enough for her brother? She'd done her best to support her dad but, when it came to Matthew, she'd always assumed he was thriving. He gave that impression, after all, but now she realised it couldn't have been easy. Trying to balance bringing up a daughter with being in the public eye, and respecting Lilian's wish to keep Olivia separate from her half-sister, Rose. The impossible tightrope the girls' mother trod, trying not to hurt either of them. Maybe her brother had struggled more than she'd realised.

'Gosh, Anna, you could be onto something there with this influencer thing . . .' said her dad, tugging her back to the present.

'Do you think so?' She smiled as the lake opened out in front of them. The idea had taken root in her mind like a wind-borne seed, and now, as her dad nodded back at her, they put their bags down on the shore while the water ahead seemed to shimmer its agreement too.

'I'm not so sure about this, though,' murmured her dad as he dipped his toe in the shallows. '*Eeesh*.'

Buttermere's steely surface swirled at their feet, and Anna shivered. The storm seemed to have sucked the last of the summer's warmth from the landscape.

'Maybe I'll wait till spring, eh?' said her dad, retreating from the waterline. 'You go ahead, it's nice just being out, taking it all in.' He lowered himself onto the pebbles and gazed out towards the mist-cloaked mountains.

Anna waded into the lake's chillsome embrace, then swam parallel to the bank in sweeping, muscle-stretching strokes. The air was still, and birds danced branch to branch in celebration that the sky was once again calm. She concentrated on her breathing, the sensation of the water supporting her limbs, and the cloud-wisp patterns above her head, but the murmuring hum of a conversation drew her attention.

It was then that she saw them.

Two figures sitting side by side on the beach.

She was about to turn round, head back in the direction of her dad, when Jackson raised a hand in recognition.

She waved back, spluttered as she sank a little, thrown out of sync by coming across him and Rose. *Of course. Where else would they have gone?* The farm was mired in the past. But here, with such a wide horizon before them, anything felt possible.

41

'Thanks,' said Anna as she took the hot mug of coffee from her father.

'Bacon butty?' he said, with a sideways glance.

'Go on, then.' She grinned, ever appreciative of someone else cooking even the simplest thing; a rare treat when you were a chef with Anna's reputation.

'D'you think I can still have one even if I didn't go in?' said her dad, already buttering two buns. They both knew he would; was as delighted to be having breakfast together as she was.

Anna nodded.

'I'll build up to it,' he said, as the sizzle-hiss of bacon filled the kitchen.

'Jackson and Rose were down by the lake,' she said, as she leaned against the counter.

She saw her dad's jaw tense.

'What is it?' she asked.

'There is actually something else,' said Robert to the bacon rashers.

Anna frowned. 'Do I need to sit down? I'm not sure I can cope with any more secrets—'

'It's nothing like that.' Robert shook the frying pan. 'I just said to Rose that she has to do what her own heart tells her to.'

Was that why she'd come to see Jackson at the restaurant, because of what her dad had said? wondered Anna.

But as her dad handed her a ketchup-coated crispy bacon sandwich, made just the way she liked it, she realised it was served with an apology.

'Thank you,' she said, smiling at him across the table, and for once it didn't feel as though Marion was missing. It was a moment for the two of them, and she couldn't have asked for more.

'Holy ravioli, what a night that was!' said Dani, when Anna came through the door later that morning.

Anna blew out a breath. 'I'm pleased to say Sally's home safe and sound, though,' she replied.

'I know, she just texted me.' Dani drummed her hands on her thighs as though whatever was about to come next required a percussion accompaniment.

'What is it?' said Anna, narrowing her eyes.

Dani's cheeks ballooned like a puffer fish with the effort of keeping the information inside. 'Maybe I should let Sally say instead . . .'

Anna nodded. Less conversation and more cookery sounded perfect.

'Or do you already know?' asked Dani, scrunching up her shoulders in anticipation of Anna's response.

She hadn't a clue what Dani was on about. 'Why don't we wait and share all our excitement with Sally?' she replied.

They had a long Saturday ahead and hadn't even got started on the prep yet.

'Okay, you're right,' said Dani. 'I thought it was the loveliest idea ever . . .' She jiggled her head like she'd just tasted the most delicious dessert she'd ever had.

Anna couldn't help being the slightest bit intrigued, but they couldn't spend all morning talking, however much that would have delighted Dani. They were already two members of staff down, so she needed her pastry chef to be operating at full speed. They were going to be more stretched than strudel dough today.

But then Jackson appeared, apron on, in the back doorway.

'I thought I gave you the day off?' said Anna, by the fridge.

He nodded. 'You did. But you're missing a KP, aren't you? Thought I could fill in . . . if you want . . . just for the time being.'

Anna smiled at him. 'That would be brilliant.'

Dani gave him a grin. Opened her mouth to congratulate him. But the news she'd tried to keep a lid on seemed to spill out like she was a shaken bottle of soda. 'You'll never guess what,' she blurted. 'Sally's named her son Jack, after you.'

42

Never in a million split-shifts did Anna think she'd be calling Flick from Grinfluence Agency of her own volition. But here she was, mobile clamped to her ear, first thing on Monday morning. Hesta was closed, as usual, and it was as though the restaurant was sleeping, the whirring snores of the kitchen equipment the only background sound as she waited for her to pick up.

Anna cleared her throat, would have thought she'd have been more likely to eat her own hat than be about to make the following suggestion, but it seemed to have been infusing in her mind all weekend like a recipe she couldn't ignore.

To her relief, Flick was immediately on board. 'I'll obviously have to speak to my client and come back to you,' she said, but Anna could hear the animation in her voice as she thanked her for the call.

Then Anna clicked to ring another number, expecting to leave a voicemail, imagining her brother listening to it 125 miles away in Manchester, and almost fell off her chair when Matthew actually answered.

'I thought you'd be at work,' said Anna.

'Not till later. Everything okay?' he said, with an uncharacteristic quiver of worry in his words.

'Yes, fine,' said Anna, and she heard him exhale.

'I thought something had happened to Dad then for a second.'

'No, no, he's all right.'

'Phew. You gave me the shock of my life; you don't normally call.'

Well, neither do you, thought Anna.

'What is it? Are *you* all right?' That tremor in his voice again; she felt touched.

'Yes. Thank you.' And then she explained what she'd been talking to Olivia's agent about.

There was a pause as Matthew digested what she'd said.

'How is . . . my niece?' said Anna, an image of her scream-emoji expression stamped in her head.

'She's obviously had a massive shock . . . I did want to tell her the truth all along, but Lili said Rose didn't know and it wasn't fair to tell one and not the other.'

Anna found herself nodding. It was so easy to judge someone else's actions when you weren't in their position.

'Lili knew how much hurt and disruption she'd caused Rose, and she didn't want to put her through any more. I did think there might be problems in the future.'

Fear could turn the woolliest reasoning into concrete logic. Anna felt for her brother, caught between being honest with his daughter and loyal to his partner.

'I was wondering,' said Matthew, 'about taking a couple of days off. Coming up for a bit.'

'To Buttermere?' Despite all the recent surprises, this seemed like the biggest shock of all.

'Yes,' her brother replied. 'To see you and Dad. Spend some time together.'

'Do you mean that?' asked Anna. 'Don't say it if you're not serious.' She was picturing her dad's ecstatic expression if she told him what Matthew had said. 'Dad'll get his hopes up, you know.' But she was the one whose face had lit up at the thought, she realised.

Flick called back before the end of the day to say that the Fire and Ice Bonfire Night Party that Anna had pitched was on in principle: Olivia had agreed to promote the event.

'Yippee!' said Anna aloud, startling herself and also Flick, who laughed on the other end of the line.

But as soon as she'd put down the phone, Anna's elation vanished faster than a plate of biscuits in Dani's presence. She hadn't spoken to Rose and Will about her idea yet – there'd seemed no point before she had Flick and Olivia's approval – but now doubt curdled her stomach. Was she interfering? Once upon a time, Rose had been keen to try anything that might boost the ice-cream business, but so much had happened since then. She might not even want to *see* Olivia again.

Flick was going to email over a proposal to Fell View – an outline of the potential event, including an appearance and online promotion by Ms Lawson and a projection of the increased visibility. It all sounded great, thought Anna, *in theory*. But life so rarely went to plan. She ought to know that better than anyone.

She drove up to the farm, her car armour against the Cumbrian cold and the frosty reception she was afraid she might receive.

The yard was deserted, no orange glow to signal anyone was home.

She rang the bell outside the farmhouse anyway, hood pulled up to shield her face from the gale which pushed its way inside the porch like an interloper.

No answer.

She'd turned to walk back to the car, head bowed against the blusters, when she heard the door open.

Will.

He didn't even part his lips, he had that little to say to her.

'Hi,' said Anna, peeling back her hood, the whispering wind filling the silence between them. 'Please can I come in?'

His fingers didn't leave the doorhandle, as though he was still deciding his answer.

'Just for a second . . . if that's okay. To speak to you and Rose about something—'

He shook his head. 'She's not talking to me.'

'Right.' Anna felt the wind pummelling her back as though urging her forwards. 'Well, it's just I had an idea – a plan to bring new customers to the farm. Increase exposure for Wild Rose—'

Will held up a palm. 'No, I'm sorry, this is stopping this second.' He jabbed his forefinger at the hallway floor. 'From now on, we're staying firmly in reality,' he said. 'Feet on the ground. No more fantasy land.'

Anna frowned. 'What do you mean?'

'Encouraging these daydreams doesn't do Rose any good. She only gets disappointed in the end.' He folded his arms. 'Better to—'

'Never try anything?' finished Anna.

'No. Live in the *real world*,' countered Will. He sighed. 'This is *nothing* to do with you.'

'Well, it is a little bit,' said Anna. 'When my niece is Rose's half-sister.'

Will's cheeks turned cherry. '*What?*'

'Yep. More in common than we first thought, eh?'

'Hang on. So, Olivia is—'

'My brother Matthew's child.' Anna nodded.

'Good god.' Will pinched the top of his nose. 'But this is what I'm saying,' he continued. 'Look how all that turned out.' He looked down at his socks. 'I thought pretending Olivia didn't exist was the best option, the only way to protect Rose, but I ended up hurting her even more.' He winced, his daughter's pain inseparable from his own. 'I love her so much. The last thing I ever wanted to do was make her feel like this. I didn't know how to handle it, blocked it all out instead. I mean, how do you even *start* that conversation?' He slumped against the doorframe, and that's when Anna saw Rose, standing behind him, listening to every word.

43

Anna had never been into the kitchen at the farmhouse before. Wasn't used to being offered hospitality of any kind at other people's homes, apart from her dad's. The pressure of providing food or drink for a professional chef tended to put people off inviting her, even though Anna would have been appreciative of anything, but Rose plonked down a pot of tea as though she was as much of a fixture at Fell View as the range, which was belting out heat like it had got used to compensating for the cool atmosphere between Rose and Will over the last few days.

Anna sat down at the long oak table.

Rose did the same opposite her, then Will took the chair next to his daughter, leaving the seat at the head of the table free, choosing to sit side by side instead.

'This is only a suggestion,' began Anna, 'but something for you both to think about.' She looked from one set of frown lines to the other, like she was reading from an autocue.

'Go on, then,' said Will, as he sloshed out tea for the three of them. 'What is it, this plan of yours?'

'A party.'

'What?' he said, the milk jug in his hand hovering mid-air. 'You think having a *party* is the answer to our problems?' His laughter ricocheted off the flagstone floor. 'This is a working farm, not a fancy restaurant, in case you hadn't noticed.'

Anna put her palms on the table. 'I know that.'

'And what exactly have we got to celebrate?' said Will, milk slopping onto the tabletop as he set the jug back down. 'We've got a failing business, for god's sake. It would be a funeral wake.'

Rose turned to face her father. 'We have to do something, or we'll lose the farm forever.'

Will pressed his fingers to his temples. 'And you think funnelling money into throwing a *party* is the way forward.' He looked from his daughter to Anna and back again.

'A Fire and Ice party,' announced Anna. She took a sip of tea, felt it scorch her throat as Will and Rose stared back at her. 'A bonfire night extravaganza with Wild Rose Ice Cream as the focus,' she explained.

'Where we watch our entire livelihood go up in flames,' said Will.

'No, an event to ignite new interest, bring in fresh customers, really launch the business with a bang,' said Anna. She saw a brief flare of excitement cross Rose's face.

'Anna could be right, you know, Dad. We need something *different.*'

'And how do you propose we do this?' Will said to Anna, glancing round at the faded farmhouse furnishings. 'Not exactly as plush as Hesta in here, is it?'

'That's why fireworks night is perfect. We hold it outside. Prove ice cream isn't just for summer. Show off some

304

delicious winter-inspired combinations.' She clasped her hands together. 'Imagine everyone gathered around a big bonfire—'

'I suppose that bit's easy enough to do, at least,' admitted Will.

Anna smiled.

'A Fire and Ice party,' whispered Rose. 'It sounds amazing.'

'And we'll make it *taste* amazing,' said Anna. 'Picture all those autumnal flavours, topped with shards of cinder toffee.'

Will licked his lips, despite himself.

Rose sighed. 'I don't have time to do any extra stuff like that.'

'I know someone who's Hesta-trained and would love to give you a hand,' replied Anna.

Will opened his mouth, but closed it again.

'Jackson's really enjoying it,' murmured Rose to Anna.

Will shot her a look. 'You've seen him?'

Rose nodded.

Anna remembered spotting them down by the shore, heads bent together like a pair of swans.

'But we're talking about the future of the *farm* here, not me and Jackson,' continued Rose.

Anna folded her arms. 'So, are we on for the fifth of November or not?'

Rose bit her lip. 'But how do we honestly make it work? It's a lovely idea in theory, but it's not going to generate profit.'

'If we pull in enough people, spread the word far enough, tell the whole of the North West what Wild Rose has to offer, I think it could have a real long-term effect.'

Rose rested her chin on her hands as though the weight of all her thoughts was simply too much.

'Plus, Olivia has said she'll promote it,' said Anna. 'Across all her social media.'

'You mean she would come here? To the event?' asked Rose, sitting up straight. 'No thanks. I don't want her pity.'

Will rubbed his stubble with his thumb but didn't speak, much to Anna's surprise.

'That's not the idea,' she said to Rose. 'I think it would be mutually beneficial. Good for Olivia's profile too—'

'We're not peasants in need of charity,' interjected Rose.

'No, that's not what I'm saying. She's changing her image, wants to use her platform to shine a light on sustainable projects that will get people talking.'

'We don't need her help.'

Will cleared his throat. 'What if it's not just about the business?' he said. 'What if this could bring you both together?'

Anna raised her eyebrows.

Rose glared at him. 'What? We couldn't be *more* different.' She pushed her chair back from the table.

'I'm only saying that, if she's willing to—'

'What, pose with a sparkler, that'll solve everything?' said Rose, standing up. 'I don't think so. This isn't a cute background for an Instagram photo – this is our *life*.'

'Well, you were all for it last time, when you thought a famous influencer was visiting the farm,' retorted Will.

'Yeah, because someone hadn't given me all the facts!' Rose shouted. 'I don't want to be the poor relation, begging for some second-hand attention.'

'Right, well, I'll tell her it's off, then,' said Anna, drinking the last of her tea and getting to her feet.

Rose put her hands on her hips. 'Olivia has already said yes?'

Anna nodded as she put her cup down. 'Doesn't matter though, can easily be cancelled.'

Rose jutted out her chin.

'Her agent had pencilled in a virtual meeting for tomorrow morning,' said Anna. 'She's sent you an email.'

'I haven't seen it,' muttered Rose. 'I'm behind with all that—'

'Never mind,' replied Anna. 'I'll let her know it's been kiboshed.' She did up her coat.

'Anna, wait, we're grateful for you trying to organise something,' cut in Will, jumping up from his chair. 'Rose is smarting . . . and it's my fault.'

His daughter slumped back down at the table, leaned her elbows on its solid top as though she could use some of its strength.

'I do see what you're saying, though,' he said, resting his hands on the back of the chair for support. 'If Olivia can add value, draw a bigger crowd, and she *wants* to, then maybe we should take her up on it.' He turned to Rose. 'You're always telling me we need to move with the times, be more modern in how we think about things.'

Rose nodded slowly.

'I know it's not easy. It isn't for me, either,' continued Will. 'But maybe we can build some bridges as well as a bonfire.'

44

'I brought brunch for afterwards,' said Robert as he set up the laptop on the farmhouse table the following morning. 'Hot Cumberland sausage buns for everyone.'

'Ooh,' said Rose. 'Glad I agreed to this now.' She grinned at her dad.

'We need to figure out how to actually do this video call, first of all,' said Anna, squinting at the screen in front of them.

'It's Zoom,' said her dad. 'We use it for book club. Really easy. I'll show you.' He tapped and typed for a moment or two and then declared they were 'good to go.'

Anna raised her eyebrows. 'Thanks.'

'No problem,' replied Robert with a nod. 'Right, I'll leave you to it – want to get started on a batch of spiced apple ice cream and try making a mulled fruit sorbet. For the party.' He smiled as he left the room. 'See you in a bit.'

Anna angled the computer so Will and Rose were more in the picture. 'I'm not sure I really need to be here either—'

But Rose put her hand on her arm. 'Yes, you do. Please stay.'

Anna hesitated.

'You're my mentor, remember,' said Rose as the laptop before them flickered with life.

'And you're my aunty,' said Olivia from the screen.

'Goodness me,' said Will as she appeared in front of him.

Rose squeezed his hand: they'd face this, and the future, together.

Anna waved, never normally so far out of her comfort zone in a kitchen, but this set-up was discombobulating. Manchester and Buttermere coming together round the Fell View farmhouse table.

'Good morning,' chirped Felicity from the square beside her client, signalling that the meeting had started.

'Firstly,' interrupted Olivia, used to being the centre of attention. 'Can I just say I'm *so* sorry for not posting anything about Wild Rose Ice Cream sooner.' She held up her hands for emphasis, bangled wrists jangling, doing their best to distract from the tentacle-like marks on her skin, the ghost of the hogweed. 'I promise I'm one-hundred-per-cent invested in this Fire and Ice party, though. It's. Going. To. Be. *Lit.*'

The last word was clearly slang Anna didn't understand, but she appreciated the fact that it worked in a literal sense too, for a bonfire event, and she nodded.

'*Brilliant,*' said Flick, translating for the benefit of everyone else.

Anna looked across at Rose, who was still staring at her half-sister, studying her features on the screen. She saw Will squeeze his daughter's hand in return.

He gave a little cough then, shuffled forward on the wooden seat of his oak dining chair. 'Erm, I know this situation is strange for us all,' he said. 'But I've learned, although it's taken a long time and a lot of encouragement,' – he glanced at Rose and back again – 'that we're stronger when we share ideas and support each other.' He looked at Anna now. 'None of us is really that different. Not in here.' He patted his chest. 'So, what I'm saying is, it would be wonderful if we could all get together on the fifth of November.' He was directing his words at Olivia now, noticed Anna. 'Your mother and her . . . Matthew too . . . and the only fireworks are the ones that there'll be in the sky.'

Rose put her arm around his shoulders.

Flick dabbed a manicured nail at the corner of her eye.

Olivia's delicate nose wrinkled. 'But we are going to have sparklers, right?'

45

The sequinned November sky was the finishing touch. The Lake District had gifted a fine night for the occasion, thought Anna, as she looked round at the scene: the Wild Rose Ice Cream stand festooned with lights, the barn doors flung wide open like welcoming arms. Inside, hay-bale benches were piled with bundles of blankets, and a live band was tuning up at the back, haloed by a circlet of golden bulbs that hung from the roof. Out in the yard, the bonfire reached towards the stars as though it believed it might burn as brightly. Festivity fizzed in the air. Everything was set for the Fire and Ice party.

'Anna,' said her brother's voice behind her.

She felt the smile on her own face before she turned and saw his. 'You came!' she said.

He nodded, beaming back at her. 'I was actually hoping to catch you before it all began . . .'

She saw Lilian over his shoulder, hanging back to let them talk. 'What is it?' Anna asked, trying to read his silhouetted features. He seemed suddenly serious.

'There's something I wanted to speak to you about.'

Anna swallowed. Was it about him and Lilian? Or Olivia? She so desperately wanted the evening to go smoothly, whatever it was needed to be sorted beforehand. 'Go on,' she said – just as Rose appeared, illuminated in the glow of the barn. 'Mum?' she shouted, emotion spilling out into the stillness of the night.

Anna glanced at Matthew, wanting to give the two of them privacy, but another set of footsteps echoed out across the yard.

Will was walking towards them from the milking shed, wearing wellington boots and a shadow-smudged expression, his mood impossible to gauge.

The air temperature seemed to dip. Even the band had fallen quiet.

He came to stand beside his daughter, feet square on the frost-glittered ground as though he needed all the strength he could gather. Then he stretched out an arm to shake Matthew's hand. 'Welcome to Fell View,' he said. 'I'm Will, and this is Rose.'

Matthew's smile said more than a sentence ever could. 'Thank you. That means a lot.' He turned to Lilian. 'We're very pleased to be here.' Then he addressed Rose. 'Congratulations on all of this.' He splayed his fingers, indicating the glinting cabinets and floodlit banners bearing the Wild Rose brand. 'It's really impressive. I've got some press coming tonight, I hope that's all right.'

'Oh, wow.' Rose's eyes widened.

Will put his hand on her shoulder.

'I couldn't have done it without Anna,' she said.

Then there was a flash of a headtorch from the field and a figure appeared. 'That's the pyrotechnics in position,' Robert

312

said to Rose. 'The rockets are synchronised so as soon as you say the word, I'll light the fuse—'

He broke off as soon as he saw his son standing there in the yard. 'Matthew!' he exclaimed; his face more lit up than any firework-decorated sky could ever be, noticed Anna. She smiled. She too could hardly believe her brother was here.

'Is there anything else that needs doing?' asked Lilian, tentatively taking a step towards Rose.

The girl looked as though she was about to shake her head, but she hesitated instead. 'Er, actually, yes, there is.'

Anna glanced round; everything was in place. The display case was full to bursting with innovative bonfire-night flavours: dandelion and honey, spiced pumpkin, even a chanterelle mushroom ice cream for the most daring, that tasted of freshly poured cider and sweet apricots. She couldn't wait for people to sample what Wild Rose had to offer. What else was left to do before everyone – including the guest of honour, Olivia – started arriving?

'Erm, just over here . . .' she heard Rose murmur as she steered her mum inside the barn.

'Look at all this – it's amazing!' Lilian declared, gazing up at the light-wreathed roof and then admiring the array of options in the glass cabinet before her. 'What was it you were wanting?' she asked, with a glance at her daughter, just as Rose reached out and pulled her close, squeezing her tightly as though she'd never let go, tears for their missed years spilling down her cheeks.

The cheers that erupted after the fireworks bloomed above the farm like fantastical flowers were almost louder than the spectacle itself. Applause reverberated around the valley as flame-flushed faces smiled at each other, the bonfire reflected in their delighted eyes.

'Anna,' said Matthew, emerging from the throng and coming to stand beside her. 'How's it going?'

She looked around at the ice-cream-cone-clutching crowd. Even the mushroom flavour had been well received, despite some initial scepticism. Rose's speech had had a raucous response, and Olivia had had a whole series of long-exposure photos taken with sparklers spelling out WILD ROSE either side of her and her half-sister standing in the middle of the picture. The night seemed to have been a roaring success, so far as she could tell. But her brother looked as though there was something on his mind.

'Is everything all right?' she asked.

He sighed. 'I wanted to say I'm sorry. For not dealing with things very well. For staying away so long.'

'You're here now, though,' she said with a smile.

Matthew's eyes crinkled at the corners, like their dad's did when he talked about ice cream. 'Thank you,' he said. 'For this. For bringing us all together. Making us a family again.'

Anna took a deep breath of bonfire-scented air and, in that moment, felt their mum there with them, in the lyrics of the band's music and the laughter of those who'd known her. Her brother must have sensed it too. He looked up at the star-spangled canopy, as though searching for Marion in a crowd.

'I think what you've done with the mentor scheme is incredible,' Matthew said, glancing back at Anna. 'The difference you're making to people.'

'Thank you,' murmured Anna, reminded of Jackson, hard at work in the restaurant. Tonight, it wasn't their mum who was missing but him.

314

'I'm not really meant to tell you this, but Lilian's got inside knowledge from her contacts in the catering industry.'

'What?' said Anna, tilting her head, anything to do with cookery always piquing her interest.

'You're up for the Special Award at the Craft Guild of Chefs.'

'You're joking?' Anna cupped her hands over her mouth.

Matthew shook his head. 'Marcus Bradley told her himself.'

'But that's the—'

'Highest accolade there is, yes. Presented to those who've gone above and beyond in their career. That's *you*,' said Matthew, with a nod.

Anna blinked. 'But they're the chefs' Oscars. I can't believe it.'

'Well, I can.' Matthew grinned. 'And I bet everyone else here would say the same.'

Anna looked round, noticed someone walking up the track towards the farm.

'I'll catch you later,' said Matthew, as a journalist came to steal him away.

Anna watched the man, standing on the other side of the bonfire, taking in the celebratory sight before him.

Jackson.

As she was about to shout over to him, he turned to leave.

Anna wove her way through the mass of mittened ice-cream eaters, trying to get his attention. 'Jackson!' she called above the noise of the rousing number the band were belting out from the amber-bellied barn.

But he couldn't hear her.

'Jackson!' she yelled again.

She managed to catch up with him before he disappeared into the darkness.

315

'Dani said she'd finish clearing up, that I should come,' he said when she was closer.

'That was good of her, considering how much she loves ice cream,' quipped Anna. But even the bonfire's phoenix-feather flickers couldn't put the light back in his eyes.

'I just wanted to know it had all gone smoothly,' he mumbled, gazing at the gathering, still in full swing. 'And I've seen that now, that Rose is happy . . .' He glanced towards the ice-cream stand, where Rose and Robert were still serving customers queuing up to try the different taste combinations.

'I'm not sure about that,' said Anna, hands on her hips.

'Why?' replied Jackson. 'What's happened? Everyone looks in good spirits to me—'

'I think you need to ask her yourself,' said Anna. 'Dad's more than capable of holding the fort,' she added, jerking her head at the stall. 'I reckon Rose would like to see you.'

Jackson raised his eyebrows. 'Really?'

Anna nodded. 'Come on.' She linked his arm, led him through the party. And her own heart squeezed when she saw Rose's expression melt at the sight of him. 'I can take over, if you like,' she offered, taking the ice-cream scoop and reaching for a cone as she came to stand next to her dad.

'The line's going to double now it's Anna Carleton behind the counter,' he said, with a grin.

But she couldn't think of anywhere else she'd rather be, she realised, as her brother waved at her from one of the hay bales as he bit into a splinter of cinder toffee and the band began another song. She looked over her shoulder, saw Rose take Jackson's hand for a dance, just as Will caught his daughter's eye across the straw-strewn floor and smiled.

Epilogue
Zakopane, Poland

The one in the big sunglasses dragging the giant suitcase didn't exactly look like his usual farm-stay guest, but he tried not to judge. He knew how unfair assumptions could be. What it felt like to be on the receiving end.

The other girl raised a hand as she made her way across the waving wildflower meadow, squinting at him in the summer sunshine.

He stood up from his chair on the spruce-slatted veranda, lifted a hand to greet them in return, then looked out over the soft pink swathes of rosebay willowherb towards the soaring Tatra mountains beyond. A view he never tired of. A marriage of craggy peaks and gentle valleys; the perfect combination. He'd only ever been in one other place as beautiful, but that was a long time ago now, in a different life.

'Welcome!' he said as his visitors came to a stop outside the wooden farmhouse, stilled by the sight of the building in front of them and its breathtaking situation, the reality infinitely more impressive than the image they'd seen on the Internet.

'Wow!' said the one with the rucksack. 'It's stunning here!' Her fingers shaded her face in a makeshift visor as she marvelled at the carving that decorated the gable above.

'Told you it would be gorge,' said the other girl, grinning at her.

'It's a radiant sun. Typical of the region,' he explained to the one who was interested, following her gaze to the highest part of the house. He strove to be a knowledgeable and informative host. Not for the five-star reviews on his website, but because this landscape was in his blood. 'See the rays shining out?' He splayed his fingers, miming the sunbeams, struck by the fact that, in reality, they weren't straight lines at all: they were invisible, like love.

The girl nodded in response, before glancing at her companion. 'I should get Dad to do one on the barn back home, for when it's grey and miserable and the sun doesn't come out all day,' she said with a giggle.

Her accent stirred memories within him. That distinctive intonation.

'That's a good idea,' said her friend. 'But an even better idea is to drop our bags and go and find a drink.'

'Let me show you to your rooms,' said their host, taking his cue. He tentatively reached for the handle of the suitcase, didn't want to suppose anyone needed assistance. He had once known someone so capable she could do anything at all she set her mind to. 'It's this way,' he said, gesturing for them to follow inside.

'So how many rooms do you rent out to tourists like us?' said the girl with the backpack and the Cumbrian vowels, more out of polite conversation than an actual desire to know, he suspected, but he appreciated the interest. This was his home and it had shaped him the same way his father had carved the motif that adorned the outside. It was part of him. His place in the world. There was only a small piece of his heart that would always be more than a thousand miles away.

'Three, normally,' he said, pulling himself back to the present. 'But my daughter is here. Home from travelling.' Today was a special occasion, and happiness fizzed in his heart, leaving no space for sadness. A smile spread across his face.

The man was beaming more than the sun symbol on the side of the house, thought Rose, thinking of her own dad as she took off her rucksack. She felt an unexpected stomach-tug of homesickness. Ridiculous. She'd be back in five days' time, and she'd dreamed of exploring beyond the hills and lanes of Buttermere for so long – and now Olivia had offered her the chance. Her sister's treat. She would soak up every single second and they could really get to know each other.

Their host set down the suitcase outside a faded fir-wood door, and her sister darted inside to have a look. Rose wasn't bothered which of the two rooms she took.

'They both have the view,' said their host.

'You choose,' said Olivia, popping her head back out into the hall. 'You're the bride-to-be, Rose, and this'll be your best hen do. I had to get in there first.'

'You are getting married? Congratulations,' said their host.

'Thank you,' said Rose.

He handed them each a key. 'So, you're celebrating too. You're welcome to join us for dinner later, if you want to. My son is cooking. The dishes Katrine missed most on her travels.' He chuckled, clearly delighted to have both his children under one roof. 'But if you have plans of your own, you must make sure you try Oscypek while you're here.' Then he turned and left them to unpack, going to check on Mateusz's progress in the kitchen.

'That's what I was telling you about!' Rose said to Olivia. 'The smoked cheese. It's a speciality. Exclusive to here.' She knew nothing perked Olivia up more than the word 'exclusive'.

'It's sheep's cheese, though.' Olivia wrinkled her nose.

'I thought you were a food influencer?' replied Rose.

Her sister shook her head. 'No, I'm Liv Wild, now. I show-case ways to live more sustainably.'

Rose could see she was serious. 'Really?'

Olivia nodded. 'Why do you think we're here? I knew you liked lakes and mountains, obvs, and this place has all that and more – permaculture gardening, eco-friendly farming.'

'Who are you and what have you done with my sister?' said Rose, plonking down on the bed in her room. Olivia came and sat in the armchair in the corner, perfectly positioned to take in the sweeping panorama beyond the panes.

'I'll show you my socials when we're eating this sheep's cheese.' Olivia stuck out her tongue.

'Ah, there she is after all,' said Rose with a laugh. 'Thought you'd been kidnapped for a second.'

Olivia giggled. 'Do you like it, though?' she asked, pushing her sunglasses onto her head.

'It's amazing,' replied Rose. She gazed out towards the hills, then back at Olivia. 'How did you think of it?'

'Anna gave me the idea.'

'Really? But I thought you kept it secret from everyone, so it was a surprise?'

'I did – wasn't sure I'd get you out of Buttermere if I didn't. You always say you can't leave the farm.'

'Well, Buttermere takes some beating, but this is pretty special.'

Olivia grinned. 'I'm glad. Anyway, it was something she said at your engagement meal. Remember when we were all a bit tipsy and Jackson asked everyone round the table where they'd go if they could go anywhere in the world?'

Rose nodded. 'I think he was wanting honeymoon ideas for somewhere different.'

'Well, Anna said Zakopane. That she'd never been, but someone once told her it was the most beautiful place you could imagine. She had a kind of dreamy expression when she said it.'

But was that because she'd been talking about the place, or the person? Rose bit her lip.

'We'll text her in a bit. Tell her it's every bit as good as we hoped,' said Olivia, standing up to survey the rest of the room.

'So, are you wanting to go into town, or shall we take our host up on his offer? It's very kind of him,' Rose added.

'I don't mind. It's your trip.'

'Our trip,' corrected Rose.

'I chose the thermal spa for tomorrow, so you decide.'

'Okay, let's do it. Let's dine like locals.'

'Then your wish is your maid of honour's command.'

'So where are you from in the UK?' asked Katrine, offering the plate of grilled Oscypek with one hand and an accompanying cranberry dip in her other.

'The Lake District?' said Rose, eyebrows raised. 'Cumbria?' she tried, used to supplying at least two answers to this question, before finally resorting to 'The North'.

'Aww,' replied Katrine, gaze momentarily misting with remembrance. 'I went there. Kendal mint cake.'

It was funny how food so often cemented recollections in your head. Rose was reminded of Anna, and all the people who came to mark occasions at her restaurant. She nodded. 'Yes. Not too far from there. Buttermere.' She smiled and took a sauce-smothered bite of the melted cheese delicacy. But beside her she felt their host stiffen as though the air was February-frozen, not summer warm.

She glanced at him, sitting in the chair next to her. 'This is delicious,' she said, but he didn't meet her eye.

'Did you go there?' Olivia asked Katrine, taking the tiniest nibble at first, before devouring the rest of her piece with relish.

'Didn't have time. It was a bit of a whistle-stop tour. But I wanted to. Dad used to live there.'

Rose's head snapped up. 'Did you?'

'Oh, years and years ago.' He looked like he was struggling to swallow. He reached for his water glass.

'When he was as handsome as me,' said Mateusz.

'How long for?' said Rose.

'A year or so . . .' murmured Dominik.

'Maybe you knew my parents?' asked Rose, eyes wide.

'Probably, it's a small place,' reasoned Katrine.

'I've never been,' said Mateusz. 'Too busy making this.' He grabbed another slice of Oscypek, purposefully reaching across his sister's plate in sibling jest.

'Will and Lilian, from Fell View Farm?' said Rose to their host, so desperate for someone to remember the three of them as a family, to know for certain it had once been real, she didn't notice the twitch in his jaw as he bit back the memories.

But he didn't reply, just pushed his seat away from the table and walked out to the veranda to seek solace from the dusk-kissed mountains, solid and unchanging, in the distance.

Katrine and Mateusz shared a look, all teasing evaporated along with the dinner party atmosphere. The kind of wordless brother–sister language no one else understood and neither Rose nor Olivia had ever experienced. Whatever was wrong with their dad concerned a time before they existed. But now he had them here, by his side, and maybe they could do something about it. They excused themselves, standing up from the table.

'I think I've upset him somehow,' murmured Rose, when there was only her and Olivia left. The mood had turned gritty, like a spoiled batch of ice cream.

'I don't think it's to do with us,' Olivia said, snapping a picture of the cheese to send to Anna. 'Have you heard from Jackson?' she asked.

'Yeah,' Rose replied distractedly. 'He'd been out foraging sweet cicely with Anna – tastes like liquorice, apparently.' But she couldn't help wondering what was going on outside, whether the family that had welcomed them into their home was all right.

'Anna hasn't replied,' said Olivia.

'It's only been about a minute.' Rose rolled her eyes, sure social media had eroded her sister's patience the same way the Buttermere fells had been shaped by the weather.

But then her own phone buzzed with a call. She pulled it from her pocket, worry making her fingers fumble as she wondered if something was wrong back at the farm.

But it was Robert.

'Hi, Rose. Um, I'm with Anna . . . she just got your text . . .' he said when she answered, as the peach streaks of sundown stretched inside, as though trying to coax her and Olivia out to the veranda . . .

He faced the blush-coloured peaks, felt their pinkness reflected in his cheeks.

Mateusz and Katrine pulled up a chair either side of him, stared at the vista before them, ever changing, shifting with the seconds, never quite the same.

'What is it, Dad?' said Katrine, her eyes mirroring the rose-gold glow of the hills.

He'd always been honest with his children, but this was hardly a conversation the three of them could have. He didn't regret anything, though. How could he? Because his path through life had brought him them.

'You can tell us,' encouraged Mateusz, his usual humour gone, face shading as he turned to look at his dad. 'You've been quiet all evening. We know something's up . . .'

The man glanced from his son to his daughter.

She nodded too.

'How can you?' he said.

'You're our *tata*,' Katrine replied. 'We love you.'

'We're adults now,' added Mateusz, 'We know what it's like to hurt here, too.' He placed a fist on top of his heart. 'We're worried about you.' He looked to his sister.

'Mum's happy,' said Katrine.

He felt his shoulders ache with the slightly lessened weight. 'Is she?'

His daughter smiled. 'Yes.'

He'd tried to be a good husband, but it hadn't been right. Not in the way he knew it could be. And Amelia deserved more than that.

'It's been five years now,' said Mateusz softly. 'You can forgive yourself. You weren't making each other happy.'

'You're the best dad,' whispered Katrine. 'But if there's something you need to do for *you*, you must do it.'

The three of them watched the last of the light fade, as though the sunset itself was warning him not to let his last chance of happiness slip away.

But the sound of their guests walking out onto the veranda jolted him to his feet. He took a deep breath of twilight-sweet air, and turned to face them, just as Rose, her phone still in her hand and her half-sister by her side, smiled at him.

'You're ... *Dominik*,' she said, as the same moon that shone over Buttermere gazed down at them open-mouthed.

Anna Carleton's Classic Wild Garlic Pesto

A fresh, flavoursome recipe featuring foraged ramsons. This simple pesto is the perfect accompaniment to pasta and combines wild garlic leaves with parmesan, lemon juice and pine nuts for a vibrant, aromatic sauce.

Springtime is wild garlic season and you'll find this fragrant plant growing between March and May in woodlands and shaded areas. <u>Important note</u>: Please always consult a pocket foraging handbook first and do not pick anything unless you're absolutely sure of what it is*.

Time: 15 mins
Makes 1 x 275g jar
Gluten-free
Vegetarian

Ingredients

    150g wild garlic leaves

    50g parmesan or vegetarian alternative, finely grated

    ½ lemon, zested and juice squeezed

    50g pine nuts, toasted

    150ml extra virgin olive oil

Method

Wash the wild garlic leaves thoroughly in a sieve and then roughly chop them.

Blend the wild garlic leaves, parmesan, lemon zest and pine nuts to a rough paste in a food processor.

Season with salt and pepper to taste, and with the appliance running slowly, add in the olive oil.

Add a few squeezes of lemon juice to your liking.

Place the pesto in a clean airtight jar and it will keep in the fridge for 2 weeks. Also suitable for freezing.

*Always check that it's legal to forage in a public area or that you have the landowner's permission. Never pick leaves growing next to busy roads or in places where dogs are regularly walked. Use all your senses to identify a plant – it might look similar to wild garlic but, if it doesn't smell of garlic, don't eat it!

Acknowledgements

This book is a love letter to the Lake District and a celebration of the flora, fauna and food that make this part of the world so special, but at its heart, it's a tribute to the friendships and connections that nurture us throughout life. I'm grateful to so many people for helping me along the way to publication, and this novel is for all of you.

Thank you to the entire team at HarperNorth for bringing this novel into the world, specifically Genevieve Pegg for championing me and my writing, and Alice Murphy-Pyle for her endless enthusiasm. Thank you to Sarah Whittaker for a stunning cover design that even incorporates Fleetwith Pike – I couldn't have asked for a better jacket to accompany the story.

Thank you to my agent Anne Williams at KHLA for being by my side throughout the whole process and believing in me from the beginning.

Thank you to my family for your unstinting support – I couldn't do any of this without you and I am forever grateful.

Thank you to Daniel Harsant for being the spark that started it all and the muse for so much of my writing.

Thank you to my friends, in particular Al Mullin for foraging with me, and Niamh Lewis for your unwavering faith in me. You are a dream team of encouragement and I am lucky to have you both.

Thank you to my readers: a novel is just words on a page until you believe in it. All your lovely messages mean the world and make it all worthwhile.